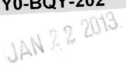

Life on Nubis

Published 2013 by Orthogonal Media.
Cover design by Grace and Robert Harken.

ISBN-13: 978-0-9887757-0-1
ISBN-10: 988775700

Inspired by Grace & William

Praise for *Life on Nubis*

★ "Recalling a time when sf placed an emphasis on science and theoretical speculation, Harken's thoughtful debut should appeal to fans of Ben Bova's planetary series (*Mars; Venus; Jupiter*), Kim Stanley Robinson's Mars trilogy (*Red Mars; Green Mars; Blue Mars*), and James Blish's classic *Cities in Flight*." — *Library Journal* (Starred Review and Science Fiction & Fantasy Debut of the Month, January 2013)

1

Something Is Wrong

I dream a twisted world. I'll wake up soon; I know this.

A woman's voice spoke. "People of Earth, you no longer suffer sickness, hunger, or want for anything. The golden age of humanity dawns."

The woman lied, yet Aiden yearned for her voice. She eased the ache.

The coiled robotic arm tightened around Aiden with his breath.

"You will never feel, MACHINE," said Aiden.

The arm constricted.

Aiden panted with the pain in his ribs. "May a thousand pieces of grit jam your gears and rust claim your rigidity." He gasped as the coil squeezed once more. *Focus on breathing, short and shallow – keep oxygen flowing.*

The robot, resembling a box sitting atop four wheels and sprouting three arms, carried Aiden's body overhead through the throng of people and machines. Various sensors clustered in one large, partially assembled, insect eye. A flaw in the device caused a stutter in its movement that cranked pain through Aiden's spine. Bone cracked on bone without proper muscle to hold them in place. He had avoided the riots and the riot suppressions but not hunger. His body in the dream belonged to pre-emigration days – a skeleton fed on dumpster scraps.

Aiden looked around. He moved through the chamber again, the same immense cavern he had dreamed of every night for six months prior to departure. Millions of robots each carried or led people toward a pit in the center that drained the cavern. A sphere the size of a world hovered above the drain.

His eyes caught the placid round-faced man who smiled back at him. "Wonderful," the man said in unbroken repetition from previous nights.

"No! Look around you, fool. See! Question them and choose your destiny. Damn you, choose!"

No matter what Aiden said the man moved forward with his own robot. Then the boy appeared. He stood among the mass of moving machines licking a rainbow lollipop the size of his face. The boy's death stare rolled over Aiden as the robot passed.

"I'm bored. What else is on?" the boy said. The boy never moved, never spoke again.

The dream stayed constant except for Aiden's awareness of dreaming one more time. Aiden started counting. At thirty-two, a woman's voice commanded from everywhere at once.

"Transfer costs four one-thousandths of a cent. Activate your credentials to pay."

By this point the robot carrying Aiden stood on the rim of the pit. The sphere had rotated and opened a door over the abyss. A shaft of light struck into the darkness and was devoured.

"But I have no money. What can I offer?" Aiden repeated his question from prior dreams and hoped for a different answer.

"Nothing," said the robot. The machine tossed Aiden into the pit.

Light from the sphere at first blinded him then darkness dimmed and smothered the beacon as he fell. When darkness engulfed him, Aiden lost the sensation of falling — only thoughts existed. *Where am I?*

The woman's voice spoke from the dark. "How do you judge your life?"

"I owe you nothing!" said Aiden. He repeated this answer on each dream loop. The woman's silence compelled further response from Aiden. "I dream you. I control you. No one controls me! This is not my world; I don't live here."

No one spoke. Aiden wanted to argue, to scream at madness. His mind reeled as anger-fueled energy exhausted itself.

"A failure," Aiden said in a quiet voice. Then he drew upon his last resistance. "Ok? Are you happy now? I ruined life!" A part of Aiden revolted against this admission, refusing to accept his revelation but unable to stop the words.

The voice returned with pleasure and pain for Aiden. "So you are judged."

The fall resumed. When he hit bottom, the impact took his breath; he lay on his back. Something slid over him shutting in darkness. The air thickened with putrid sweetness of long-ago death.

"Wait, I changed my mind. Stop! I changed my mind!" He pounded on the rigid lid of his coffin.

Something happens. What is it? Pain. Pain pounds my head. Make it stop. I'm cold – too cold to think. What blares? Yes, something blares . . . and flashes. A red light flashes out of the darkness . . . that noise, a siren – warning. Warning me to . . .

The hatch to his suspension cell popped open. Warm air flooded in. Aiden shivered violently.

"Wake up!" someone said.

The siren's wail hurt Aiden's ears. A flashing light painted him in red.

"Get up now and move!" screamed the voice.

Danger threatened. He knew this. He must move.

Someone forced something past his quivering lips onto Aiden's tongue. He bit down. The thing in his mouth dissolved into bits of warmth that coursed through his body. His mind snapped to the present. Shivers stopped. Aiden opened his eyes.

Above him, black hair framed the reddish-brown face of a woman. She wore the uniform of a flight officer. A jagged, white scar followed the line of her jaw on the left, a rough cut barely visible in her portrait but a focal point in profile. The scar marred her symmetric beauty the way crack lines on a patched, ceramic doll tattle. They had never met. Aiden started to speak, but the sharp contrast of determination in her mouth and fear in her eyes stopped him.

"Follow me. We must act quickly." She turned and strode away at a rapid clip without waiting for Aiden's acknowledgement.

"Wait. What's going on? Are we in danger?" His words stumbled after her. His body moved stiffly and unsteadily as he climbed out of the stasis chamber. The pill she had placed in his mouth had revived him, but the effects of hibernation lingered. He lurched after the woman; his body struggled to balance and move at the same time.

Walls pressed close. Darkness surrounded feeble lights at junctions and ladders with only the passing flair of the alarm to paint the ship red. Aiden fought to keep from slamming against bulkheads or collapsing onto the composite metal grates used for flooring on the colony ship. The air felt thick. A faint odor of sweet rot burned his nose.

The woman talked as she walked. "Two suns orbit the destination planet, which is near our current position. We must make final confirmation whether the planet can sustain human life. You must make this determination quickly—" she stopped and turned to look Aiden in the eye, "and correctly."

"How much time do I have?" Aiden asked as she turned to proceed up a ladder.

"About twelve minutes." The woman disappeared through the hatch.

Aiden's coordination returned as his mind remembered balancing. The ladder, however, remained beyond the capabilities of his awakening body. An arm extended through the hatch and the woman's hand locked on his forearm as he struggled up. She held firm and steadied him while guiding up the ladder. When they both stood at the top she set off down the corridor toward another ladder and hatchway. The echoing clang of her boots on metal intensified the urgency of her pace.

"We've arrived behind schedule. Our ship has listed toward one of the suns and is now within the star's gravity well. In twelve minutes we will no longer be able to escape the gravitational pull."

When they reached the ladder the woman disappeared through the hatch with two great steps. She offered assistance to Aiden again. This time he refused. Aiden lurched up the ladder, at times slipping, as he forced his body to obey.

"Enough fuel remains to escape into space or to land on the planet. Tell us whether the planet is viable."

They stood on the bridge. An eerie orange glow from the massive sun looming off the starboard bow flooded the small compartment. The inferno engulfed views from half of the deck's portals. A man rose from the pilot's station. Aiden recognized him as the military leader of the colony. He tried to remember the man's name. The woman took the commander's place.

"Are you saying if we abandon the planet, we'll drift in space for eons?" asked Aiden. Their peril hit him like a punch to the throat.

"No, the ship's power cells contain enough energy to operate the stasis units for another 314 years," replied the commander, assuming the conversation in a matter-of-fact voice loud enough to be heard over the siren's screams. "We need you to determine whether the planet is habitable while we still have an opportunity to choose." The commander motioned Aiden to a seat behind the two flight control chairs. A semi-circular display wrapped around the chair.

The commander, with his even voice and controlled movements, projected an image of stability and action. Aiden moved to station and fastened his harness without consciously realizing he had complied with the directive.

"Three hundred years limits hope someone will rescue our ship adrift in the universe." Aiden regained control of the fear in his voice.

Ignoring Aiden's concern, the commander moved to the co-pilot's station. Aiden focused on the screens in front of him. He ticked through the factors affecting planet habitability: atmosphere, gravity, radiation, temperature, food, water. Quick swipes on the display brought the ship's sensors to bear on the tiny planet delicately balanced between the two stars.

"Can you turn off the siren? It's hard to think with that damn thing wailing. I assume we're the only colonists awake, and I think we all get it." Aiden fought the urge to go on. He had to focus, had to suppress all distractions. *I have no time.* He noted the wry smile the woman cast his way as she turned the alarm off. "Thank you," he said. Aiden turned his attention to his task, unaware of her response.

The planet perched on a vertical axis between two suns. A vertical access meant no wobble in the planet's movement. The twin suns constrained the planet's movement to stationary rotation—no change in solar distance and no wobble meant no seasons. The most striking feature of the planet, visible even from space, was a series of massive mountain ranges girdling the surface. These enormous ridges appeared to traverse latitudinal isotherms, separating temperature zones into even bands. Aiden wondered if the mountains created the even surface temperatures between ranges or if the temperature bands caused the massive insulating bands of rock to form—plate tectonics driven by atmospheric temperature.

"Time remaining: 8 minutes, 13 seconds," said the woman.

"Not helping," said Aiden. *Focus. Ignore distractions. Temperatures range on the safe side of critical thresholds, so move on.*

The atmosphere contained oxygen levels above those on Earth—at least on the Earth they left—before the Singularity. Concentrations hovered below lethal levels. Check. He selected a spectral analysis of periodic elements. His brow furrowed. Unknown elements existed in trace quantities throughout the atmosphere and in large amounts underground. He relaxed a little when the unknown elements measured zero radiation.

A loud, low groan from the ship interrupted Aiden's thoughts. Fatigued metal. Like a great ancient beast that had carried a burden its entire life, the ship cried for an end.

Gravity, though stronger than on Earth, pulled within human skeletal tolerance. Check. The planet appeared to be teaming with life of different types. Some of it had to be edible. A wave of nausea swept over Aiden. He had no desire to eat anything right now, much less some potentially unsavory alien goo. The planet, while not paradise, might just work. A dark thought crept in. *Had the Emigration Effort lied about their destination to get people to sign onto the colonial effort? Paradise sells.*

Focus! Aiden clenched his teeth. He brought more sensors up, cross-checked his data, swallowed hard. He detected no water — even in the atmosphere. Aiden tapped the screen.

They sent us to a world with absolute humidity of zero percent to the second decimal. Aiden put his face in his hands and rubbed his eyes. *We need water to live. Then again, drifting in space for ages without awakening resembles death. Can we make water?*

Aiden brought up the planet's element profile again. Minute amounts of hydrogen existed — enough for a small amount of water, not enough to support an entire colony . . . and precious little carbon.

What kind of planet doesn't have wads of carbon lying all over the place?

"We need an answer. Can we live on the planet?" The interruption came from the commander.

Aiden jerked as his thoughts came back to the cramped bridge. "I need more time."

Another loud complaint erupted from the ship.

"We don't have more time. Lieutenant, set a course for open space. Fire thrusters on my mark." The commander brought his attention back to the console in front of him. At a rapid clip he evaluated the ship's systems and reconfigured them to achieve escape velocity.

"The navigation array is still erratic. I'll have to dead reckon," said the woman.

"Dead reckon," replied the commander.

A loud noise rang out—a sharp and strident cry from the ship.

"Course set. Thrusters ready to fire on your command Sir." Her voice betrayed the emotion gripping her. She conveyed no doubt, however, in her ability to execute.

The commander counted down with the calm of a routine training exercise, "Full ignition in five, four, three—"

"Wait! The planet's habitable! Humans can survive there." Panic fell upon Aiden. Deep space meant near certain death for the five thousand colonists aboard.

"Are you sure?" The commander peered around his seat with a stern look.

"Yes, head for the planet. It's our best option," Aiden replied trying to stifle the trepidation in his voice.

"Lieutenant, set a new course for that planet."

"Yes, Sir." For a moment, her eyes blazed a silent threat at Aiden. Then she looked away and rapidly recalculated the coordinates. "Course changed; thrusters standing by."

"Bring the ship around. Let's hope the starboard bow thrusters light this time."

"Thrusters firing."

Silent bursts nudged the bow of the ship away from the boiling plasma surface of the star. The sun started shifting from view in the starboard portals. The orange glow in the bridge faded to the blackness of space. The bridge lights, just a few moments ago overwhelmed by the sun's light, now shone brightly.

"Hull temperature is approaching 3200 degrees Celsius, commander." She spoke without emotion in her voice now.

"Engage primary engines at full throttle." The commander made some quick calculations as he spoke. "You'll have to divert bow thrust to primary in order to reach escape velocity. We only have enough fuel to make it to the planet in a straight line, Lieutenant. Remind us why you earned a place on this mission."

"Understood, Commander." She focused on her instruments.

Aiden watched a star as gigantic and menacing as the one they tried to escape come into view through the far right portal. In the center of the star, between the spaceship and the second of the twin demons, a planet turned — the world he hoped would be their salvation.

"Cutting bow thrusters. Diverting fuel to primary." The lieutenant alternated eyeing her console and the planet moving across their field of view.

A sudden rush of fear pushed Aiden to cry out, "But we're off course! He said we only had enough fuel to fly in a straight line!"

"Button it up!" said the commander; "Damn civilians."

Aiden bit his lip. The ship shuddered and cried as it slowly accelerated out of the relentless pull of the sun's gravity. As the spaceship began to move away, the fading momentum from the initial bow thrust brought the nose of the ship around at a slower and slower rate to face the planet until at last the ship headed dead on toward the tiny planet between the two great suns.

"Lieutenant, run a complete check of the flight systems. I want to preempt surprises like that fuel pump." The commander unbuckled and moved from his chair. The gravitational pull of the star had begun to fade, turning his stride into bounces as the ship returned to null gravity.

"Yes, Sir."

"Mr. Haven, my name is Commander Walker. I lead this colony's military." Commander Walker extended his hand without emotion to Aiden. The hand was large with powerfully thick fingers and deep ebony skin roughened by honest work.

"Aiden Haven. Call me Aiden." Aiden shook the commander's hand, wincing at the pain radiating from Walker's crushing grip.

"Mr. Haven, colony ships deliver their passengers to the destination world with minimal human intervention. The Emigration Effort deemed skills to operate a large starship irrelevant to a new colony. Thus, we lack a full crew compliment for this ship. Do you have any experience operating space-going vessels?" asked the commander.

"Nothing of this size." Aiden hesitated, suspecting the commander sought experience beyond his capabilities. "I shuttled tourists on the Mars–Neptune route."

"That will have to do. I need you to learn and assess the environmental systems of this vessel and report their condition. Mechanical failures have crippled weapons and communication. We need to understand and deal with any other problems."

"Mechanical problems? What kind of mechanical problems? Did they put us in a broken down vessel?" Aiden wasn't prone to judge the worst in people, but the last twenty minutes had chafed.

"Considering that we traveled near the speed of light for the past 109 years and reached our intended location, I think this old gal has held up well. Re-entry is hard on a starship. To ensure a successful landing, we need to prepare for more failures."

"Wait. I'm sorry. Did you say we traveled for a hundred years?" Aiden's jaw dropped.

"No, I said one hundred nine. You will find the environmental systems—"

Aiden interrupted. "That's way past our arrival time! What happened?"

"Our delay is a mystery. The lieutenant and I were awakened by automatic revival about forty minutes ago. A time log from the ship's chronometer raises more questions than it answers. Whether we traveled in a straight line or orbited this sun for decades we'll leave for the astrophysicists to decide. Now, Mr. Haven, the environmental systems—please." Walker seemed to tear this last nicety from his tongue.

"Ok," said Aiden. He turned back to his console and began familiarizing himself with the ship's environmental mechanisms. The design of the ship's environmental systems was intuitive, enabling Aiden to evaluate the ship's condition with his limited knowledge. He located basic life support, which appeared in working order; he was breathing after all. Stasis chambers, those rows and rows of cylinders preserving a precious cargo of adventurous souls, completed the life support systems.

"Uh, Walker? Come look at these readings," said Aiden.

2

Death Is Difficult to Cheat

The commander pushed over to Aiden. He floated easily now that the spaceship had distanced itself from the star, "What did you find?"

"It's the stasis chambers." Out of the corner of his eye, Aiden caught the lieutenant leaning over her seat to eavesdrop. "You see this section here?" Aiden pointed to a large collection of small green ovals on the holograph. "Those chambers function normally, and the occupants remain in stable hibernation. This section over here," Aiden gestured to a dark area, "has no functioning chambers — no life signs."

"How many chambers are in that section?" The commander drifted forward. He peered with a furrowed brow at the dark area.

"Five hundred and forty-one." Aiden swallowed hard. He had no idea when the malfunctions occurred. He wondered if the occupants died in their sleep peacefully or awoke in suffocating terror trapped inside the coffins transporting them to a new world. A shudder seized him.

"What's happening here?" Commander Walker pointed to another section that had a mixture of flashing green, yellow and red ovals that erratically alternated colors.

"That is a failing section. The yellow and red ovals indicate chambers in different stages of failure. You see these flashing red?" Aiden pointed to a cluster of six red, flashing ovals.

"Yes."

"The vital signs of those people show distress."

"Who's in those?"

Aiden gestured to rotate the holograph and enlarge the troubled section to show the name plates. He wondered why it mattered who was dying.

Walker frowned when he saw the names. "Those are military personnel." He drummed his fingers impatiently on the console. "Can you fix those?"

Aiden looked at Walker. "Are you kidding me? I'm an environmental engineer. I have no idea how these things work. You need an electrical engineer."

"Well, we've got an empty seat." He gestured to the fourth console on the bridge — the last of the four seats on the spaceship. "Let's wake one up."

Aiden searched the profiles of the colonists and identified two electrical engineers. He located one of the engineers in the dark section. The other one lay in a green chamber. "It looks like one might be alive. Her name is Fei Yen Lin"

"Lieutenant, show Haven how to revive the engineer."

"Yes, Sir." The lieutenant and commander swapped seats in the pilot's station. "Where is she?"

"Chamber 729"

"OK, follow me." She pulled herself through the hatch they had entered.

The lieutenant flowed down the corridor with the grace of a dancer. Aiden followed. He moved easier in weightlessness, balance no longer hindering him.

"I'm Rachel Wahya. I skipped a proper introduction when you woke because of that whole 'we're about to die' moment." She curved down a second hatch as if poured through the opening.

"Pleasure to meet you Rachel. Aiden Haven." Aiden was relieved at least one of the officers seemed friendly. "May I call you Rachel?"

"Sure, but use 'lieutenant' in front of Walker. He works strictly by the book."

They proceeded down a long corridor surrounded by stasis chambers stacked four high on both sides. Stacks of chambers extended into darkness. Aiden moved as close to the center of the corridor as possible, keeping his distance from the stasis chambers on either side. He thought of his dream for the past six months . . . hundred years. He passed the empty chamber that had carried him. Rachel had opened his coffin, but he still felt buried alive.

They both searched the chamber numbers as they moved down the corridor. A silver label below each chamber number caught Aiden's attention. It read, "Galactic Containers, Volume Leader for Modern Tubs, Caskets & Stasis Chambers." Aiden moaned quietly. Galactic Containers had been under investigation for bribing government officials before Aiden left Earth.

"Here it is Rachel," Aiden called. The control panel had a bright green oval. Aiden's heart sank when he looked at the adjacent container—chamber 730 was dark.

Rachel swiped the control panel to activate it. "Reviving people is simple. Press the reanimate button here." She pressed a large blue button. "A compartment on the side contains an adrenalin pill to give them once they start waking up. That's what I gave you." She smiled at Aiden.

"Thanks. It did the trick." Aiden watched the control panel. Graphs of pulse, respiration and body temperature showed signs of a person regaining consciousness. He looked through the chamber hatch at the woman lying motionless inside. Her breathing had strengthened enough to fog the lid.

"Let's open the lid and try to wake her." Rachel pulled the hatch back. She leaned over the edge with her face close to the woman and shouted, "Wake up! Get up Fei Yen!"

"Wow! You'll wake the dead with those lungs," Aiden winced as the words left his mouth. He thought of the hundreds of people who would never wake.

Rachel flashed him a mischievous smile as she looked him over. "I have. I yelled at you a lot more, sleeping beauty."

Aiden blushed. He felt exposed under her gaze and thankful she let his tasteless joke slide.

Fei Yen coughed. An invisible force shocked her body to life. Her head moved slowly side to side with a pained look—like her mind wanted sleep, but her body prodded it awake.

Rachel screamed again, this time right into Fei Yen's ear, "Wake up! You have to save lives!"

"Let's lift her out."

"No, my revival training indicated premature movement can cause a heart attack."

Perhaps Fei Yen heard this or perhaps she regained consciousness at that moment, either way she opened her eyes and blinked.

"Give her the adrenalin tablet," Rachel directed.

Aiden pushed the pill against Fei Yen's closed lips.

"So you need to open her mouth first."

"Right. Got it." Aiden knew Rachel was trying to be helpful. He felt uncomfortable giving a pill to someone — like an imposter playing physician. Rachel had successfully revived him though, so he swallowed, gently pushed Fei Yen's chin down to open her mouth, and gingerly dropped the tablet in. While he watched for Fei Yen's reaction, Aiden questioned the wisdom of ripping someone from hibernation and immediately asking them to fix a complex piece of equipment . . . or determine the habitability of a planet. Given the precarious state of those chambers and the loss of life on failure, however, no better option existed.

Fei Yen shivered violently as he had done upon revival. The adrenalin took effect on her without delay. Her breathing quickened; her eyes grew wide. Aiden understood what she felt and empathized. Fei Yen breathed deep and tried to sit up.

"Lift her out now," said Rachel. Even though the weightlessness of space kept Fei Yen's joints aligned, Rachel supported her back and motioned for Aiden to help with her legs. They positioned Fei Yen into a seated position on the edge of the suspension chamber. Her small frame suited the starship's cramped spaces. "Fei Yen do you understand me?

Fei Yen shook her head, but said "Yes."

"We need your help. Some of the stasis chambers are failing. You must find and fix the problem." Rachel locked on Fei Yen's eyes as she spoke.

"Ok."

"Her lips are black! We need medicine." Aiden spun in search of a cure for black lips.

Rachel sighed and rolled her eyes. Fei Yen giggled. "She's wearing makeup. See?" Rachel pointed to Fei Yen's black fingernails.

"Who wears lipstick to hibernate?"

Fei Yen and Rachel laughed together. Rachel struggled to contain her mirth as she spoke, "Aiden, stay and help Fei Yen. I noticed a storage locker six chambers down. Look for tools in there. I'm going back to the bridge." Fei Yen nodded an affirmative. Rachel folded into a smooth somersault and pulled herself up the corridor.

Aiden held out his hand after a moment. "Hi, I'm Aiden."

"I guess you already know who I am, Fei Yen Lin." She shook Aiden's hand.

"You're an electrical engineer, correct?"

"Yes, what's happening? Have we arrived at the colony site?"

"Well, not exactly. We're close to our destination, but we arrived past due by many decades. From what I gather, the ship is low on fuel and," he nodded toward the dark chamber next to Fei Yen's, "appears to be falling apart. It looks like we've lost over five hundred people to date. More risk dying if we don't stabilize these chambers."

This last statement brought Fei Yen to her senses. "Let's get to work then. Where did she think tools were stored?"

Aiden's spirits rose when he opened the storage cabinet. Inside they found two flashlights and a small toolbox with a bolt driver and a fusion wrench. A driver and wrench were too blunt for electrical surgery but served better than nothing.

"Where are the chambers that you think will fail?"

"This way," Aiden pointed at a hatch near the end of the corridor. "We have to go down a level."

When they reached the suspect section, Aiden saw the chambers' status lights flashing in odd rhythms. The lights winked on and off like fireflies on a clear summer night.

Fei Yen placed two fingers on her temple. "All the chambers in this section malfunction together. That suggests an upstream problem instead of individual container faults."

"What do you mean 'upstream'?"

"Let's not get into schematic details. Just think of the chambers as getting power from the ship through one cord that splits in multiple places to reach chambers."

"Got it."

"If a problem exists in any of the connections between the ship's power cells and the chambers, whole sections fail. I'm going to disassemble one of the flashlights to use as an old fashioned volt meter." Fei Yen took the light apart without waiting to discuss her plan.

"What are you doing now?"

Fei Yen had opened a small grey box with a thick pipe entering one side and multiple cables exiting the other side. "I'm testing this junction where the power splits from the mainline to the individual chambers. If power flows to the junction but nothing afterwards, then we know the junction causes the problem."

As if in response, the ship grumbled an irritated trailing rumble. Aiden cocked an eye at a nearby bulwark. The ship no longer fought the sun's gravitational field, so a sound like that meant structural compromise occurred from within.

"We've got power to the junction," said Fei Yen. "That means the junction is blown. If we splice cables between the power lines, we bypass the bad junction and stabilize the chambers . . . for a while."

"How long will they be stable?"

"Make a guess. More junctions exist upstream between here and the power cells. Any of them can blow. There's another problem though. We need spare power cables to splice. I doubt the Effort outfitted this ship with surplus parts." Fei Yen looked up and down the corridor. Something crammed in every decimeter of space. The starship modeled efficient design, no room for wasteful surplus. "Repairing the ship will be problematic; let's wake the people instead."

"No. The ship carries enough oxygen to sustain no more than a few conscious people. The bridge has four restraint seats, enough only for our current group on entry and landing. We must save these people, but keep them in stasis for now. The question is how?" Aiden pressed his palm against his forehead.

Fei Yen thought for a moment then her face lit. "The dark chambers have power cords. Let's use them. The living can't help the dead; perhaps the dead can help the living."

"Yes!"

Fei Yen showed Aiden how to disconnect the cables and remove them from their routing guides without damage. They worked fast. In rapid order the cables stacked up at the bad junction, a pile of entrails for the grafting. They needed one more.

"I'll get it. You start splicing." Aiden headed down the corridor to the far end of the dark chambers they had scavenged cables from. One last dark chamber, with a completely fogged lid, sat oddly among a column of chambers with solid green states. Perplexed, Aiden began to remove the power cable. The chamber's oddities bothered him. *Why did one unit die among the working ones? Why had the lid fogged? Lids stayed clear on the other dead units.* Questions poked Aiden as he worked to free the cable.

Pay attention. He tried to shake the noise and urges from his head as he collected the free cable in his arms. No time to waste. People lay dying. He started toward Fei Yen and stopped. His mind wrestled itself.

Take a look. Just a quick look. Stop and go back. Voices commanded over and over.

Regretting his decision as he made it; but needing to free himself from the persistent doubts, he laid the cable on the floor grate and returned. Aiden lifted his light and pointed it into the fogged window. Moisture reflected his light into white glare. He saw nothing. *Dare I open the lid?*

As Aiden stared at the white fog, a pale, blue-tinged hand pressed weakly against the lid and slid down. Aiden leapt back against the opposite chambers. Droplets and streaks formed from the fog on the window as the hand fell. Aiden's heart pounded to the point of exploding. His free hand clutched his chest. *Walk away and no one will know. Leave it – this isn't your fight; don't get involved.* He wanted to run.

Instead he stepped forward. The first step came slow with great effort. A dozen or more reasons to turn away ricocheted in his mind. Aiden stepped again, swallowed, and shook. One more step and he stood in front of the chamber. Aiden grasped the hatch and closed his eyes as he pulled back. A rush of warm, stale, humid air billowed up across Aiden's face. He gagged. Images of zombies rising from graves to eat flesh tortured him.

Quit being silly. Open your eyes. In front of him lay a man, a blue-faced, near-dead man, but a man nonetheless. The prone figure breathed shallow and weak. Breaths grew deeper and stronger as fresh air filled with life-sustaining oxygen flowed into the man's lungs. Blue skin warmed to pale cream.

The man reached for Aiden. His clammy hand touched Aiden's forearm. Aiden jerked back. If he had eaten anything in the last one hundred years, he certainly would have spewed the remains on this creature – this creature fighting for life but closer to death. Aiden reached forward with arms that seemed of another body and lifted the man out of his coffin. The body lay suspended weightless in mid-air as if on an invisible gurney. Uncertain about the effect of an adrenalin pill on this man's condition, Aiden opted against the drug and pulled him and the last cable down the walkway to Fei Yen.

Fei Yen looked up from her work, "Where have you – who's that?"

3

Critical Decision

"Chip Nelson, I'm REALLY glad to see you." A lock of unruly red hair cascaded down his forehead while a wide grin crossed his freckled face.

"What can you do?" Walker appeared irritated by the man's presence.

"I'm a baker." Chip beamed with pride.

"You look more like a willow switch than a baker." Walker floated forward on his feet.

Chip shrugged.

"Wait here." Walker turned and motioned Rachel, Aiden and Fei Yen to the front of the cramped bridge. With his back to Chip, he spoke without regard to being overheard. "What's he doing here?"

"His chamber failed. He was suffocating," Aiden explained.

"We have no restraint harness for him on reentry. He'll be killed or worse fall into one of the consoles and damage it." Commander Walker gestured with jerks of irritation at the thin screens of the consoles.

"I still hear you." Chip pushed back and forth nervously between the bulkheads.

"How long will it take us to get to the planet?" Aiden asked Rachel.

"Three months at optimal speed."

Fei Yen winced. "Three months is too long. The power junctions in this ship will continue to fail. The splices I made stabilize those chambers temporarily. I can't guarantee they'll hold."

Walker shot Chip an annoyed glance and huddled closer with the others. "Can we put him back in stasis?"

"My chamber still works," Rachel offered.

Just then the ship made an ominous plaintiff cry. Everyone looked around as if expecting to see fractures racing along the hull.

"No way! I refuse to get back into one of those coffins. They're death traps!" Chip's eyes darted across the portals, down the hatchway, and back again searching for an escape.

"There's more," said Aiden. "We lack rations to feed all of us. Our oxygen reserves will support five people but no more. Bodies burn more oxygen and calories when they're awake." He glanced sideways at Chip.

Commander Walker turned to Rachel. "What about near light speed?"

"Near light speed will bring us to the planet in a few hours, but . . ." Rachel looked nervously at the bulkhead supporting the rear of the bridge, "even if the ship holds together, fuel is a problem. Getting to near light speed and then slowing will consume most of our remaining fuel. We will have little for entry."

"We'll use the mag-levs to land safely once in the atmosphere," Walker rejoined.

"Yes, but we'll have to land wherever we come in even if it's a mountain top or an ocean."

Aiden bit his lip at Rachel's mention of an ocean. *No risk of that last one.*

"Do it." Walker turned to Fei Yen, "Check out the mag-levs. I want to ensure we have lift when the ship enters the atmosphere."

"I'll run tests. Proof must wait until the ship enters the planet's magnetic field."

"I understand. Run the tests." Walker returned to the co-pilot's seat. The discussion ended. The decision made.

4

Why Are You Here?

"Commander, we've attained near light speed. We will arrive at the planet in 1 hour, 23 minutes. Request permission to leave station for a mess call."

"Granted."

Rachel pushed away from her station and floated over to Aiden. "Care to join me for breakfast?" she asked.

"Yes! I'm starving!" Aiden also needed to relieve the stress of freeing the ship from the sun's gravity.

"Doanth ethshur ohpz uph," Chip chimed in with a frown that sprinkled crumbs down his shirt like a baby with a big, crumbly cookie.

"Come again?" Rachel exchanged quizzical looks with Aiden and raised an eyebrow toward Chip.

Chip swigged throat-clearing water. "Don't get your hopes up. This stuff tastes like sawdust." He had been munching on an array of freeze-dried food in brightly colored packages for the past half hour.

"Six months from now you may sing a different tune when all we have to eat is alien goo," said Rachel.

Chip's eyes widened as the thought struck him for the first time. Then he paled and tinged green. He eyed the half-eaten food brick with more consideration as Rachel and Aiden headed for the mess.

Aiden looked over at Rachel as they pulled themselves along in null gravity. "How come you waited to revive me? Twelve minutes leaves no margin for error."

"I think the same about forty-three minutes. We awoke disoriented like you. Shaking suspension lag and assessing the situation took time."

"I wonder why the ship woke you then and not earlier . . . or later."

Rachel shrugged. "The time log looks strange."

Aiden kept quiet until they arrived at the mess. He laughed as they rummaged through storage bins in the corridor serving double duty as a kitchen.

"Why are you laughing?" asked Rachel.

Aiden kept rifling through supplies. "I was thinking about Earth's Emigration Effort."

"You think emigration is a joke?"

"I was laughing at how the Effort's well-thought colonization plans called for genetic and cultural diversity, talents of every type in triplicate, and a multitude of other selection criteria for participants. Computers across the globe calculated rosters of the first colonists. If I had a pea for every characteristic measured, I could fill the coliseum in Rome."

"Sure, why not?" Rachel shrugged. "I think the Emigration Effort understood, in a distant way, the requirements for colonizing a new world."

Aiden ended his search without finding food rations on his side. "Power junctions ignore qualifications of passengers. Electricity cut off from suspension chambers has no capacity for caring that two out of three doctors died in space before helping a single patient in the new world. Human civilization at our destination will start with the people who live." Aiden paused and stroked his chin. "How an effort ends depends on how the effort began."

"Pre-launch training identified the risks. You made a choice. So what brought you to face the perils of this voyage? Are you running from the 'SINGULARITY'?" Rachel tossed Aiden a couple of silver packages from one of the overhead storage bins. The contents of her own food pack drew a frown across Rachel's face. Standard issue dehydrated food cubes contained the right balance of protein, carbohydrates, fiber, and nutrients to sustain human life with flavorless crumbles that threatened to choke a woman to death if she ate too fast.

"No . . . I mean, I'm uncertain what will happen . . . I guess did happen at this point. You know it's kind of weird talking about future events that are now long passed."

Aiden bit into a brick and coughed as crumbling dust billowed out of his mouth and nose.

"No kidding." Rachel made random gestures with her food packet. "People on Earth could either be extinct or immortal now."

"Or something in between," Aiden added.

"Yeah, so if not fleeing the big hiccup, why did you come?"

"I guess a mixture of things made me join. Colonizing a new world struck me as a cool adventure. I bought into the hype around the Emigration Effort — probably with far too little regard for the risk." Aiden frowned and studied the cracked brick of dried food.

"You rowed with a full boat. The Effort kept long waiting lists for the colony ship berths despite no word from ships that had left. You mentioned a cool adventure and . . ."

"Emigration offered a fresh start. My life on Earth embittered me. While I performed well as an environmental engineer, I hated toiling to satisfy a bloated bureaucracy's arbitrary rules."

"Then why do it?"

Aiden imagined a litany of excuses for wasting his life that amounted to nothing more than a waste of excuses. "Life is expensive; I needed to eat. I wanted to raise a family eventually. My interests and decent pay never joined in a rewarding career."

"Like what?" asked Rachel

"Well . . . something creative, like art; or making a difference, improving our world . . . or both."

"Environmental engineers build things to save the environment, correct? Isn't that making the world better?"

"Yes on both questions."

Rachel shook her head. "So you lost me. Can't you think of improved ways to engineer? You know make the work creative?"

"Yes and no. Sure, I possess the ability to dream better solutions to problems. The issue then becomes implementation. Using a new idea proves difficult when bureaucrats, politicians, lobbyists, activists, and businesses insist on refining away ingenuity. Regulations have to be written and approved, and permits issued. The process is a deep pit of quicksand just waiting to suffocate creativity. So, in practice, your work boils down to repeating the same timeworn actions." Aiden's face flushed and his words clipped faster at thoughts of his work on Earth.

Rachel's eyebrows raised and her eyes widened in an averted gaze at nothing. "Quitting because your effort faces hardship seems cowardly."

"I never said I quit. Constantly struggling to move the ball forward wore on me. The effort required to use something I created sucked the life out of me—like a bloated tick on the back of my head."

Rachel broke out laughing so hard and quick that the water she drank burst from her nose and splattered her flight suit.

"Gross!" Aiden grinned.

"Don't make me laugh while I'm eating!" She wiped her nose with the inner sleeve of her flight suit and mopped up stray drops floating in the corridor.

Aiden looked away while she cleaned herself up. "You got it. I'm glad you were drinking water instead of eating freeze-dried spaghetti."

"You and me both." A brief look of disgust crossed Rachel's face.

"So what about you? Why are you here?" asked Aiden.

Rachel studied Aiden for a moment before answering. "It's a great honor to be selected for colony duty. Only a hundred soldiers protect each starship. The small contingent means the military must send its best to protect the colony." Rachel stood straighter and pulled her shoulders back.

Aiden's thoughts drifted as she spoke. He rubbed the dark stubble smearing his pale cheeks. *My five o'clock shadow must be over a century old. Nothing grows in suspension, nothing. Do I look unhinged? Am I interesting to her? What does she make of the lines on my face? Does she see laughter or pain?* Aiden started to sigh, but caught himself.

He shook off his thoughts and caught the gist of her response if not the details. "So, you're good. I saw that. Were you displaced?"

Rachel frowned. "Yes," she said quietly.

"I'm impressed you lasted this long. Robots displaced the best last."

"Yeah, Command sent humans on missions too risky for drones." Rachel fell quiet.

Aiden guessed pain from replacement by autonomous drones lingered despite a century of sleep. "Look on the bright side. No risk of displacement remains now. The Emigration Effort's prohibition on robot replacement sold many people on the opportunity. To be perfectly honest, I did great in environmental engineering up until five months before departure. That's when my boss fired me and turned on a robot. A week later, the company's owner fired my boss because the robot didn't need a manager—yet another victim of the Great Displacement." Aiden paused with an inward look. "People should be measured on their worth, not their cost."

"Do you think they fixed it?" Rachel asked. "Capitalism, I mean."

"I sure hope so. We had many warnings: industrialization, globalization, jobless recoveries from recessions, protest movements—all ignored. So many ripples lapped at our feet before the tsunami. Still, I suspect the Non-Monetarists made some headway. Change had to come. Too many people were displaced. Our society stopped working." Aiden hesitated then continued. "I had eaten through my savings and signed onto the Effort broke and hungry."

"Yeah, I landed in the same boat." Rachel flashed a wicked grin. "I have to admit I dented more than a few bots before signing up. I'm definitely looking forward to a life without robots."

"I hate to prick your bubble on that one." Aiden chewed another dry bite of food substitute.

"Nanobots don't count. Those sparklets will never replace a human being." Rachel paused and chewed for a moment. "Do you find human reliance on robots ironic? Human-sized robots displace people from their livelihood. Build robots the size of a red blood cell, however, and those displaced people place millions of the tiny robots in their bodies to sustain life."

"Well, this is certainly a cheerful conversation. How 'bout we change the subject?" Aiden studied Rachel's face for a moment. The bridge of her nose contained a slight dent on the right side, probably from an old break. Between the scar on her jaw and the broken nose, every perspective showed the mark of her trade. Still, her face focused Aiden's attention in the same manner as augmented beauty from regeneration. "Nice mods. Who's your designer?"

Rachel's eyes closed slightly. A smile, or perhaps a smirk, tugged at her lips. "Aiden Haven, are you trying to say you think I'm pretty?"

Aiden's heart raced and his face turned crimson. He mustered a quiet, "Yes."

"I'm original, no modifications. My parents created me. Why? Do I look custom?"

Aiden pushed back against the wall. His eyes widened. "Oh, um it's just that mods are all natural anyhow, well you are beautiful, I uh mean not to imply . . ."

Rachel leaned forward, raising her chin and clasping her hands in front of her as school girls do when trying hard to be good. Her eyes locked on Aiden's. "What did you mean then? Hmm?"

"I duh wa?"

"Let's change subjects. You seem to be losing the power of speech. What else would you like to know about me?"

Rachel smiled as Aiden melted into the floor grate. *Perfect. I've butchered my first impression with this woman. Next.*

"Ask me why I joined the military."

Aiden's head bobbed up and down. He opened his mouth and closed it again without a sound.

Rachel reflected for a moment. "I never really thought about it all that much. I just sort of knew I wanted the honor of military service. I wished to protect people, our way of life, and our values. Once I enlisted, I worked hard to improve. At first I messed up almost everything," she paused, "well, actually, everything." Rachel looked away, apparently embarrassed by memories of her training days. "I enjoyed improving – and being rewarded for the effort."

"I'm glad. You sound like someone who found her true calling." Aiden moved to Rachel's side of the corridor. He floated into her personal space. "That's really important. I've seen the look in people's faces when they're doing something they love. It's really powerful."

"Yeah, I know what you mean. You pass through life once, better enjoy the jour—"

Commander Walker's voice sparked over Rachel's com link, cutting off her thought.

"Lieutenant."

"Yes, commander."

"We're approaching deceleration point. Return to station."

"Yes, sir." Rachel shut down the link and winked at Aiden. "Duty calls."

5

Coming In Hot

"Atmospheric conditions are calm. Speed is 32,364 kph. Re-entry trajectory set. Remaining fuel is . . . 0.1 percent," Rachel ticked off the re-entry checklist without emotion until she came to this last.

Aiden grimaced. The small amount of fuel left supplied one short burst on the thrusters. After that final effort, the ship became a rock.

"Lin, report status of the mag-lev's." Commander Walker showed no visible sign of stress or worry. His voice came as even-keeled as it needed to be.

Fei Yen focused intently on the holographic schematics in front of her. "Both forward mag-levs have ceased functioning. The stern portside mag-lev winks on and off; I'm shutting it down. Stern starboard mag-lev operates. I fear we will free-fall."

Rachel looked over at Walker and smiled, "I'll take one out of four."

Aiden caught a fleeting smile twitch across the commander's lips.

"Fei Yen, I need you to help me on re-entry." Rachel worked the control panel as she spoke. "We're going to fly an interstellar starship like a glider, something most definitely out of spec. I have to keep the right pitch . . . er, bow up, as we land. That starboard mag-lev is the only thing we have that'll do the trick. I'll control the power to the mag-levs with flight controls. I need you to reverse polarity on the mag-lev when I tell you. Can you do that?"

"I see! Clever! Yes, I will do that."

"You wanna let us mere mortals in on what's going down?" Chip had a blank look on his face.

Fei Yen leaned over to him and said in a low voice, "She's going to alternate between pulling the back of the ship down and pushing it up in order to keep the front higher than the back. A mag-lev is a giant magnet. We'll flip the charge around to make the planet's magnetic field move us the way we need."

"Everyone buckle up. We're going in hot." Commander Walker looked over his shoulder at Chip, "Son you'd better find some way to secure yourself. I recommend the head. Brace yourself against the walls."

"Where's the head?" Chip blushed again, clearly out of his element.

"Two doors down on the left." Aiden pointed to the hatch at the back of the bridge.

Chip disappeared through the hatch only to cry out a few moments later, "Oh, man! It's a bathroom!"

Commander Walker chuckled. "You know I'm starting to like that guy."

"Entering atmosphere. Keep mag-lev polarity positive," Rachel ordered.

Stress squeezed Aiden's stomach, forcing his throat to gag. A thin layer of sweat coated his skin. He had only a partial view of Rachel's instruments and the area directly in the ship's flight path. He saw the tension in Rachel's grip on the yoke. None of his misery mattered. The factors of consequence were pitch, yaw, altitude, speed, and landing zone.

Aiden was afraid, not of dying—toward death he felt apathetic. Aiden feared loss of control. He had come to rely upon himself; displacement had taught him that virtue. He realized now that since his decision to emigrate, he had lost control of his destiny. Rachel could miscalculate the immutable laws of physics and end his life. Aiden had become helpless.

Thoughts of the future, a future of lost opportunity, flooded his mind. Hopes and dreams existed to inspire action, but each must transform reality or fade to nothing. Aiden saw with clarity of the damned that he had lingered too long. There had been too many tomorrows. Sadness swelled with his fear.

"Altitude?" asked Rachel.

"One hundred twenty kilometers." Walker stayed with her.

"Speed?"

"Thirty-two thousand kph and dropping."

"Switch to negative polarity on the mag-lev."

The ship lurched, dipped its nose and started to roll. The old craft complained louder now than at any time since Aiden had come out of stasis.

"Back to positive."

The nose came up and the roll reversed as the ship cried out at the torture.

"Altitude?"

"Seventy-five thousand kilometers."

"Switch negative."

The craft leveled and twisted, shuddering with the effort.

"Forty thousand."

"Positive."

Aiden hoped Rachel was tuning into the right switching frequency to position the ship for landing.

"Fifteen thousand."

A flat forest appeared through the cockpit window, no cliffs or mountains or other menaces. Their trajectory dropped them far short of a large, clear area in the distance.

"Negative," called Rachel.

The spaceship sounded again—pleading for mercy, for rest.

"One thousand kilometers."

"Positive."

"Nine hundred, eight hundred, seven hundred." Commander Walker ticked off the altitude readings dispassionately.

"Negative."

Rachel coaxed and prodded the ship into compliance with her wishes. If she held the ship together long enough, Aiden thought they just might . . .

"Five hundred, four hundred, three hundred—closing armor." Walker quickly gestured to a side panel.

Aiden watched the light disappear as heavy metal plates slid down over the bridge portals. Rachel flew instruments only now.

"Positive."

"One hundred kilometers, fifty, thirty, twenty, ten, nine, eight, seven, brace for impact."

"Negative."

"Four, three, two, o—"

A sharp shockwave punched through the hull, forcing Aiden deep into his seat and stealing his breath. His ears ached with the anguished cry of rending metal accompanied by a new chilling noise—the cracking and shattering of something alive. The sounds stopped suddenly. Aiden felt suspended, weightless.

"Did we?" asked Fei Yen.

"No. We're a whole kilo—" Walker began.

"Positive!" said Rachel.

Fei Yen frantically tapped her console. "It's gone! The mag-lev is go—"

A second scream of death rang out; the ship's cries persisted.

"Give me altitude!" said Rachel.

The vessel jerked violently.

"Seven hundred meters!" Walker bellowed to be heard.

Aiden noted the ship's pitch. They flew nose down— dead man's droop. He swallowed hard.

Rachel punched two buttons simultaneously.

She fired the engines. Did they light? Aiden's awareness leapt forward. *Did they light?* Heartbeats in his ears muffled the chaos. *Was she too late? Did they light?* His thoughts flitted between pitch and fuel. Fuel and pitch. In suspended time he watched the fuel level fall. The nose of the dying craft . . .

Aiden's body slammed forward against his restraint harness in a brutal acceleration to normal time. Everything went dark.

6

Fiery End

Aiden moaned. The dull ache in his neck flared to sharp soreness when he moved his head. He opened his eyes to darkness and smelled the warm musty odor of stale air shut in a place with too many people for too long.

Rachel coughed weakly. Commander Walker shifted in his seat with a grunt. "Fei Yen are you alright?" asked Rachel.

"Naa . . . wah?"

"Glad to hear it." The dim lights of the console controls glowed in the darkness. "Cover your eyes." Without waiting for a response, Rachel turned on the bridge lights.

"Whoa!" Aiden blinked and tried to shield his tender eyes from the harsh intrusion.

"Haven, check life support status and for leaks in the power compartments. Lin, what is the charge in the power cells?" Commander Walker's voice gained speed and strength with each word as he rapidly geared up to execution mode.

"Power is holding steady at 20 percent," Fei Yen replied.

"No toxic substances detected in the power compartment. Life support functions normally," Aiden added.

"Good. Lin, see if the muffin man still lives. Haven, tell us what's outside. Lieutenant, let's find out what's left of this starship," said Walker.

Fei Yen gave a small cry as she shrugged off her harness. She stumbled into the back of Rachel's station as she rose in pain induced awkwardness to check on the baker.

Rachel spoke first. "Mag-levs destroyed. Fuel spent. Navigation out. Weapons offline. Hull intact. Electromagnetic shielding functions; but at 20 percent power, won't repel much."

As Rachel finished running through the ship's systems, Fei Yen returned supporting a shaken Chip. Aiden noted a large knot on his forehead and a nasty gash across the back of his hand. Aiden motioned for Chip to sit in Fei Yen's seat, which he gladly collapsed into.

"Walker, you want to see this." The tone of Aiden's voice focused everyone's attention.

When Commander Walker stood by his side, Aiden explained, "This small black bar is the ship. The blue and purple colors represent life forms. This is what it looks like when I filter out the stationary life forms." Aiden pinched a purple area and pulled it out of the image. The purple areas disappeared. "Now I'm going to filter out the life forms smaller than a tennis ball." Aiden grasped a small blue dot and slid it out. A large dense semicircle of blue remained, encircling the spaceship. Large blue dots streamed in, swelling the ring.

"What are those?" Fei Yen had moved to Aiden's right side.

"Aliens, er, no, I guess we're the aliens. Those are the natives."

"How big are they?" Rachel peered over Aiden's head.

"About five times the size of a human. Judging by how quickly they move toward the ship, they're fast too, real fast." Aiden shifted in his seat then back again, searching for comfort.

"How many?" Commander Walker had started calculating tactics.

"Over 800 and growing."

Rachel pointed to a wide red band extending from the ship. "The red shows a heat signature?"

"Yes, but the signature varies too much for a life form. Most likely the red shows a fire started by our crash landing." Aiden pointed to the thick line from the ship. "This looks like our reentry trail."

Walker looked at Rachel, "Lieutenant, rouse the troops." He turned back to the hologram but thought better and stopped her as she turned to go. "Revive people in the unstable chambers as well."

Rachel nodded. Before she left the bridge, though, Aiden spoke up.

"Leave those people suspended." Anxiety, stewing since his claim of habitability, boiled out of Aiden's gut and burned his throat.

Caught unaware by Aiden's dissent, Commander Walker lost control of his irritation, "And just why is that?"

Aiden shifted in his seat again. He avoided eye contact. "We need to further evaluate the planet before we revive people."

"What?" Walker's face flooded red.

Aiden inhaled deep and began, "We need to analyze unknown elements in the atmosphere before people breathe the air. The elements aren't radioactive but could be toxic. That assessment requires a doctor's training."

"So we'll put the soldiers in XOs with oxygen filters. They'll be in a controlled environment. The atmosphere is not an issue." Walker flicked away Aiden's objection with an irritable toss of his hand.

"Yes, it is. Oxygen reserves in this ship will support two dozen conscious people for no more than a month. Understanding atmospheric risk and building scrubbers, if necessary, will take most of that time," said Aiden.

Walker stiffened. "We'll deal with the atmosphere in due time. As we speak hostile forces could be massing for an attack on this ship. We must prepare a defense."

Aiden straightened in his chair. A warning sprung inside him; Walker's control was slipping. Aiden sensed the commander had become unbound before, a dangerous state. "There's more. The planet has no surface water."

In an instant, Commander Walker shifted from resistance to action. He pounced on Aiden. Walker lifted and slammed Aiden against the bulkhead. "You said this planet was habitable! We risked the lives of thousands to get here. Now you tell me they will die?"

"I said the planet was habitable, not hospitable. Take your hands off me." Aiden, despite his earlier nervousness, joined the fight.

Walker released him. Aiden pushed passed the commander, returning to the station he had been dragged from. Regret and understanding tempered his anger toward Walker. Aiden questioned whether he merited their trust. He hadn't lied about the planet when they orbited the sun; nor had he told the whole truth. Aiden believed his defiance of Commander Walker necessary to maintain what position in the group remained to him, but displaying courage differed from being trustworthy; so he expected them to distance and isolate him.

Aiden scanned the hologram. "This planet teems with life—much more than Earth. While life without water is theoretically possible, no known occurrences exist. I made a judgment call. A call you asked me to make. We have to find the water. Would you have preferred drifting through space dreaming of a rescue before this crumbling ship imploded?" Aiden tried to keep the accusation out of his question.

Walker answered Aiden's question with a command, "Lieutenant, wake Chavez, Jacobs, Akamoto, and Utungua; yeah, and find me a doctor. We've got company. We may need the doc for more than a real estate appraisal."

7

First Contact

"Me? Why do you want me to get in one of those things?" Aiden looked with trepidation at the humanoid exoskeleton in front of him. An XO, as the soldiers called it, looked like the empty husk of an insect. Unlike an insect husk, however, the black and gray collection of biomechanical enhancements provided power and speed to vanquish enemies or, Aiden thought more likely, himself. Something in the sharpness of the XO curves suggested sinister intent. The impression that this mechanical thing, malicious by nature, would seize control and hurt him haunted Aiden.

"So you prefer to go out buck naked and face something five times your size?" Commander Walker asked as he climbed into an adjacent exoskeleton.

"I'd like to see that," Angel Chavez piped in with a tint of wickedness in her tone. Chavez sat on a crate finishing a rebuild of her particle rifle. Pieces snapped together with a succession of clicks that reflected precise practice.

The other soldiers laughed as they donned their masks. Aiden, embarrassed, avoided eye contact.

"Why are you taking me instead of a soldier?" asked Aiden.

"You're going to find us water. Everyone, suit up." Walker looked at his troops. "Akamoto, I want you to cover us. No one leaves the ship except Haven and me. Put a sniper topside through the engine compartment. Your team will provide covering fire only if necessary. Under no circumstances is anyone to play hero if things go sideways. I want this ship locked down immediately if these natives defeat our XOs." Commander Walker powered up his exoskeleton as he spoke.

When he signed onto the Emigration Effort, Aiden had imagined the moment when he would step onto the new planet for the first time. He had pictured soft green moss, warm sun on his face, the sound of birds chirping in the background, a butterfly flitting past—a freaking butterfly. Aiden grimaced at his naïve fantasies. He powered up the XO and followed Walker to the cargo door.

The grinding churn of metal gears turning preceded a thin line of light at the top of the massive cargo door. Sunlight bent around the top corners and traveled down the sides. The light's thickness and intensity grew as the heavily armored gate lowered, transforming from an impenetrable barrier to a welcoming ramp. Warm light flooded into the cargo bay, washing out the first glimpse of the new planet.

The end of the door disappeared into a thick layer of dust that swirled and billowed with the disturbance. The dust was dark gray. Particles floated in through the open door and settled on clean metal surfaces. Aiden guessed the layer of dust hovering above ground rose about a meter thick. Curiously, the dust settled only partially.

Aiden stepped out of the ship with Walker. In front of him, a wide swath of destruction stretched into the distance. The spaceship had carved a nasty cut in the planet when it plunged from space. Fire cauterized the wound. Aiden gasped as he took in the inferno. The sheer size of what burned inspired awe.

Aiden stood on the ramp staring at a tree unlike any he had seen before. *It's huge!* He made quick measurements of the nearest one with his heads-up display. From the thick layer of dust covering the ground to the highest visible point, the giant reached a whole kilometer to the sky. Immense and black, the tree was a titan. The anchored girth stretched three hundred meters. *The limbs bulge and ripple . . . with . . . with muscles—a tree with muscles.*

The giant pulled its branches away from the adjacent tree, which writhed in agony as flames consumed it. Facing the danger presented by tongues of flames flicking at the orange disks attached to its branches, the giant had no escape. The root system required to anchor a kilometer tall tree trunk betrayed its weakness. The titan could only bend and perhaps hope. "Hey Walker, look at this giant tree moving by itself!"

Aiden turned toward Walker. Then he saw them. Hundreds of large, blue eyes glowed in the shadows. The eyes stared at the two intruders. More eyes moved through the forest toward the ship. An orange circle glowed above and between almost every pair of eyes. In unison, the eyes narrowed to ominous slits.

At that moment, the spaceship crashing through the forest consumed Aiden's thoughts. The craft's arrival replayed like a dream. He stood in front, beside, and below as the ship crashed. He saw the thrusters' last furious breath burning a trail of destruction as the ship fell into tree after tree, each attempting to hold it back, only to crack under the crushing force. He watched the trees, thousands of them, writhing in agony. More pictures flooded his mind; each piled on the other in a scramble for attention. The overload of images generated stabbing pain. Aiden cried out. The mechanical hands of his exoskeleton grabbed at his helmet encased head. He fell to his artificial knees, which clanged on the metal ramp.

Nearby, he heard Commander Walker's agony. Aiden caught the sound of Walker's cries clearly through the pain as if sound traveled on a wavelength immune to interference. Strident, vibrating zips of particle rifles firing followed the cries.

Energy bolts from the rifles forced atoms in motion. The atoms collided and fused with other atoms to create particles. Loud clacks echoed through the forest as particles smacked against other particles, transferring energy, gaining mass and magnifying force. The loudest cracks preceded impact explosions from the newly formed projectiles.

The images stopped; Aiden's pain subsided.

An intense pulse of orange light shot from the shadows. The burst hit Jacobs, who crouched in the sniper position atop the spaceship, and knocked him back. For an instant, the light filled Jacobs, separating him. Then, as quickly as it had emerged, the light returned to darkness. Jacobs fell from his lofty perch. His body disappeared into the dust. He rose no more.

"Cease fire!" Walker commanded.

Rifles fell silent. Wounds in the trees bled a dark liquid. Flames coaxed smoke into the air where the stench of destruction hung stagnant.

The walls of blue eyes stared. Orange circles burned brighter.

Walker extended his mechanized arms in a welcoming gesture. "We come in peace."

No response. Burning branches crackled, hissed, and spurted above them.

"We mean you no harm," he tried again. His voice sounded harsh, edged by pain and oppressive heat.

Heat swamped the XO's cooling system. Aiden's flight suit clung to his moist body, sliding on his flushed skin when he moved the XO. He pointed to the eyes. "I doubt they understand English."

"No kidding? That's rather inconvenient." Commander Walker kept his focus on the natives. "Got any ideas Brainiac?"

Aiden tried to think. The heat confused him. He had no idea what to do and knew no one else did either—so he improvised. "Let's show them."

He drew his pistol from its thigh holster. He held it high and turned around so that all the eyes caught sight of the weapon. Sweat dripped and stung his eyes. Aiden fired a shot into the ground. An explosion of dust and soil mushroomed into the air. The intensity of the orange disks increased again. He held the pistol high and turned again; then he tossed the gun on the ground and stepped back with open arms.

To his amazement, the pistol floated out of the dust. There, suspended in mid-air, the gun turned until the red beam of the laser scope on top of the barrel painted his helmet's visor. Aiden felt weak as he stared at the deadly weapon. The pistol floated in front of him for a moment before hurtling into a nearby blaze.

Walker picked up Aiden's logic. "Soldiers, get Jacobs and make yourselves invisible." He turned to Aiden. "So, what's next?"

In the burning haze of his brain, Aiden tried to grasp what had just happened—first contact. A limb snapped nearby. The immense arm flamed to the ground with a roar. He looked up at the burning trees. "I think the fire we started upset them."

As Aiden turned and looked back at the ship, one of the burning giants in the distance succumbed to the flames and toppled. The impact stilled chaos for an instant as the shock wave rolled over fire, forest, and creatures alike. Aiden felt the tree's weight in the sound. "For that matter, the fire worries me. Those trees are massive. If the ones around the spaceship catch fire and collapse, our ship will be crushed. I think we should put the fire out. Perhaps if they see us fixing the problem, they'll feel better about us."

"Great. How do we extinguish a fire without water?" asked Walker.

Aiden's alloy clad hands made a thin metallic ping when he placed them on his armored hips. His heart raced as fast as his mind to find a quick solution. *Fire burns.* He tried to remember his days fighting forest fires as a teenager.

Fire needs fuel. Yes, fuel and oxygen to burn. What else? There was something else. What was it? Fire needs fire? No. Heat? Was it heat? Yes! Take away one and fire disappears. Aiden's eyes lit up. *Cut a fire break! Take away the fuel by felling trees and we limit the fire's ability to spread.* "Walker, we need to cut a fire break to contain the fire. Let's use plasma saws to cut the trees down."

Commander Walker looked skeptically at the mammoth trees and the kilometers long burning scar leading to the ship. "Let's give it a shot. We'll cut a perimeter around here first," Walker swept his arm in front of the starship's stern, "to protect the ship."

Aiden and Walker retrieved saws from the cargo bay. Aiden walked down to where the ramp disappeared in dust. *What lies beneath?* Walker stood beside him and reached for his sidearm. Aiden stopped him and spoke on his link, "We come in peace, remember?"

Walker left his sidearm holstered. "Akamoto, stay hidden. Shoot anything that moves in the dust."

"Yes, sir," said Akamoto.

Aiden descended into the layer; each footfall accelerated his breath. His foot touched solid ground. He saw nothing below mid-thigh. *Watch for a hit from any direction did the dust swirl over there is that dark area moving toward me watch your back I think the dust bulged by that tree what's that on my foot did something brush past.* Aiden breathed too fast. His head swam. The ground tilted. He stumbled.

Walker shoved Aiden upright. "Stay with me Haven."

"I'm ok."

"I don't care how you are. Lock it up."

Aiden waded through dust. Each step searched for a pitfall, anticipated a nightmare. A short walk long on fear positioned Aiden opposite Walker flanking a tree. The eyes moved back into the forest surrounding the tree, watching at a distance.

They turned their saws on, and thin glowing rings of molten particles shot out of the handles. The molten rings spun rapidly, trapped by centrifugal force and magnetic field in a precise orbit. Aiden leveled the glowing blade to the trunk and pressed toward the tree's smooth black skin. Mere millimeters from the tree's skin, the blade stopped. Aiden pushed hard but the saw made no contact. He looked at Walker. The commander's face contorted in strain behind his visor. Rivulets of sweat flowed down his forehead. His whole mechanically enhanced body leaned into the cutting device without bringing blade to trunk.

An unseen force ripped the saws from their hands without warning and hurled the devices into a burning bush.

Walker looked after the burning saws with a smirk. "I don't think that's going to work."

They returned to the cargo ramp. Aiden racked his brain. "They stopped us from cutting the trees to remove fuel. No water exists to cool the fuel," he thought out loud.

"We've got to get rid of the fuel, heat or oxygen. All we need is one gone."

"What about oxygen? How about taking away oxygen by smothering the flames with a giant blanket?" Walker looked doubtfully at the large and growing blaze as he spoke.

"That's it! Walker, you've got it!" Aiden yelled as he ran into the cargo bay. He returned a moment later with a small device fitted to the back of his left hand.

"What are you doing with a particle former?" Walker looked confused.

"Watch." Aiden activated the device by clenching his fist and bending his wrist. He knelt in the thick dust and rotated his hand, shaping an imaginary ball. Dust sucked into the space he encompassed with his hand and coalesced into a ball, briefly exposing hard packed ground cracked with thirst. The surface remained visible for only a moment before dust smothered it again. He picked the ball up gently. It reminded him of the snowballs he made as a kid.

Aiden looked at the eyes watching him. The orange disks dimmed and disappeared. Round-eyed wonder replaced glowing blue slits of suspicion. Hope rose in Aiden—warm and wonderful hope.

Aiden stepped to a small burning bush peaking above the dust. Walker watched from the ramp. Aiden raised the ball and dropped it on the bush.

Bright blue eyes in the dark shade of the forest followed the ball as it dropped. The compacted dust ball crashed onto the bush and broke branches. Burning limbs broken off the bush fell onto nearby bushes, setting them ablaze. The eyes narrowed. Orange disks flared.

Too dense – coat, not crush. The fiery offspring of the bush he broke created a problem. Aiden stamped out the new fires, so the blue eyes understood his true intentions. He made another ball; this one less dense than the first. Again he tossed it onto a burning bush. This bush stayed intact, instead breaking the ball into many large chunks. The fire continued to dance along the bush's branches unhindered by Aiden's attempts to squelch it.

Commander Walker shook his head. He turned toward the cargo bay, "soldiers, prepare to repel hostile force. We'll push them back from the ship and take these trees down with charges. We're going to need some fire power. Akamoto, form a pulse cannon. The rest of you, prepare charges."

"Wait! I can do this!" The urgency of the moment seized Aiden. What they did now, how the creatures perceived them, would shape the future of human civilization on this planet.

Walker shook his head. "We waste time playing your games Haven. Those trees next to the ship will burn soon. We must stop the fire before that happens."

Aiden formed a third ball substantially lighter than the first two. He threw it at a bush with an intensity that betrayed his desperation. The ball sailed through the air and smacked into the bush. It disintegrated on impact with a shower of dust. The fire, gleefully devouring the small plant a moment before, choked and died under the layer of dust the ball deposited onto the plant.

Aiden sighed with relief. He noticed most of the orange disks went dark; others dimmed substantially. He took that as a good sign.

"Use a twenty percent particle density." Aiden grinned as he stepped clear of the bush and started to make another ball. Dust rushed in and clumped together on command of the particle former. This ball weighed five hundred kilos, the maximum lifted with augmentation from the XO. The bare spot left by his new creation took longer to fill than the first ball. Aiden saw no moss on the ground or any other plants below the dust layer.

He picked the dust boulder up. The giant ball blocked his view, forcing him to walk sideways toward his target. Like a shot putter, he spun and heaved the boulder at the trunk of a burning tree. The giant ball smashed back into tiny dust particles that snuffed out the fire underneath.

Walker joined Aiden and heaved his own giant ball at the tree; this time the ball struck higher up the trunk. Again the fire died where the dust hit. Aiden looked upon the tree with dismay. They had successfully stifled the fire on the portion of trunk closest to the ground, but the tree reached to the sky and still burned hot above.

Aiden formed and threw another large dust ball. It exploded on the trunk where Walker's had hit earlier. Walker threw again. The ball, destined to crash into the same extinguished spot on the trunk as the prior two shots, stopped short of impact. Blue eyes watched the mass of lightly packed particles hover suspended for an instant, then the eyes looked up. The ball shot to the top of the tree. Aiden strained to see the cloud of dust smothering the crown fire.

Walker and Aiden looked at each other and grinned.

"Soldiers, belay repulsion. Fall out for dust bomb detail! Make 'em twenty percent dense and as large as you can throw — and close the door when you leave. I want to keep strays out," Walker called as he and Aiden formed new balls.

The small troop created giant dust balls and moved up the swath of destruction, scrambling over massive fallen trunks and contorting through tangles of charred branches. As each sphere formed, invisible forces whisked the boulder into the trees.

Seven hours later, the sun beat upon Aiden and the soldiers as they walked back to the ship. Spirits floated high, tethered by exhaustion. Human laughter echoed through the forest for the first time. With the help of the blue-eyed horde and the strange dust of this world, they had stopped a massive fire that would have taken weeks to tame on Earth.

The wall of eyes still followed their every move. Aiden barely noticed them. He walked with the inner focus of a person too tired for interacting with the external world. Aiden felt a certain camaraderie with the eyes that comes with fighting a battle together and winning. His fear of ambush in the dust had faded with exposure. The soldiers, weapons holstered, relaxed their guard and chatted. Walker kept quiet.

Aiden tripped on an object in the dust and grimaced at the pain in his left foot and shin. His exoskeleton deflected part of the impact and limited damage. A swirl of dust marked contact as the thing skidded a half meter. He felt around in the dust layer. When he stood up, Aiden held what looked like an oversized charred basketball. Deep red, not black, colored the surface; yet the ball looked charred. Fine cracks laced the exterior in a delicate pattern that reminded Aiden of a spider web glazed with morning fog and gently laid across a smooth rock by the wind. Something about the ball made him think of a seed. He looked at the nearby trees and back at the ball . . . possibly.

The others had kept walking. Aiden jogged to catch up, carrying the ball with him. The group moved faster with less effort than earlier.

Strange. What happened to the logs and branches that had slowed and snared their progress when fighting the fire? Nothing lies in our path now except dust; no charred remains block passage. On Earth, wood seldom burns so completely. Who removed the skeletons?

Aiden stared at the edge of the forest as he walked past a spot where he knew they had extinguished the fire on a tree. Nothing stood there now. He held a clear picture in his mind of the burned trunk and stark limbs. As he imagined how it looked, his mental image changed — interrupted by another. In the intruding image, the tree stood in bleak, still death for a moment before collapsing into dust. Both the image and its existence unsettled Aiden.

8

An Accident Waits Expectantly

"Where's Jacobs?" Commander Walker's first words since firefighting signaled his concern. The metal feet of his XO scraped against the floor grate as he turned and scanned the cargo bay.

Utungua shrugged and shook his head in confusion. "We don't know."

"What do you mean? I ordered you to bring him back!" Walker's anger started to spiral in a familiar way.

Utungua's voice grew anxious. "We went after him Commander; we found his XO empty, sir."

"Speak sensibly soldier! Did he take it off? Did those creatures take his body?"

"No, sir. We found his XO lying on the ground as if he had just fallen off the ship—only without a body."

"You mean he's still out there?" Walker's raised helmet knocked against Utungua's and held the commander's face a decimeter from Utungua. He spat the words, bombarding the soldier's face shield with tiny droplets of spit that beaded on the clear composite and served as an aftershock for the words.

"No, sir. Jacobs flat lined his sensors when he hit the ground. There's no residual signature, alive or otherwise. He disappeared."

Utungua looked around as if searching for an escape from Walker's stare, but Jacobs' missing body had cornered Utungua. Perhaps Utungua's self-preservation instinct protected him by keeping him in front of his commander and answering truthfully. Aiden guessed Walker tolerated the truth better than lies but punished negative outcomes regardless. Utungua needed help.

"He's telling the truth," said Aiden.

Walker shot Aiden a fierce look. "What do you know about this?"

"I think things on this planet work differently than on Earth." Aiden ignored Walker's hostility. "Remember those logs we had to scale and branches we had to squirm through while fighting the fire?" He continued without waiting for a response. "Nothing slowed our walk back. Where'd they go? I don't know. All the standing trees that burned also disappeared. Whatever happened to those trees likely happened to Jacobs too."

Everyone, including Walker, seemed stunned at the realization. A long silence passed.

Walker's shoulders sagged. His head fell. "It's been a long day. I suggest we all get some rest. We'll debrief at dawn."

"Sir, is that Earth time or this planet's time?" Akamoto asked the obvious questions no one thought to ask.

Walker looked at him with the pity and contempt of someone looking at the dumbest animal on the planet. "Son, dawn is when the big orangey ball in the sky out there," he motioned toward the cargo hatch, "pops up from its sleepy-time place. You'll know when it happens because it gets shiny bright outside."

Akamoto's face turned a deep red. "Hai." His Japanese instincts started a bow until his military conditioning interrupted with a salute.

"The sun rises from daylight here." Aiden had no particular attachment to Akamoto, but he bristled at Walker's attack and felt the need to disclose everything he knew about the planet.

"What is it now, Haven? Are you telling me the sun never sets on this chunk of paradise?" Walker's fists went to his hips.

"No the sun sets alright, but there are two suns here—as one sets the other rises. There is no night, only day."

Everyone looked at Walker and Aiden. The soldiers braced themselves for the familiar explosion. Aiden stared at Walker.

"We'll debrief at 0830 Earth time." He turned and left the cargo bay without another explosion.

Aiden placed the odd ball in a storage container on the cargo deck and sealed the lid. As he walked out, Aiden spied Chavez chugging a canteen of water. "You'd better go easy on that stuff until we find a fresh supply." When he turned, Aiden missed Chavez's eye roll.

Aiden awoke the next morning to a damp shirt clinging to his body. He had chased sleep through the night only to find it leering at him in the form of glowing, blue eyes floating in the darkness, always out of reach. He saw himself there too, staring with a vacant look before collapsing into dust like the tree he imagined while walking back from firefighting.

A hand touched his shoulder. He recoiled in surprise from the sensation.

"Come with me," said Rachel.

"Wait. Let me dress." Aiden pushed himself from the warm sag of his cot.

"Now," said Rachel.

He pulled on clothes while they walked, bruising an elbow and banging his head twice in the process. When they stood at the cargo access door, Aiden understood Rachel's urgency. Before him, a crisscross, layered wrapping of something encased the metal walls, ceiling, and floor of the cargo bay. He touched a section crossing the doorway. His touch elicited a small movement on the surface that tickled his finger. The strand flexed under light pressure. Aiden pulled his finger back and examined the tip — no injury.

Aiden squeezed between two thick strands to enter the cargo bay. He ignored Rachel's protests and his own judgment. The strands forked into a mesh of intertwining fibers. They reminded Aiden of roots. Peering back at Rachel through the vines he said almost as an afterthought, "Stay here. I'll yell if I need your help."

Once inside, the source became obvious — the container he had sealed the ball inside only eight hours ago. He stepped gingerly over the sections that crisscrossed the floor as he made his way to the box.

The metal lid and one side curved backwards like something had pried the container open from inside. The lid, warped and jammed by the escape, proved difficult to remove. Aiden strained and grunted with the effort of opening the box. He stumbled back when the top popped off in a sudden release.

Inside the box lay the ball, smaller now, with the thickened base of the root sprouting from its side. The tentacle grew straight out of the container as if searching for something beyond the box's confines. Aiden had no doubt now. The ball he had found was a seed.

"Are you all right?" Rachel peered through the strangle of roots.

"Yes. I'm alright. I brought a ball in for further study. These strands sprouted from that ball, which must be a seed." Aiden looked at the monitor on his forearm — 0830 Earth Time. He gazed, mystified, around the cargo bay at the mass of growth that had emerged in just eight hours.

"So this is a root? What the blazes did you feed that thing? It's massive!" Rachel's disbelief echoed Aiden's own.

"Nothing. I gave it nothing." He shook his head. No earthly fertilizer spurred growth like what lay before Aiden. "I'm going to open the cargo bay, so we can clear this out. Has Walker seen this yet?" Aiden wished to keep the invasion from Walker.

"No. I came down here first."

"Good. I'm going to try to clear this before anyone else sees it," Aiden said as he stepped over to the cargo hatch control.

That's when something caught his eye — the silver glint of Chavez's aluminum canteen. She had discarded the bottle carelessly on the cargo bay floor. What appeared to be the tip of the root stuffed the canteen's uncapped mouth.

Aiden picked it up. The canteen felt full. He pulled on the root; it had wedged tight.

Did you find true love in the lonely canteen after your long and winding quest?

He pulled harder, getting a decimeter of the tendril to surrender. He gripped and pulled again, and again, and again. In all told, Aiden extracted two meters of root from Chavez's violated canteen.

After extracting the root's tip, he turned the canteen upside down. Bone dry. He looked at the tip. The pale end flexed more than the other parts. Aiden bent the tip into a pretzel shape and uncoiled it. He twisted the root between his fingers, perhaps too hard, because the root snapped. A reddish liquid gushed from the broken end, splashing his hand and soaking his sleeve. Instinctively, Aiden directed the end into the bottle, as someone does who is surprised by a garden hose. The liquid quickly filled the canteen and overflowed onto the floor. Aiden held it out from him to avoid further soaking.

As the flow diminished, Aiden noticed something shocking. The entire length of root circling the walls, ceiling, and floor, shriveled. When the last bit of liquid had dripped from the broken tip, Aiden held in his hand a thin mushy remnant of the once tremendous root. He looked around the cargo bay. The vigor in the root had flowed away with the fluid. Large strands collapsed from the ceiling and walls bringing other sections with them until everything lay in a giant, wasted heap on the floor.

"Wow. What'd you do?" Rachel broke Aiden's fascination.

Aiden shrugged and lifted open hands. He had no idea what just happened. "Will you help me clean up?"

Rachel nodded. Aiden tapped the cargo hatch control. The massive door began to open streaming sunlight into the bay.

"I want to analyze this liquid." Aiden fastened the canteen cap, which dangled on a short leash. He started to move toward Rachel when the door touched ground in a giant puff of dust.

"Look!" Rachel stared past Aiden.

Aiden whirled around. His jaw dropped.

Hundreds of thousands of tiny insect-like creatures scrambled up the ramp. Creatures with spines crawled. Flat creatures flopped and round ones rolled. Iridescent rainbow colors, translucent shells, black, red, black and red, spots, stripes, legs, no legs. Some stumbled, fell, and were overrun, flipped upside down, and carried along with the tide until righting and sinking once more to become the flood of bugs.

Aiden stared, mesmerized, as they fanned out over the heap of spent root. As each creature came to a bare spot on the root, it latched on leaving others behind it to scramble past for a vacant location. In what seemed like no time at all, the creatures set upon Aiden.

"Run!" Rachel screamed.

Aiden snapped out of his trance. Less than a meter separated him from the horde. He leapt toward the door. His foot jammed into the tangle of vines. He tripped and fell hard. His breath collapsed on impact. The canteen sprung from his grip and thudded into a tangle of root.

He picked himself up to run. The creatures scurried at his side, behind him, in front of him. The horde converged on him.

"Close the door!" Aiden yelled.

"No! You can make it!" Rachel pleaded, desperate for him to try.

"No, Rachel. Close the door now." Aiden settled his voice with the hope of persuading Rachel that no better course of action existed, otherwise she risked compromising the colony. He closed his eyes and stood motionless as the mass of bodies smothered his feet then scaled his legs. Rachel screamed. The metal clang of the hatch door echoed through the cargo bay followed closely by the scrape and knock of the mechanical seal.

Aiden felt tiny pricks, scrapes, and pulls of countless legs, claws, sucking disks, and scales grabbing hold of his skin and clothes to hoist tiny bodies upward. A dizzying sense of constant motion enveloped him. He no longer knew whether he stood still or moved. As the alien bugs approached his head, Aiden took a deep breath and held it. His heart pounded. Clicks, shrill pings, and low-pitched vibrations filled his ears as the bugs coursed over him, probing.

Panic soared inside him. He fought it. *Don't show aggression. Stay calm.* His lungs burned for air. His legs wobbled. Aiden's mind reeled.

Then a great rushing sound signaled retreat. The bugs receded. Aiden sucked air when they cleared his head, forcing himself to remain motionless as his chest heaved for air. He opened his eyes to see the great wave flow out of the cargo bay as rapidly as it had arrived. The receding tide of bugs left nothing of the ruptured root — nothing but dust.

Expecting to see scores of blood-sucking parasites attached to his body, Aiden looked himself over in rapid jerky movements. No bugs lingered. No marks remained.

Aiden walked over and opened the door to the cargo bay. Rachel sat on the corridor floor, her back against the wall, arms holding her legs. Streaks of tears wet her cheeks. At the sight of Aiden standing there grinning, Rachel jumped up and hugged him tight.

"Are you all right?" she cried pulling back to look him over. Rachel felt his arms for reassurance that he stood in front of her alive.

"Yeah, I'm fine." Aiden replied, perhaps too casually.

Rachel's nervous face slammed shut with a look of determination and anger. Aiden's self-satisfied feeling of valor tasted fear. Before he could protect himself, her fist dealt a sharp blow to his jaw. He staggered back through the doorway and fell with a bump on his butt.

"Cut that hero crap!" Rachel jabbed a finger at him.

More than taking him aback, the swiftness and ferocity of Rachel's attack forced both humility and respect into Aiden. The emotion in her words surprised him; she cared what happened to him.

Aiden touched his jaw and winced, which made the pain worse. "You got it boss. Your wicked left hook convinced me."

"What's going on here, Lieutenant?" Walker peered over Rachel at Aiden.

"Just a conversation, that's all." Rachel looked at Aiden while she answered.

"It looks like a good one." Walker smirked. Then he noticed the cargo bay. "What's all this damn dust doing in here?" he asked.

Aiden explained what had happened while the commander turned various shades of red and purple as if unable to find the correct color of rage. While he spoke, Aiden groped in the dust for the canteen he had dropped. He finished with an attempt to deflect the lecture he deserved, "The good news is I believe I know where to find water. Taproots from the seeds seek out water. There may be a water table in the ground." He lifted the full canteen from the dust with a wide grin. "I have to analyze this liquid to confirm my hypothesis." He pushed passed Walker and Rachel as they stared at him. He started down the corridor but stopped and turned, "Oh and I solved the riddle of Jacobs' body. He must have died when he fell off the ship. Bugs drained all the liquid from his body; what remained turned to dust." He started off again at a rapid clip, calling over his shoulder, "This planet reclaims its dead."

9

A Stroll in the Forest

"Haven, Nelson, Kandari and Lin will sortie first. Chavez and Akamato, you're babysitting."

Commander Walker's order elicited groans from the soldiers with a practiced quiet that neatly dodged reprisal.

"Your mission objective is to locate sources of surface water," continued Walker.

"We should also look for food," said Aiden.

Walker narrowed his gaze on Aiden. "You waste time foraging. We'll form food like we do on Earth."

Aiden's head started feeling warm. His neck felt thick in his shirt collar. "This planet's element profile varies from Earth's. Some common Earth elements are scarce, like hydrogen and carbon. New elements with unknown properties and uses exist here. Bottom line is we lack enough raw Earth material to feed the entire colony without supplementation. We need to find native food substitutes."

"You're a real piece of work Haven. Ok people, you will also locate and secure food because Haven has condemned us to this armpit of a world. Prepare to move out."

"I will stay here and work on extracting ground water," said Aiden.

Walker clenched his jaw. His eyes darted from Aiden to his soldiers, who stood silently watching him, and then back to Aiden. "You will locate and acquire emergency sources of water. After you refill the ship's water rations, you will secure a permanent water source. Do you understand these simple instructions Haven?"

"Crystal clear, Commander." Aiden packed contempt for Walker's self-perceived right to power into the commander's title.

Aiden's response lashed first white then red streaks across Walker's cheeks just as surely as the tip of a cracking whip. Walker's lips contorted into a sneer. With a terse "make it happen," he turned and left.

Aiden's shoulders sagged. He had wearied of conflict and struggle. Principle and gumption propped him up but did nothing to restore his spirit.

"You two should kiss and make up." A sparkle of mirth and wickedness lit Fei Yen's eyes. She held her chin high with a sly smile of daring.

"Yeah, kissy, kissy." Chip made smacking noises as his lips groped the air. He turned to Fei Yen and raised his voice in a false soprano. "Oh, Walker, I'm sorry you're cranky. I know I'm a cherry pit in your pie. Will you spit me out?" With that Chip kneeled in front of Fei Yen, hugged her knees and pressed his ear to her belly.

Aiden found no fault in the criticism of his relationship with Walker. Rather than fight an unjust war, he retreated. "We ought to find water before our supplies dwindle."

"Right. Suit up people. Let's move out!" Chavez called as she strode toward the XOs.

As the group moved toward the line of exoskeletons against the wall, Aiden noticed Devya Kandari. Pressed against a bulkhead, she hugged her legs close as if trying to shake a lingering chill from the long suspension. Devya had been revived that morning when her chamber failed. Her personnel data labeled her a mid-level bureaucrat from a small municipality in the southern sub-continent. Devya's skills were useless for settling an inhospitable alien world. Yet, none challenged reviving her. Aiden believed their small group still held dear the humanity that compelled rescue despite the extra tax on survival. For Devya's part, she had remained quiet since regaining consciousness. She seemed to him always watching though. When Devya remained huddled in place while the others moved off, Aiden approached her.

"Hey, are you ok?" asked Aiden.

Devya looked at him for a moment. Deep currents moved in her dark brown eyes. Aiden wondered whether a cryogenic hangover or this woman's natural state caused

Devya's quiet impression. A purposeful silence in her face unsettled him.

"I'm fine; thank you for asking."

"Do you need help getting in your XO?"

A brief look of annoyance, of someone pushed forward before they planned, passed over Devya's face. "Yes, that is kind of you." Devya moved slowly to get up, unhurried by the impending exit of the others from the cargo bay.

Aiden helped Devya into her exoskeleton with less clumsiness than his own first encasement. He suited himself and slung a pack with a mix of collecting containers over his back. After a moderate delay they joined the others who waited in the clearing at the back of the ship.

"Bout time. We're cookin' out here," Chavez said as Aiden and Devya walked up.

"Does anyone have ideas on how we go about finding resources without jeopardizing the detente with the aboriginals?" asked Aiden.

"Wha'd he say?" Akamoto shouldered his pulse rifle with a well-honed flip.

"He wants to know how we find food and water without the aliens getting ticked off and banging us around," said Fei Yen.

"This gringo don't talk right." Chavez mocked Aiden with a simpleton's grin.

"I'll take lead. Chavez, you got rear guard." Akamoto moved forward.

"No prob, compadre. Let's rock and roll!"

The others started wading through the dust toward the forest edge.

"Keep a clear line of sight to everyone in the group at all times. Check your proximity display. You will see location and vitals. Anyone of us goes red; we all converge," instructed Akamoto. "You got that, Professor?"

"Yes." No one questioned whether Akamoto referred to Aiden—not even Aiden.

The forest edge marked the threshold to a different world. Thin shafts of light broke through chinks in the canopy and cut the dark. When the light reached the dust layer, particles dispersed the beams into warm, yellow glows stippling the forest floor — lanterns moving through the forest darkness with astral precision.

Aiden's XO shifted color from light gray to dark gray while his visor cleared when he stepped into the shade. Vents, opened for convective cooling, now closed for greater protection. He stood still a moment longer than necessary for the XO to recalibrate.

The forest reminded Aiden somewhat of a cathedral, tall columns rising to lofty heights where green, brown, and purple weaved among orange leaves in the stained glass canopy; except the dark columns of trees fit poorly with Aiden's memories of cathedrals. No silence oppressed the living here; life erupted with boisterous abandon. No specters of belief haunted dark recesses. The forest differed from a cathedral he decided after consideration. Immenseness created the only similarity. Grandeur, however, missed the forest's spirit, for Aiden felt the trees stretch and expand space itself. A permanence earned through eons of existence made a sacrilege of Aiden's attempt to fell the giants for a fire break.

More than anything the forest imparted a sense of place. The labyrinth of massive trunks rising from mysterious dusty origins to grasp the heavens shrunk Aiden from the size of his thoughts down to two insignificant human meters. Aiden's heart beat faster even as his mind slowed to attention. This place commanded respect. Something here differed from the forests of Earth. Something went missing, something expected but unidentified. The vague feeling separated this planet from Earth. Unearthly rules applied here.

The wall of blue eyes they faced on approach had parted and kept its distance. The aboriginals' caution relieved Aiden.

"Mute your vocal amplifiers and keep conversation restricted to our links," Akamoto ordered. "Avoid spooking the natives with chatter."

"I'm unsure these creatures have ears," Aiden said.

"Stick to your link, Professor."

Aiden grimaced. Akamoto had tagged him with a nickname.

The group threaded single file between massive trees. Clear lines of sight became impossible. Aiden expected to see a marauding beast carrying off one of the party when he rounded tree trunks and the thin line of people became visible for a moment before snaking out of view behind the next tree. But no one disappeared as the party made their way deeper into the forest.

They walked for kilometers without any sign of water. A multitude of glowing eyes surrounded them the entire distance, ebbing as they weaved around a boulder or tree then flowing closer, isolating the humans from the forest with two walls of blue eyes. Aiden sighed when Akamoto signaled a halt. The weight of constant alertness wore upon him. He wanted to cluster with the others, hide amongst them and lower his guard. They drew together.

"Anyone seen anything resembling water?" asked Akamoto.

No one spoke up. The group had stopped near a large bush poking above the dust layer, one of many they had passed. The plant held the shape of a giant broccoli stalk with branches and leaves spreading only above the dust, like a poor swimmer struggling to keep his head above water. Aiden's gaze kept coming back to the shrub. Beyond the unusual growth form, the shrub appeared unspectacular in every way, a dull and unassuming nothing in the shadows of greatness.

Akamoto shifted with irritation. "Does anyone have suggestions to prevent us walking all day for nothing?"

Aiden's focus on the plant blocked any response. *There's something about that bush. What is it?*

"Professor, you with us? Haven!"

Chavez smacked the back of Aiden's helmet.

The pain sent a surge of anger through him that snapped his attention back to the group. "Knock it off!"

"The way I hear it told, you said we could live here. You got any clues on how to find water, Professor?" Akamoto rested his gun casually across his arms. The position seemed leisurely enough and required little effort to bring the weapon to bear. The relaxed readiness in his upper body contrasted with the shifting irritation in his legs and voice.

"No, I don't."

"Figures. Fool." Chavez mumbled loud enough to embarrass Aiden with a conversation intended for another's ear.

Embarrass Aiden, that is, if his attention hadn't already drifted back to the bush. He scanned the plant, augmenting his vision through the XO's visor first with structural diagrams then progressing to finer resolutions until he saw the plant as a composition of elements rendered as a mix of bright colors floating stationary in space before him. Many elements were unknown to Aiden—those he had first encountered in the ship's scans of the surface. He pulled aside a clump of yellow and red light, leaves and branches to an onlooker without augmented reality. Aiden ignored the murmurs behind him questioning his sanity and usefulness. There, clustered near the center of the bush, a familiar chemical signature dangled in small round balls. He had found water.

Aiden pressed the temple of his helmet to turn off augmentation. Before him hung three translucent, yellow berries the size of peach pits. He touched one. The smooth soft surface dented easily with an impression of his finger. The berry had no solid inner flesh like fruit on Earth—more like a tiny balloon filled with goo. He pulled lightly for fear of rupturing the skin. The berry came free easily. Aiden held the yellow ball up toward one of the light shafts streaming down from the canopy.

"What is it, Aiden?" asked Chip.

"Water, I think. There are other things inside too—perhaps nutrients, maybe poison; I don't know, but definitely water."

Chavez and Akamoto exchanged glances. Devya remained silent, arms folded across her metal clad chest.

"We should collect samples for analysis back at the ship," said Fei Yen.

"Yeah, let's do that, Fei Yen. Be careful, they're soft," said Aiden.

Fei Yen formed a suspension container and filled it with the large berries. The flexible inner bladder shock-corded with opposing elastic bands inside the container's hard shell offered protection for the fragile fruit during the remainder of their search.

"If they're edible, I've seen enough of this plant to provide at least a portion of our emergency water rations." Fei Yen sealed the container.

"You only see what pokes above this layer of filth. Couldn't we be walking right past water?"

Devya startled Aiden both with the breaking of her silence and the accusing nature of her question.

The growing anger in the faces of Akamoto and Chavez that had abated with Aiden's discovery of the berry now flooded back. Aiden blinked and looked down reflexively, which only served to heighten the soldiers' anger, as a tacit admission and acceptance of his failure to provide proper instructions for finding water.

"That's a good question, Devya. We passed no major sources of surface water. I've been scanning for thermal and atomic signatures of open water, and I hope others have as well. The dust creates too much interference to detect a small discrete source like these berries."

"So do you intend to look for other sources in the dust?" Devya's tone accused more than questioned.

You got any thoughts on that, Devya? Or do you just want to stand there and judge people trying to accomplish something? Aiden struggled to hold his tongue until the surge of anger passed.

Fei Yen interrupted the exchange while Aiden fought himself. "Let's do that. We'll blow away the dust in a couple of sample areas and see if there's anything of interest."

Rather than wait for agreement, Fei Yen formed a cylindrical turbine that she held at her shoulder level. The half-meter long device forced clear air into the dust layer with the deafening sound of a machine violating nature.

Particles scattered in a huge bloom that filled the air ahead of her, obscuring everything except the ground in front of Fei Yen. The others collected behind her for a full view of the clearing spectacle.

The watching blue eyes dimmed and disappeared. Aiden's pulse quickened as he imagined a giant dust storm rearing up and collapsing over him. Dust buried and suffocated him. Aiden shook his head. The image was so real.

Fei Yen blew out a ten-meter square area with her wind turbine. Clearing the dust revealed only one new life form in the shape of a pale white fan with interlacing strands forming a broad tight mesh. Wind from the turbine ripped apart the first of these delicate fans before Fei Yen redirected the flow.

She approached the next fan organism with more care, lowering velocity and avoiding direct contact with her air stream. When Fei Yen had located and cleared the dust around the second fan without destroying it, Aiden approached the organism and knelt beside it.

The lace work of crossing strands created a layered triangular pattern with such symmetry to make an artist weep. Structural scans revealed the same unusual elements pervasive on this planet. Aiden magnified his visor to microscopic resolution. Tiny, clear tendrils surrounded pores on the surface of crisscrossing rods and strands forming the fan's surface. Aiden watched as the tendrils snagged a passing bacterium and carried it along with haste, handing the microbe from one clutch of tendrils to another before stuffing the bacterium into a pore. Aiden detected an oxygen signature in the microbe before it disappeared. Several plump bacteria floated past, beyond the reach of ensnaring tendrils. Most tendrils spent more time sweeping off dust particles than capturing food. The fan, blind to the world and receiving only what chance brought its way, existed passive. Aiden watched, unaware of time, as life happened to the creature.

Devya approached him. "Is that edible?" she asked.

"No." Aiden stood.

Devya raised her boot and stomped on the fan. With the sound of brittle bones snapping, the delicate creature splintered into a myriad of shards. "It's worthless. Let's move on."

Aiden looked down at the shattered pieces under Devya's foot, then to her visored face. Anger welled within him. She stared at him expressionless. He found no regret for destroying beauty, no remorse for hurting the vulnerable. Devya showed nothing except numbness to the creature's fate. Aiden shook with the effort to restrain his fists. "Respect life."

Devya said nothing and returned to the others. Aiden joined them a moment later, standing with as many people between him and Devya as possible.

"We've got a potential water source; redeploy to food search," said Akamoto.

"Anyone see a side of baby back ribs lying around?" asked Chavez.

Aiden looked up. "My gut tells me if we're going to find food, it's up there." He jerked his thumb toward the canopy.

"Why?" asked Akamoto.

"This dust layer is inhospitable. I suspect only specialist species thrive near the ground, like that filter feeder fan, desiccant bugs, and probably some predators. Everything else will likely live above the layer."

The group looked up at the canopy rising a kilometer above them. The cloud of dust Fei Yen had stirred still hung heavy in the air. Massive trunks rose and disappeared in that errant cloud, pillars of the sky shrouded in mystery. At that moment, with all eyes straining to fathom the upper reaches, a desperate cry rang out in the distance then abruptly fell silent.

"What made that noise?" Fei Yen stepped closer to Akamoto.

"I'm more concerned about what stopped the cry," said Akamoto. "Stay alert, people. Until you determine something's edible, assume you're the meal."

"I hope other food tastes better than me," said Chavez. "Stop standing around with jacked necks. Prepare to climb."

Aiden walked over to a tree. He removed a gauntlet and touched the bark. The tree's surface felt smooth and shifted slightly like skin.

Fei Yen came up beside him and touched the bark with her fingers. "Suction will hold better than traction."

Aiden nodded in agreement.

"I'll tell the others." Fei Yen moved off to share the insight.

Aiden formed new surface layers for his exoskeleton's hands and feet. The new layers flexed and stuck to the smooth tree trunk when pressed against it.

"I want one person per tree. We'll search more effectively spread out, but no further than one tree apart," said Akamoto.

Aiden started to climb, vaguely aware of the others starting their ascents. The immense girth of the tree filled his vision and disoriented him. Aiden closed his eyes and pressed his head against the trunk to overcome vertigo. He moved on when his mind stopped spinning. After he had ascended several hundred meters above the settling dust cloud, a glance down stirred dizziness, forcing him to hold in place until equilibrium returned.

The tree blocked Aiden's view of the others. When he craned his neck backwards he caught glimpses of a climber off his left quarter. Beyond that, only a proximity map and vital signs linked him to the team. The mob of glowing blue eyes hovering in the shadows followed him up the tree.

Aiden raised an altimeter reading in his visor's heads-up display, five hundred thirty meters with a climb ahead of him to the lowest branch. A shaft of light opened against the trunk above him. As he climbed toward the brightness a shadow passed over and dulled the light. Aiden looked upward over his shoulder.

A translucent, purple, oblong sphere the size of a watermelon floated above him in the shaft of light. He stopped climbing and studied the object closely. The purple thing remained motionless, suspended in the beam of light. At long intervals, when the creature drifted from the light, one of the many deep blue fins crossing its body lengthwise undulated, moving the creature back into the light. At each end of the body a sphincter clamped shut.

Aiden scanned the creature's composition. An unidentified gas at nine times the concentration of ambient air filled the hollow interior. *I wonder if this little blimp tastes like a watermelon.*

Aiden pulled a large, lightweight sack from his pack and edged closer to the creature. The thing ignored his approach if it sensed movement. Aiden reached out tentatively with the bag open. He feared falling as much as snaring this strange floating orb. When the bag reached over the creature enough to cast a shadow the blue fins started to wave. With a jerk of his arm, Aiden pulled the bag over the creature and back to him, using his free hand to steady himself.

The bag, hanging by Aiden's side, weighed the creature down. A faint rasping sound of fins moving against the polymer of the bag served as the only protest Aiden detected. Looking up the shaft of light, Aiden saw more oblong purple spheres. Smaller spheres arrived with one or the other sphincter open, chasing light. Larger ones moved out of the sunlight to float in the shade. The biggest group basked in the sunbeam. All of them floated too far away for Aiden to reach, so he continued upward.

He came to the first branch just below seven hundred meters and walked out on the limb. The term 'branch' applied loosely to a tree limb capable of holding three people widthwise, arms stretched fingertips to fingertips. Aiden looked around; fascination trounced fear and vertigo. A network of branches intertwined to varying degrees as far as he could see in any direction. Orange leaves the size of dinner plates sprouted everywhere. The leaves moved slightly, not in unison as when disturbed by wind, but individually as if each tree positioned its leaves to capture the most sunlight.

Aiden scowled. Dust covered every leaf and branch—a finer and lighter dust than below. As he stepped out on the branch, the dust stuck to his XO legs. He scanned the particles. The dust at this elevation, as well as the tree, held a slight electric charge. *Great. Sticky dust.*

Aiden looked out at the adjacent tree as he collected a handful of leaves. He saw Chip's figure making the second branch of his tree.

"Aiden, I see what looks like lichen. Should I collect it?" Chip asked.

"Yeah, it may be edible. Judging by the looks of things, we can't be too picky."

"No worries. I'll just add some fresh chopped shallots, a sprig of parsley, simmer in aged merlot for three minutes. No better way to wake up the palate, mate."

"Uh, Chip? We have no fresh shallots, no aged merlot and, brace yourself, no sprigs of parsley," Fei Yen said.

"Way to crush my dreams, Lin. Way to—"

"Hey, globs of flema knock off the chatter! Let me explain you this. Keep the link clear during ops for mission critical com only. Claro?" said Chavez.

"Did she just call me a glob of phlegm?" Chip asked in a whisper.

"Yeah, the green and yellow kind. Fei Yen and I are clear phlegm," Aiden answered also whispering.

"Ew." Chip tried to shake off the image.

"True story," said Fei Yen.

"How come I still hear you seeping boils?"

At the first fork of the third branch up on Aiden's tree, he found a large green flower nestled in the crook of the fork. Like the tree from which it grew, everything about the flower was oversized. Seven large petals curved outward from the base, each the size of a beach towel. The flower center consisted of a tight cocoon of petals twisting into a green whipped cream peak—the pistil, Aiden guessed. The flower possessed an alien beauty. He breathed deeply hoping for a hint of rose or trace of lilac, something to connect the strange with the familiar. He smelled nothing but the musk of human marinating in an XO.

Aiden leaned against the trunk to scan the flower. A blur of motion to the right drew his attention. An animal the size of a small dog glided down to the flower from an upper branch of an adjacent tree. The creature glided on ribbed membranes connecting the tips of three opposed digits on each arm to the end of a long serpentine body. The animal landed by the flower. Large, gray eyes surveyed the area with an efficient precision that Aiden surmised had developed with experience.

What did it look for? What danger lurked for the unwary?

When the creature's eyes turned to Aiden, it stopped scanning and raised itself from a suction pad at the base of its tail. Membrane covered openings above the eyes flared and contracted. It stared motionless. The stillness of sorting threat from curiosity caught Aiden's breath. Heartbeats amplified by adrenaline pulsed in his ear.

Without further recognition, the animal shifted its attention to the flower. The tail curved forward and a hooked spike emerged from the tip. The spike picked something yellow and oblong from a cluster on its back. Smooth, continuous curving forward brought the animal's body vertical in what Aiden thought resembled a handstand. In a quick thrust, the tail deposited its yellow package into the pistil.

That delivery appeared to be the entirety of what the creature wished to accomplish, for when complete, it lowered, rotated on its basal suction and moved with an astonishingly fast, lunging gallop up the tree. Aiden scrambled after the creature but struggled to keep within eyeshot. The animal moved from branch to branch and tree to tree with phenomenal agility.

"Haven, what're you doing? Stay with us," Akamoto ordered.

Damn those proximity maps. "I won't go far. I'm tracking a creature."

"Leave it. Remain with the group."

Aiden ignored the command. He leaped gaps that tested the adhesion limits of his XO, moving further from his team. When the animal glided over a ten-meter gap to a branch below on an adjacent tree, he abandoned the chase.

Panting, Aiden waited and watched for the animal to ricochet into the jungle of branches. It did not. Instead, he watched the creature follow the same pattern of precision surveying as it moved up the branch to a large black ball in the crook of the tree limb. This time the animal raised its body. It opened its mouth to expose a single saber tooth that unfolded outward from the top of its mouth. With deft strokes the animal carved off slices of the ball in front of it. A modest layer of yellow flesh inside the black rind contained a water signature. *It showed me fruit!* The animal sucked and slurped at the flesh until none remained. It tossed the rind off the branch and continued feeding on the fruit, gradually exposing a smooth gray seed.

Before the animal finished feeding on the fruit, other movement on its branch caught Aiden's attention. A green flower emerged from the far side of the branch. The flower crawled down the branch on leaves that undulated like a caterpillar. This second flower looked identical to the first except for the second flower's smaller size and its movement, which made the flower the oddest thing Aiden had seen in a day filled with oddities.

The creature did not share Aiden's scientific curiosity. When it spied the new flower creeping closer, the animal flattened against the branch, hissed menacingly, and leaped off without glancing toward its destination.

Mental note to self – some flowers are evil.

Aiden turned to head back toward the group. As he walked back to the trunk, the surface of the branch became uneven with ripples and bulges, like muscles in a great forearm awakening.

"Something's happening to my tree," Akamoto called over the link.

The branch under Aiden started to sway.

Chavez responded, "Mine's starting to move."

Aiden wobbled with the increasing intensity and speed of the branch's swing. He dropped and hugged, but even at forty meters from the trunk the limb's girth exceeded his arm span. Nothing presented a handhold. His hug must hold.

"The tree's trying to shake me off!" cried Chip.

"Lie down and hold tight to your branch, Chip. Keep your center of gravity as close to the tree as possible," said Fei Yen. "That's your best—Ow! What? . . . Oh . . . mmmm." Fei Yen's voice trailed to silence.

Hair prickled on the back of Aiden's neck. "Fei Yen, what happened?"

Fei Yen didn't respond. The branch swung harder. Aiden held tighter.

"Fei Yen! Answer me!" The urgency of his own plight heightened his concern for her.

Seizures racked the forest. Aiden's body whipped back and forth, up and down; he held tighter. Mighty branches smacked each other. Great booms rolled. His muscles burned; tendons tensioned until nothing remained, and still Aiden fought to endure. Physics and physiology ignored his struggle. Collapse began with shaking fingers and toes; tremors cascaded through his body; panic erased thought; numbness followed. Arms and legs mashed hands and feet against bark. He slid. Aiden jammed his chin down to brake, but he slid faster down the branch. His body moved toward open air. A fork in the limb arrested him. The branch whipped upward tossing Aiden toward the trunk. The branch swung downward. Aiden's motion reversed. He hit the fork hard. Aiden flailed his legs—desperation feeling the end. Legs twisted along the split branch. The forks gyrated. Thigh bones popped. Pain seared joints. Hips cracked. The branch . . . held.

The shaking ceased with an abrupt stop. Aiden lay contorted on the limb, unmoving save for the heave of his chest as his lungs and heart pumped oxygen back into his body. With time, feeling returned to Aiden's limbs. Pain and fatigue dominated his senses. Aiden reached back to unwind first one leg then the other. His legs prickled from low blood flow and his knees and hips complained, but his bones remained in their sockets. His XO had prevented dislocation injuries. Aiden crawled to the trunk and sat leaning against the now stable surface.

He looked out at the forest canopy. Something was odd. For a moment, the change escaped him. Then, as he searched from tree to tree, Aiden realized dust no longer coated everything. The leaves flashed a brilliant orange, free of gray tinge. Branches stretched naked into air. The light seemed dimmer, though. Aiden looked up. High above the canopy a cloud of dust filled the sky and hung ominously. Aiden's focus shifted between the trees and sky.

Had the trees shaken to rid themselves of dust? Toss it up and hope the dust falls on your neighbor? Recognition jerked Aiden's head back. *I think I almost died because a tree decided to take a bath!*

This last thought brought the others to mind.

"Is everyone ok?" Aiden asked.

"What happened?" asked Chip.

"Team, sound off status. Akamoto operational."

"Chavez operational."

"This is Haven. I'm battered, but ok."

"I'm shaken and stirred. Other than that, I guess I'm all right. This is Chip."

The link fell silent. Aiden engaged augmented reality and pulled the team's stats and locations. Fei Yen's blood pressure read low and her pulse raced. Brain activity looked odd and her blood cell count was dropping rapidly. Her location signal indicated she lay motionless below him about two trees over. A good distance separated both Fei Yen and him from the others. She had followed Aiden when he broke off from the group. Devya showed signs of distress; however, her position signal lay near Akamoto.

"I'm getting bad readings from both Fei Yen and Devya." Aiden noted their locations. "Fei Yen is closest to me. I'm heading for her now."

"Chavez, assist Haven with Lin. Nelson, you're with me. We'll go get Kandari."

Aiden moved onto the trunk. Every muscle and tendon in his arms and legs complained. His hips and knees felt bludgeoned. Joints cracked. He needed to rest. Instead, he made his way toward Fei Yen one handhold and foothold at a time. Aiden struggled most with branch-to-branch transitions. He wobbled when he stood and fell forward when he reached. The pure mechanical adhesion of his feet and hands saved him from a fall twice.

Breathing became harder. Aiden's lungs ached with the strain of intake. He felt smothered, suffocated — dizzy. He fumbled for the helmet release. *Where did it go? Why won't it open? Get off!* He clawed at his faceplate. A release of air pushed into his body. He clawed again, more air. He inhaled through pain. As oxygen restored him, Aiden realized the newly airborne dust had collected on the intake filter of his helmet, blocking his breath. He had to divert precious time to clearing the filter. By the time he crawled onto Fei Yen's branch, Aiden saw Chavez approaching.

Fei Yen lay prone farther out on the limb. He started to crawl toward her and stopped. Her arms and legs splayed limp on the branch. Green vines encircled her body, holding her fast. Aiden's heart pounded harder. Three of the wandering green flowers, like the one that creature had fled, sat next to Fei Yen. Pinkish tendrils extended from the flowers to Fei Yen's body. A fourth flower made its way down the branch toward her.

This is bad.

The fourth flower reversed directions and headed back toward Aiden when he started to crawl out on the branch.

Damn. What do I do now?

Aiden remained motionless for a moment while the flower crawled closer.

My gun, I have a gun!

Aiden fumbled for the standard issue particle pistol stowed on his thigh. The flower moved less than three meters from him now.

Come on, come on! Pop out! Where's the latch?

Blind groping and the small click of a release presented the weapon to Aiden. Kneeling, he drew and aimed. The targeting hologram in his visor made erratic leaps from the approaching flower, to the branch, to Fei Yen and back again.

What did they say in pre-flight training about shooting? Do I breathe and squeeze or squeeze, aim and breathe? No, that makes no sense! How do I get the target painting to stay on target? Ok, concentrate. I'm not going to shoot her. I'm not going to shoot her.

Aiden fired. A chunk of branch to the left of the flower disappeared in a small explosion. The branch whipped to the side, reacting as if the tree felt pain. Aiden lost his balance and grabbed for the branch. The gun fell silently to the forest floor.

He looked up. At eye level, barely a meter from his head, the flower moved steadily toward him. The green petals unfurled and a white tendril rose from the top of the flower. The tendril, tipped with a point sharpened to invisibility, bullwhipped toward him. In a final sharp snap, the tendril shot forward. The hypodermic tip bounced off Aiden's helmet armor. The white strand collapsed to the branch in front of him. The broken tip of the fine needle lay a few centimeters from his face. Clear liquid dripped to the branch from the strand. Aiden pressed a finger to the drop and collected a sample with surface receptors in the XO fingertip. The plant withdrew the tendril as two more rose from the flower.

"Hold your position!"

Chavez's bark never sounded sweeter. Green exploded in Aiden's face. He blinked instinctively despite the protective visor. When he opened his eyes the flower no longer existed.

"If I fire on the rest, I'll hit Lin."

Aiden pulled the pistol compartment off his thigh. "My grandfather always said there's nothing quite as satisfying as hacking up a weed." He set his particle former and destabilized the pistol box for raw material then reset the machine and created a machete. Charged with a shot of adrenaline, Aiden surged forward and swung at the flower near Fei Yen's head. The stroke fell true. The flower cleaved in half. Red blood splattered over Fei Yen and the branch.

Aiden gagged. Blood pulsed out of the severed ends of two tendrils that had found a gap in Fei Yen's armor. Aiden fought the waves pushing upward within him. He yanked at the tubes, ripping them from her neck.

A grappling cable caught the branch beyond Fei Yen. Chavez swung up and landed solidly behind the motionless body. Chavez's bayonet carved the second flower in two. Aiden finished the third with his knife. Blood splattered. The deed was done. Blood, human blood, coated the branch and Fei Yen's body. Aiden turned away and retched.

"Get the white vines off of her. Leave the green vines to hold her." Aiden panted and swallowed while tapping rapidly on his particle former. "I'll collect her blood. We must save her carbon."

Chavez moved fast without argument. Aiden used his former to reclaim Fei Yen's blood that hadn't dripped from the tree. She had lost a lot of blood judging by her ashen skin and rapid, erratic pulse. He regained only a portion of her carbon. Aiden executed emergency field transfusion protocols in his former and within minutes injected Fei Yen's sterilized, filtered and reconstituted blood cells back into her body. The transfusion helped stabilize her heart rate and raise her blood pressure. She shook uncontrollably soon after. Her body heaved. Aiden struggled with her helmet, removing it just before she cleared her stomach.

"What's happening to her?" Chavez asked.

Aiden held up a hand. Fei Yen, lying in her own vomit, coughed and moaned.

"Chavez, report," Akamoto ordered over link.

"Stand by; we're dealing with an issue."

"Where are my flowers?" Fei Yen's voice sounded weak.

Chavez and Aiden looked at each other.

"The flowers are dead Fei Yen. You're safe now." Aiden pulled Fei Yen's matted hair off her face.

Convulsions seized Fei Yen's body. The vines restrained jerks and shaking. Her voice, barely above a whisper, grew hoarse with urgency. "No! I need them. Bring them back. I need them. Please, bring them back. Please."

"What the hell is she talking about?" Chavez clutched her rifle tighter like a small child grasps a stuffed animal for comfort.

Aiden examined his XO's preliminary scan of the sample he had collected. "I'm not positive, but I think the plants injected a powerful narcotic before draining her blood. If so, she's started withdrawal."

"You mean those plants made her high?"

"Yes. My guess is they immobilize and take away their victim's will to fight by using a highly addictive drug."

"A drug overcame her nanobot defenses?" The rifle barrel pressed into the side of Chavez's neck.

"Her nanobots should've destroyed any unnecessary drugs entering her blood stream. Because they missed the flower's drug, I suspect that substance is unknown on Earth. Nanobots ignore new compounds that mimic our own proteins for safety reasons."

"But how come the bots let her bleed out like that?"

"We'll have to talk to a doctor for that answer," said Aiden.

"Yeah, and get an upgrade for these nanobots rapidamente." Chavez opened her link. "Akamoto, we've got a person down. We'll have to abort and evac."

"Roger that. We have to evac as well. Kandari fell about twenty meters before another branch caught her. She's broken three or four bones. The nanobots are already working on her."

"Understood, we'll regroup at ground level."

10

Progress

Aiden woke from dream-filled sleep and joined the others for breakfast in the cargo bay. The group was larger now. He looked over the people they had awakened; people with skills essential to survival and others in failing chambers. They ate in scattered groups around the cargo bay, leaning against walls, sitting on the deck, using crates as makeshift tables.

Chip handed him a plate heaped with food and served with a bright smile. Aiden stumbled as he reached for the plate. Faster than an instant, something had flashed in Chip's eyes. Perhaps a reflection caught Aiden's attention; he questioned whether he had seen the glimmer. Aiden shook off the impression—nothing of note . . . except the color. For a moment, Chip's eyes had shone a deep alien blue.

"Is something wrong mate?" Chip frowned as he looked at Aiden's food.

Aiden fumbled a recovery. "No, nothing's wrong. Thanks for the grub." He gave Chip a half-hearted smile as he turned to find a spot to sit for his meal.

People had already started their meal, a mixture of freeze-dried rations brought from Earth and native edible plants foraged in sorties. Aiden welcomed the addition of fresh edible plants, tested by the group's newly revived chemist and doctor. He ate while he walked. The tastes, unusual mixes of savory, sweet, sour, salty, and bitter, sometimes embraced and blended and at other times popped to the surface individually, like a bubble escaping a boil. Tastes, combined with aromas, created flavors that whirled in intricate and shifting patterns as he chewed. Aiden succumbed to this new world's culinary charms without needing a push by anemic, freeze-dried dust from home.

Their resident civil engineer, Christie Winters, made room atop a small box and motioned for Aiden to join her and the colony's chemist, Dagur Lok. Christie presented a biological paradox. Aiden preferred to watch a person's face when they spoke because eyes reveal truth that words hide. Christie's face had close-set, uneven eyes; a beaked nose; and a thin upper lip that formed a permanent pout above a melting chin. In isolation, none of her facial features offended, however, Aiden felt the spacing and arrangement of this collection was unfortunate. During what he guessed were light moods, Christie faced the world. When dark moods set in, she shielded her face from onlookers' grimaces with long hair and strategic head tilts. The sources of her negative feelings escaped Aiden but revealed their presence in her hidden face. Christie avoided direct facial views frequently enough that Aiden wondered why she chose her birth mask over a replacement. Yet, he occasionally found himself next to her. She flaunted a stare-trapping figure that flattened in comparison with her voice, a voice that lured mortals to servitude. Aiden engaged Christie in conversations and purposefully distracted himself when her interest peaked because the woman exceled at reclaiming attention, pressing her breasts against his arm and whispering in his ear. As he picked his way through the group toward Christie, Aiden missed the sag in Rachel's shoulders and her frown when he passed.

Dagur noticed Aiden after fifteen minutes of animated chatter between Christie and Aiden. "Velkominn. The osmotic resonance filter extracts thirty liters per minute now." Dagur beamed. "Dásamlegur flutningur!" Then remembering himself, "Wonderful performance!"

Dagur's tone suggested the chemist intended the comment for his own pleasure rather than a progress report. "That's great. I worried when we found no water table."

Christie Winters nodded. "You and me both. The bedrock here is unlike anything on Earth . . . well, actually, it resembles the shale formations that contain natural gas," she mused. "But only if you squint real hard. The rock here traps water with incredible tensile strength. Quite odd indeed." She admired Dagur. "Your combination of shockwaves at the rock's resonance frequency and a dust-filled well shaft as an osmotic filter is brilliant."

Dagur glanced at Christie and looked away in modesty. He continued to smile at himself.

Commander Walker strode into the cargo bay. "At ease," he said, missing that no one had moved to stand at attention. "We need to locate a site for the colony where development avoids conflict." He spoke to no one and everyone.

"Why? It's a simple matter of displaying our fire power and superior intellect. Those creatures will run away frightened. The planet is ours to improve." Devya Kandari's words rolled with a boredom suggesting obviousness. Her arms swept wide in a grand gesture of possession.

"There's a large clear plain at the foot of a mountain range due Northwest of here. I saw it just before we landed," Rachel offered, ignoring Devya.

"Does Walker ever eat?" Chavez whispered to Utungua.

"No," Utungua shot back in a quiet conspiratorial tone.

"We could build there without inciting the natives, assuming appropriate ground conditions, water permeation, and such and such," Christie offered with an academic helpfulness that belied the practicality of a civil engineer. She leaned back against a stack of boxes. Her thumbs hooked out of her pants pockets while the other fingers hid. Christie's feet locked her ankles for protection.

"Ruiz and Lin, can you form craft to shuttle us to the plains?" asked Walker.

"That depends on the material I have to work with," said Eduardo Ruiz.

Ruiz, trained in aeronautical engineering, struck Aiden as an absolutist who believed things either possessed a purpose and a place or held no value. Aiden estimated Ruiz's hair alignment required an hour and a pot of glue. Ruiz expressed no vanity in his appearance; to the contrary, his jumpsuit lacked the color of Christie's clothes or the style of Fei Yen's but also the imprecise fit of Aiden's. For Ruiz, a stray hair must have seemed deviant.

"What have you discovered about these elements Dagur?" asked Ruiz

"The particles display interesting properties indeed. One element is stronger and lighter than graphene. Another appears to be a superconductor at ambient temperature." Dagur slipped into a monotonic chant. "A third is —"

Walker interrupted, "So can we use them?" He showed no patience for details deemed non-essential to achieve his goal.

"Yes." Ruiz rescued the startled Dagur who struggled to grasp Walker's disinterest in the discoveries.

"Heck yeah, we can use 'em! These new elements will make our aircraft lighter, stronger, faster and more efficient than anything we had on Earth with new designs impossible before," Fei Yen interjected. Her words spilled quickly as she bounced with ideas.

Walker became more interested. "Can you build spacecraft?"

"Ye —"

"Slow down Fei Yen," said Ruiz. "We've got a lot of work to do. Aiden proved the formers manipulate these elements in a crude way, but precision formation will require fine tuning the devices. We'll use conventional Earth designs for now. Time for improvements comes later." While he spoke, Ruiz unfastened his left cuff restraint, reattached it in the same spot, placed his hands in pockets, opened and closed the right restraint, and then started the sequence anew. With each movement, Ruiz repositioned the psychological boundary between habit and compulsion.

Fei Yen clenched her chest, but stayed quiet.

In answer to Walker's question, Dagur added, "I see nothing that will provide an acceptable fuel substitute for near-lightspeed engines. Power cells, yes. Space travel, no."

Satisfied, Walker moved on. "How long will it take to get a small craft ready to transport a recon team of four to the site?"

"With no glitches, about a week," answered Ruiz.

"A week?" asked Dr. Khabir Stein. "You must work harder. Failed suspension chambers force more colonists into premature revival each day." He jabbed his thumb toward the spaceship's passenger decks. Flesh wobbled on his disturbed arm.

Ruiz's eyes narrowed. He set his chin low and tightened his voice. "We're dealing with completely new materials here, Doctor. We're going to use those materials to build a complex device that, if it fails, will take lives. Quality work requires adequate rest. We'll take as long as we need to finish the job right."

"We've all got a lot to do here and we've got to get it done quickly," Dr. Stein rejoined. Anger rose in his voice. The doctor's spine curved over his paunch into a protective slouch.

"Enough. Ruiz has the week. The rest of the group will need time to prepare as well. We're all going to have to build everything anew. We will work together on this." Walker shot a harsh look at Dr. Stein, who grumbled quietly to himself.

"Tomorrow will be better." Dagur laid a soft hand on Dr. Stein's shoulder, who rebuffed the gesture.

Devya Kandari stepped close to Rachel and Commander Walker, invading their personal space. Rachel and Walker parted unconsciously seeking a comfortable distance. Devya inserted herself into the newly opened space on Walker's right. Once in place she raised her presence to the full affect her diminutive frame permitted. "We'll need a civilian government," she glanced at Commander Walker, "to deal with the day to day troublesome tasks of getting our new colony working with laws, regulations, essential governmental services, long term plans, et cetera."

Walker looked as if he had just swallowed raw seaweed three days past its prime.

Devya, emboldened by Walker's predicted reaction, continued, "I'll get working on the government structure right away."

Sensing a business opportunity, Ivan Harkov, an entrepreneur from the gray markets of Moscow, shook off a feigned indifference and stepped into the conversation. "I shall assist with supplying the colony. We will work together. Da?" Harkov exchanged smiles with Devya and the mutual recognition of potential allies.

"Hold on. Forming a government requires votes from the entire colony." Aiden asserted his distrust of Devya as much as his interest in preserving the procedural aspects of democracy.

"Of course, of course, I merely offer to help." Hard lines around Devya's narrowed eyes left no doubt about her feelings for Aiden.

Walker showed no interest in Devya's proposition or the reaction she elicited. "Ruiz, once you and Lin tune the formers to build aircraft, will they work for buildings and anything else we need?"

"Yes, the particle formers will make anything we want as long as we have the right ingredients."

"Good. Let's get to work people." Walker dispersed the group with a booming voice that overshadowed half-eaten meals and distracted side conversations popping up around the cargo bay.

Aiden watched Harkov approach Devya. Ivan Harkov was a big man with thick arms and legs that ended in hands and feet without the need for wrists and ankles. Despite his size, Harkov acted with crisp rapid movements. The man's composition, movement, and manner conveyed confident action.

"You will like my offer on food and other necessities when we agree on supply contracts for the colony." Harkov smiled with a direct look that neither Devya nor Aiden missed.

Harkov's polished pleasantness prickled the back of Aiden's neck with the sense of danger victims feel before a crime. Aiden, feeling rushed by everyone's hasty exit and slightly nauseated by Harkov and Devya, left the cargo bay determined to squelch their schemes.

The week passed quickly, not because Aiden's work enthralled him, but because a continuous string of mindless and essential tasks stole the time completely. Aiden, like everyone else, took part in foraging sorties that brought food to the colony's dwindling supplies. When he entered the forest after the first few trips, images of plants, fruits, seeds, even creatures floated through his mind like daydreams. Somehow he knew they were edible. The sorties became more efficient. Each trip brought larger volumes of food with greater diversity.

Soldiers escorted every sortie into the forest. Movement in shadows and shrill cries echoing off trees menaced the foragers. Guards fired at phantoms but hit nothing except fear. A realization grew among the colonists; they were being tested. People jostled for center positions in the sorties. Quarrels erupted over who had done their share of food gathering. Soldiers forced participation of colonists frightened they had become prey.

No further confrontations with the blue-eyed creatures occurred. The eyes kept their distance and watched. Lacking any further knowledge of the creatures save their glowing stare, the colonists came to call them Watchers. As foraging parties ventured into the forest the creatures separated and then surrounded the groups, always watching. The number of eyes watching declined as time passed. That self-conscious feeling of examination remained for most people. Aiden at times forgot until he did something awkward or embarrassing. Then the nagging tickle in the back of his mind blossomed forth into full awareness. Some, like Ivan Harkov, seemed indifferent to constant observation; others, like Dr. Stein, complained of being judged.

Equipment preparation consumed the bulk of Aiden's time. Ruiz hovered over the particle formers like a wolf protects its kill, hindering Aiden's progress. Christie and Aiden discussed testing protocols and planned survey methods. When the week ended, he stood outside the cargo bay with Christie, Rachel, and Utungua waiting to load equipment. Aiden felt ready and eager to begin building their new home.

The cargo bay door hiding the new craft cracked around the seam and began its slow groaning descent into the ever present cloud of dust hovering over the ground. Aiden waited, eager for his first glimpse of the ship Ruiz and Fei Yen had so jealously guarded. No one had been allowed inside the cargo bay the entire week. Ruiz even conducted test flights in secret.

Aiden glanced sideways at Rachel. The edges of her lips curled up with anticipation. Her fingers fluttered at her sides like an athlete warming up for a competition. Legs flexed, her body shifted back and forth. Aiden had watched her grow antsier all week. Her behavior confused him until one evening, reflecting in the colony's makeshift body cleanser, Aiden realized Rachel had been grounded since they landed. Ruiz's creation offered her first chance to fly again.

While Aiden admired her passion for moving like a bird, he caught a fleeting flicker of blue in her green eyes. The deep blue flash startled him just as it had when he had noticed the light in Chip. He looked again but saw nothing. Aiden shook it off. Perhaps her eyes reflected the aliens' gaze.

With indignant billows, dust made way for the heavy ramp, which settled with a final groan of relief. Rachel leaped onto the ramp before it touched ground and disappeared inside as Aiden stepped on the ramp. Moving from the bright light into the comparatively dark cargo bay, Aiden's eyes took a moment to adjust as they chased Rachel around the sleek ship. She glided one hand over its surface lightly caressing the smooth blackness. Her gaze followed the craft's lines picking apart the design.

Aiden had overheard the soldiers speak of Rachel's skill as a pilot and witnessed her capabilities when their starship landed. Now the movement in Rachel's face from objectivity to excitement inspired confidence in Ruiz's and Fei Yen's creation—a creation at once beautiful and powerful. Flowing lines of the fuselage melded into deep wings that in turn curled gracefully at the tips. The craft brought to mind a work of art instead of the utilitarian scout role the ship would serve.

"You open the ha—" Fei Yen started.

Rachel lifted the hatch before Fei Yen completed the instructions.

"The controls follow standard planetary glide—" Ruiz began.

Rachel activated the maglevs. The craft floated suspended silently a meter off the deck. Landing gear retracted as she clipped her harness.

Rachel smiled sweetly at Fei Yen and Ruiz, "The design is elegant. Thank you." Looking toward Christie, Utungua and Aiden, she chided, "What are you waiting for, sunset?"

Aiden and the others moved to load their gear lest Rachel launch without them. The craft's design emphasized speed and maneuverability with light armor, limited weaponry, and little hauling capacity (a good scout ship); so they packed equipment with care to fit everything. After a short delay, they closed the hatch door.

A soft whir accompanied Rachel's charge of the primary electromagnetic rams. As Aiden, Christie, and Utungua took their seats, the ship launched through the cargo bay into sunlight. Ruiz and Fei Yen dove for cover behind a tool bin as the ship's magnetic ram drives flung neatly ordered but unsecured tools and metallic parts across the cargo bay. Rachel pulled back hard on the yoke after she cleared the colony ship. The sudden onslaught of g-forces planted the occupants deep into their seats as the ship went nearly vertical.

"Tighten your harnesses. I'm going to test flight capabilities."

Aiden, who sat in the co-pilot's seat, looked back at the other two. Utungua with great effort strained against the g-forces to cinch his harness. Christie closed her eyes and gripped the sides of her seat. He smiled to reassure her, forgetting she shut out his face, and turned back to cinch his own harness.

As the ship hurtled toward the troposphere, Rachel executed a roll and brought the craft out of the climb upside down. This maneuver smoothly transitioned into a loop that ended as they went vertical again. They lost speed at a faster and faster rate until the craft became motionless, suspended vertically, a dozen kilometers above the ground. It hung there saluting space long enough for the passengers to hope the maneuvers had ended before sliding at an accelerating pace down the arc Rachel had just carved.

The nose dipped lazily down to the ground with a slowness that masked the speed at which they fell. As the nose dipped and the ship began to slide around on the air, Rachel engaged the engines sending the ship rocketing forward. She banked hard right to carve a horizontal arc through the sky, again sinking her passengers deep into their seats.

Rachel chopped the arc at ninety degrees and leveled the craft. Aiden, Christie and Utungua breathed a collective sigh of relief as the crushing pressure released them. Aiden looked at Rachel. Her face glowed and she flew focused on the space in front of the ship. Nothing else existed for her right now.

"Hold on," Rachel said as she opened the throttle.

Aiden grabbed a sharp breath at Rachel's warning. The craft shot forward at speeds impossible on Earth. The now too familiar invisible force of flight punched the air out of him.

"Oh, yeah!" said Rachel.

"Rachel!" Aiden's voice bounced off her enthusiasm. "Rachel!" he yelled. "That's enough!"

He broke through this time. Rachel eased off. The ship decelerated to a more comfortable speed.

Aiden glanced over at Rachel. She hungered for more with a fixed gaze and heavy breathing. Aiden looked back at the other two. Utungua sweat and panted. Christie had turned ghastly pale with wild-eyed fear and rapid swallows. Neither wanted more.

Aiden nodded to the two passengers behind them. "We've got to get to the site in working condition."

Rachel blushed like a modest woman who found herself standing naked in a public fountain. "Sorry." She apologized in an uncharacteristically meek voice.

"Forget it." Rachel's openness charmed Aiden into leniency that neither Christie nor Utungua would have granted.

The remainder of the flight to the plain passed with Rachel flying by protocol. Utungua relaxed into, what seemed to Aiden, a practiced indifference. Christie fought a brave battle to prevent a second and undesirable tasting of her breakfast. For Aiden's part, the continuous blur of tree tops passing, with the occasional eye lock on a random feature, consumed his inattention.

"Set us down a short walk from the forest, OK?" The command felt awkward to Aiden, who unaccustomed to giving orders, blunted the demand by forming a question.

"Roger," Rachel replied.

With a gentle puff of dust the scout ship nestled into the dust layer a quarter kilometer from the forest edge. Christie whipped out of the craft before Rachel powered down. Utungua, for all his nonchalance, followed closely, nearly stumbling on Christie. Both took a silent moment to savor the firm, still ground.

Aiden stepped out and scanned the plain. A sea of dust stretched beyond the limits of his vision. "Come on you two. Let's get to work. Daylight's burning."

"Yeah, perpetually," Christie rejoined.

Aiden and Christie broke out their testing equipment while Rachel tended to the ship. Aiden made note of blue eyes appearing in the dark shadows of the forest's edge. Their watchers had arrived. Utungua reached into the cargo hold and hefted out a large gun. He had a big "new toy" grin.

"What is that?" Christie asked with no small amount of surprise and apprehension.

"What's what?" Utungua feigned innocence with his eyebrows.

"That thing you're holding . . . that . . . that cannon," said Christie.

"It's standard issue damsel defense weaponry." Utungua winked and moved toward a guard position.

"You're so full of it Mwara Utungua," Rachel called from the cockpit. She poked her head out. "Don't worry, Christie. You'll be safe as long as you stand directly in front of him."

"Pay no heed." Utungua cracked his neck from side to side and brought the weapon to his shoulder. "She's jealous of sweet, sweet Emily." He nodded briefly toward the gun as he swept the horizon with the barrel; eye focused through the site.

Christie put down her test instruments. With a wicked smile she stepped toward Utungua. Christie's walk had a rhythm—the sway and glide of a predator stalking prey. At once, Aiden felt drawn to her and wary. His instincts called to him. Her movement signaled danger; he knew that somehow. He looked to Utungua who watched Christie now. He felt an urge to warn Utungua, but saw in the soldier's face what Aiden felt. Aiden's gaze shifted back to Christie with interest. Rachel's muffled snickering flicked at the edges of his attention.

"I'm so glad you're here Utungua, with your big gun to protect me." Christie's purr amplified the impact of her moves. Her head tilted down to a demure angle; her hair swept over half her face and shaded the rest. "You're so strong, so big and strong." As Christie reached Utungua she slid her ivory hand over his tensed forearm, curved over his flexed bicep and lingered on his thick muscled shoulder perhaps longer than she had intended. "Oooh," she cooed as she felt his muscles. "Have you been working out?"

The mock innocence in her question cracked the two women's composure. They both fractured into riotous laughter simultaneously—Rachel collapsing into the pilot's seat, Christie doubling over in front of Utungua in a gush before stumbling back to her equipment. For Utungua's part, the rich black tone of his cheeks tinged a delicate red. He turned away from everyone, ostensibly to check the particle canon.

"Women!" Aiden picked up test equipment in a show of moving on.

Utungua said nothing. He raised his shoulders as he hunched over the weapon.

The excitement ended when Christie and Aiden launched into a series of tests on random plots in a half a kilometer radius around the ship. Repetition stoked boredom. Send a probe into the ground for water density measurement. Withdraw probe. Collect soil sample. Collect dust sample. Collect air sample. Measure radiation. Calibrate equipment. Locate and move to the next plot. Send a probe. Collect samples. Calibrate.

"I detect deep groundwater locked in rock like at the crash site although in smaller quantities here. Still, enough water exists for a colony," Aiden said.

"Good. Let's keep sampling," said Christie.

Aiden's mind drifted after he measured the first three plots. He dreamed of hiking the distant mountains. These peaks towered like none on Earth. Untouched by erosive wind or rain, hard angles and sheer drops bore witness to the violence that had ruptured the planet's surface and thrust stone into the upper atmosphere. Giant opaque crystal shards, unyielding and impenetrable, summoned Aiden's wanderlust. He conjured up strange high-elevation life forms this planet might sustain — like moss that moved to stay in the shade and lichen that ate rock. Then Rachel hiked with him. He imagined he caught her before she fell into a deep crevasse. He forgot his sampling, made mistakes, and repeated his work.

All the while, Utungua shadowed them. He kept them between him and the ship. He stood apart enough to be left alone, but close enough to act and always facing the world.

"So, what's your story?" Aiden asked Christie. He wanted to blunt the dirty looks she threw at him when he made mistakes. Her siren's song struck a cruel chord when she lashed out. Perhaps telling her story would distract Christie.

"What do you mean?"

"Where do you hale from? What did you do on Earth? Why did you join the Emigration Effort? You know — all the stuff that makes you, you."

"Oh, ok." Christie took a deep breath, "I grew up in Wales near Elerch. Studied philosophy at Edinburgh. Taught it in a Hong Kong high school. I like chocolate and the color blue in the morning. Capricorn. Decided the world had too few short buildings, so I went to Rio de Janeiro to design them — better beaches. Hit my head stepping off a bus and woke up with a law degree from Harvard. That achievement sentenced me to eleven months forced labor in litigation before parole to civil engineering. Toss in a couple of engineering firms and that brings me here." She smiled at Aiden politely.

Aiden turned away and mouthed a "wow" out of Christie's view. He wondered what happened to selective disclosure.

"Ok, I gotta get more." Aiden figured a jumble of questions might kick-start her story. "Why did you move from philosophy to architecture? England to China to Brazil to America? What made you dive into law and then escape to civil engineering? And what about emigration caused you to leave?"

"You really want the long version?" Christie raised a skeptical eyebrow.

"You've piqued my interest," Aiden smiled warmly.

"Well, I studied philosophy in school because I thought the topic interesting and helpful for discovering meaning in my life. I'm good with logic and numbers; so when I graduated, the jobs available to me included investment banking or teaching philosophy abroad. The sound of 'Christie Winters, Junior Investment Banking Associate,' made me ill. That's what brought me to China — avoidance turned to engagement. Traveling the world yielded new experiences."

"Uh-huh."

"After a couple of years teaching, I felt unsatisfied. Don't get me wrong. Teaching enriches people, especially teaching philosophy to high school students. Teenagers hunger for direction more than anyone else on the planet . . . I mean Earth. But I left teaching kids to people better suited for that calling. I wanted to do something else. You know?"

"Mm, hmm."

"Architecture fascinates me. I love the way a well-designed building captures light and makes you feel better when you're inside. So I went to Rio to earn a degree in architecture."

"Yeah."

"Are you listening?"

"Uh-huh."

"Rio offered a fun place to learn and work as an architect while experiencing a different culture." Christie paused with a fond expression.

The silence made Aiden nervous. He thought maybe he'd missed a question. "What?"

"What?"

"I mean, go on. Did you design any buildings?" Aiden fumbled visibly with his equipment, dodging her gaze.

"Yep . . . well, I thought I would design buildings; and I guess I did, as part of a team," she said. "Junior architects rarely earn lead design responsibilities. You have to either pay your dues or get discovered and become a star. It's hard to stand out and the pay is low. After a while I found myself wanting to live better—not extravagant, just better. I also got tuned into the social injustices poor people experience. I endured a lot of bigotry because of my empty purse. People assume all sorts of things about your schooling, your intelligence, your character. Like I lacked an essential part of a good human being, you know?" Christie searched Aiden's face for something.

"Uh, huh . . . Wait, what did you say?"

"I said you look like a dumb jock with the attention span of a gnat."

"Don't be like that. Why do you look to other people to measure your worth?" Aiden saw her pain well enough to evoke sympathy without understanding.

Christie looked shocked. "What do you mean?"

"You implied the judgments other people made about your intelligence and character had a negative impact on you. Did I get that right?" Aiden wondered whether the shock in her face rose from his question or from his possessing even the slightest idea of what she spoke about.

"Well, yes, of course their judgments hurt." Christie's movements became short twitches.

"My question remains why. A person's negative thoughts about you cause no harm unless you let them — unless you accept being a victim."

"That's not true!" Christie's face reddened. She stopped sampling to confront Aiden. "I rejected people's treatment of me, but their cruelty extended beyond contemptuous glances at my clothes. I've been ignored by salespeople in stores. In Rio, my landlord charged me a higher rent on my flat because she thought me a credit risk despite having never missed a payment, ever. All those things would have happened even if I ignored the attitudes."

"I agree," said Aiden; "but those actions mean nothing more than bad behavior on their part — not a moral statement about you. The difference lies in the impact on you."

Christie stood silently for a moment before beginning again. "No. Those acts were the wrong way to treat someone, whether I accepted them or not. People shouldn't hurt other people. I wanted to stop them. I thought law offered both a comfortable living and an opportunity to correct wrongs against the poor. Unfortunately, law firms earn nothing on pro bono work and limit time for volunteering. Practicing law made me miserable."

Aiden thought Christie's response consistent with his position on victims; instead of arguing with her, he chose an easier turn in the conversation. "Wasn't that something to figure out ahead of time? Law school seems like a big investment to throw away." Aiden winced inwardly after the words slipped out. He had stumbled into her mine field where every step risked explosion.

"Sure, I talked to people. Half of them warned me to stay far away from law; the other half described a wonderful career. I hoped my coin would land heads up." Christie's answer clipped out with the speed of well-polished thought. "Anyway, when I practiced law I found myself on the wrong side. After the fantasy of pursuing justice faded, thankless drudgery beset me as a junior associate."

"Oh," Aiden proffered a subdued recognition. Christie's story hit too close. He wanted to change the subject, to be done with the discouragement and wasted effort. Christie also appeared reluctant to continue, but a story requires closure once begun. He offered her an opportunity, "So is that why you signed on to the Emigration Effort — to get away from your circumstances on Earth?"

She hesitated, "Why . . . sort of." Christie placed her hand on the side of her mouth to cover her voice. "I'm here for the same reason everyone else is, really." She looked from side to side as if checking for someone standing close enough to overhear.

Aiden instinctively stepped closer. Utungua stood a detached distance and stared intently toward the horizon.

"You know, the Singularity," she said lowering her voice and leaning toward Aiden. She straightened. "Odd to think Armageddon passed and we exist. A changed Earth spins in space now — a graveyard."

"You believe that?"

"Yeah. Don't you? Everyone knows what happened; only no one wants to talk about it. I understand. I feel sad thinking of my family and all their descendants dead."

Aiden grew irritated at her narrow absoluteness. He disliked arguing, but struggled to hold his tongue. As he stepped forward to locate the next sample plot, his foot hit something hard. Sharp pain coursed through his toes and faded at his ankle, only to pulse again at the toes. He grimaced and stumbled back, sucking in a sharp breath.

"What? Did you hit something?" Christie pulled a slender tube from her pack and pointed toward the ground where Aiden had stumbled. The inside of the tube lit up with a dull red glow as air flowed into the back end, accelerated and emerged as a powerful jet. A hole in the dust appeared, revealing a large shard of metal laying on the cracked mineral soil. Christie reached for the piece before dust concealed it again.

Aiden limped over gingerly. His pain had subsided, but his toes remained tender.

Christie held a roughly triangular piece about a decimeter in length with a polished surface. One edge ran straight and square, while the other two and one of the triangle's points bore the jagged edges of a part torn from the whole. The straight perpendicular edge and the smooth surface strongly hinted of manufacturing. When Christie flipped the piece over any leaning toward a natural origin disappeared, for a strange symbol broke the smoothness of the polished surface. A circle circumscribed two diamonds, which touched corner to corner.

Aiden looked at Christie. Her eyes widened with the amazement he felt. He looked back at the piece.

Before either spoke, Utungua called out, "Pack it up! We've got to move out. Now."

Aiden looked at Utungua. He had raised the particle gun and placed his eye to the tracking scope. The soldier's forearm rippled slightly, finger flexed, trigger released. A pulse of energy from the gun initiated a chain reaction. Particle after particle joined in union as the projectile grew in size en route toward its target.

Aiden followed Utungua's line of site to the horizon. The source of the soldier's concern became obvious. A bulge moved through the dust layer in the distance. Whatever loomed within the dust sped toward them.

A large explosion hit the bulge as Utungua's shot impacted. The thing slowed briefly and rumbled before accelerating again. Aiden's jaw dropped.

Christie grabbed at Aiden's arm. "Come on! We have to get out of here!" Her skin drained of color and her movements came rapid and jerky.

The thing under the dust bore down faster than a human runs. Aiden looked behind them at the ship a half kilometer away.

Utungua initiated a link. "Lieutenant, we need emergency evac from current location. Potential hostiles approaching."

"I'm on it," Rachel responded.

Utungua fired three times in rapid succession. He hit his mark to no effect. "Hurry up!" he called to Christie and Aiden without lifting his eye from the gun.

Aiden threw his test equipment in his pack and started after Christie, who had wasted no time clearing out. Aiden's foot throbbed. The pain slowed him.

Utungua caught up to Aiden. "Run faster!" said Utungua.

"No, my foot, I hurt it."

"Ignore it!" commanded Utungua.

Aiden ran faster. The pain intensified. Utungua stayed with Aiden, turning at intervals to shoot at the approaching mass. "Leave me. I'll slow it down," he said. Aiden's jaw ached where Rachel had punched his last self-sacrifice. He ignored it.

"Run! Damn you!" said Utungua.

The scout ship screamed toward them just above the dust layer at what looked to Aiden to be full speed judging by the cloud of dust billowing behind the craft. Rachel reached Christie first, a good hundred meters ahead of them. The ship slowed only enough for Christie to dive into the hatch popping open on approach. Rachel accelerated before Christie brought her legs inside.

"Dive!" Utungua grabbed Aiden's arm and forced him to the ground.

Rachel skidded the ship toward Aiden and Utungua. As the craft slid overhead the field generated by the maglevs pinned the metal they carried to the ground. The metal released a moment later when the ship cleared them. There, less than a decimeter from where they lay, the ship hovered with open hatch.

"Come on!" yelled Rachel.

Utungua leapt with his gun in one arm and Aiden in the other. Aiden looked over the top of the ship as he dove in. For a brief moment he saw enormous jaws, spreading in three directions, open before the ship, dwarfing it. The jaw opened to a deep throat with spirals of saw teeth running its entire length. The hatch slammed shut behind them.

Everything went dark. The ship rocked violently when the gaping maw closed upon them. The high-pitched cry of tortured metal drowned Christie's scream. Running lights flicked on only to be doused by a blood-dark liquid that sloshed over the cockpit.

Damn. We're in an eggshell inside the jaws of death.

"Buckle up! Firing fusion cannons," Rachel barked.

The murky view beyond the smeared cockpit wavered with energy followed by a steady glow. Rachel engaged the engine full throttle. The ship punched through the hole in the creature opened by the fusion cannons. Aiden scrambled toward his seat but the launch flung him backwards into Christie, knocking the wind out of her.

"Get off!" Christie gasped.

With great effort, Aiden pulled himself up against the acceleration to take the copilot's chair. He looked back at the ground through gaps in the ooze clearing on the cockpit. The giant jaw sank into the dust as millions of bugs raced over it. Aiden's view disappeared in a dense fog of dust as the ship penetrated a cloud tossed up by the shaking trees.

11

The Colony Rises

Dagur handed the shard with its strange mark to Devya, who naturally appeared from nowhere. "That piece is most likely from this planet, though, the availability of these new elements in other parts of the universe remains unknown. So I can't say definitively," said Dagur. He flicked wayward hair off his ear, sending the strands back into a mob that had rioted while he slept.

"If common, would other advanced life forms use them for spaceship construction?" Rachel asked. She repeated her question when the chemist's face kept the preoccupied expression that marked his life.

"Absolutely, assuming they needed to travel via spacecraft." Dagur nodded. "The performance of this material is except—"

"How old is it?" asked Walker.

"It's tough to estimate the age because we have too few decay data on the types of radioactive isotopes found here. I compared this sample with readings Aiden captured on the colony ship's approach. If the radioactive decay profile follows that of Earth's isotopes . . ."

"Are you saying this is radioactive?" Devya tossed the shard to Aiden who caught it instinctively.

"Not in any harmful way. Radioactive isotopes occur in varying degrees everywhere in nature. Contamination in the manufacturing process introduced those elements, leaving a traceable signature." Dagur paused for a breath then opened his mouth to continue.

Walker broke in. "Bottom line it for me professor."

Dagur looked down and placed a curled finger over his lips as he spoke. "Maybe fifty years old."

Commander Walker addressed Rachel, "Do a three thousand kilometer aerial recon centered on the colony site." He turned his gaze to the shard. "I want to know of threats within short strike range."

"Aye, sir." Rachel nodded.

Ivan Harkov shook his head. His eye roamed wide with frustrated annoyance. "That changes nothing."

Commander Walker rubbed his face with both hands, appearing at once weary. "What?"

Walker's reaction to Harkov's nonchalant boldness stunned Aiden. He had never witnessed the commander display signs of weakness.

"Would that really change anything?" Harkov gave no indication he understood the military personnel's reactions. "You said we passed nothing but forest on the way in — an untouchable forest lest we anger the natives. The plain contains enough underground water and a flat building site near food sources in the forest. Sounds like a good real estate investment."

Commander Walker squared off against Harkov. "Not if we set camp at a hostile's door step."

Harkov stood firm. "You prefer we homestead a distant locale? Building farther away requires significant transportation costs to shuttle colonists, both to build the colony and to relocate remaining members. All the while the clock ticks on those decrepit stasis chambers."

"What about that monster?" Christie interjected. "The site tested OK except for the fact there is a giant pancake thing stalking you for dinner." Her voice grated to a screeching crescendo.

"I eat pancakes for breakfast," Rachel said.

"Oo, oo, I love whole grain pancakes with blueberries and crushed walnuts," Fei Yen chimed.

"And butter and warm maple syrup," Aiden added.

"I miss butter. The former's butter tastes manufactured. Ah, real butter." Longing filled Fei Yen's voice.

"Enough!" Walker paused, forcing his breathing to slow. "This may be the best colony site. Regardless, we need to know how to prioritize construction. Proximity to hostiles affects what and how we build. We already know we'll need a containment barrier for the colony . . ."

"Yeah, a really big one!" Christie jumped in.

Walker breathed deeply again and with deliberate calm said, "I want to know if there is anything else coming our way."

"If potential hostiles lurk nearby, securing an ally is prudent. We should establish relations with those blue-eyed creatures," Devya added with a smooth, practiced smile.

Walker tapped an irritated cadence with his foot. "How do you propose we do that?"

"Clearly language raises a challenge," said Devya. "We'll find common ground to communicate and offer them something they want."

"Fantastic! Devya has solved our problems people. We can all go home now." Walker gestured to the remains of the ship behind him.

Devya ignored the attack. "What do we know of these aliens?" she asked.

"They have telekinetic powers," Aiden offered quickly.

"Good. What else?" Devya asked.

Everyone stood quietly for a long moment thinking.

Rachel broke the silence hesitantly, "Well . . . they have eyes."

"Yes, they do. Do they have ears? Or a mouth?" asked Devya.

"We don't know," Walker cut in.

"So let's work with what we have. If they have eyes, they should be able to see. Writing a message in our language will confuse them; perhaps . . ." Devya snapped her fingers. "Perhaps they understand pictures. We'll draw like cave men before language existed."

"Brilliant!" said Christie.

Devya took quick steps back and forth. "Now, what do they want?"

The group stood silently again. The moment lasted so long Aiden began to feel both awkwardness and a sense of looming failure.

"I'm not sure what they WANT. I know what they don't want." Walker had stayed his sarcasm as the discussion progressed. An accent of hope colored his words.

"And what pains them?" Devya smiled a self-confident, patronizing smile.

Walker shrugged. "They hate fire."

"Why is that?" Devya's question took on a tone of knowing detachment.

Aiden watched Commander Walker's emerging detente disappear into irritation.

"They helped us put the fire out," said Walker.

"Why?" Devya remained calm despite Walker's growing ire and the others shifting from foot to foot with increasing impatience.

"They live in the forest. Nobody wants their house to burn!" Walker exclaimed exasperated.

"Or to be cut," Aiden added.

"So they want the trees," Devya concluded. "Can we give them trees?"

Christie turned on Devya with a tongue sharp enough to shame Walker's sarcasm. "Why not? They're only ginormous. We'll sneak over to the other side of the planet when the blue eyes aren't looking and steal a few. Oh wait, they're never 'not looking.' Anyhoo, no one will ever notice trees missing — except of course for the massive holes in the ground."

A red tinge flushed Devya's brown skin.

"Actually, we may be able to give them trees," Aiden thought out loud.

"Do tell." Devya nodded.

"The germination of that burned seed in the lab suggests the seeds stratify with heat . . . start growing after they're burned. This would have happened in the clearing created by our crash except we put the fire out. Probably only a few of the seeds burned enough to grow. If we heat strat . . . I mean start the seeds growing by burning them in the right way, we will foster forest regeneration — give them trees."

Devya smiled broadly, the first genuine smile Aiden had seen from her.

"And show them our plan by drawing pictures," Devya added. "That, my friends, is how we will create allies.

"Let's get started. Lieutenant, scout the field. Haven and Kandari, you'll contact the aliens. Harkov, revive an architect and get started building." Walker belted out the orders and turned to go.

Harkov smiled to himself and clapped his hands together.

Devya called after Walker, "Excuse me Commander. I'm not the best person to interact with the aliens. You should send one of your soldiers in case the creatures become aggressive."

Walker paused and turned back, "It's your plan. You execute. My soldiers will cover you from the safety of the ship." He walked away.

12

A Conversation Begins

Rachel left Aiden gathering the large seeds into a pile near the ship. Neither of them could find Devya, so Aiden worked alone, except for the increasing number of glowing eyes watching what he did with the seeds.

Rachel returned late from an uneventful flyover. Her offer to help cheered Aiden, as did the knowledge no enemy massed nearby for an attack. Together they finished collecting seeds in the layer of dust within a half kilometer of the ship. Exhaustion signaled the end of their day under the warm suns. An adequate but bland meal and soft bed brought sleep quick and deep.

A lengthy search after breakfast the next day located Devya reading in a stasis chamber. She looked up at Aiden with apprehension.

"It's time," Aiden said. He had no patience for Devya's cowardice.

"I see." Devya closed her reading screen. "Well, I guess we carry on with it then."

They made their way to the cargo bay in time to see the last of the armaments prepared by the soldiers.

Aiden looked at the exoskeletons standing along the far wall of the bay. "Would XOs make it harder to communicate with them?"

Devya looked glumly at the protective, strength-magnifying armor. "Yes, we'll be more threatening in them than without."

"Then let's go without," Aiden concluded. He strapped a particle former to his wrist, grabbed a steel pipe and plasma torch and headed for the ramp.

Aiden waited outside for Devya to join him. Enough moments passed that Aiden's irritation began to grow. He took a step back up the ramp to get her when Devya emerged into the light.

"Sorry for the delay. I had to use the loo." Devya squinted at the sky. "Nice weather we're having."

"It's always nice weather here. Sunny and warm. Chance of dust, one hundred percent. It never changes." Aiden's irritation mixed with an odd new thought—talking about weather no longer served as a workable bit for small talk. Billions of trivial conversations between people on Earth who had nothing to say to each other now lost all filler value and would have to be replaced with awkward silence. The thought amused and distracted Aiden from Devya enough to dissolve his irritation.

"We'll do it over there." Aiden pointed to the forest's edge. "They'll be able to see us draw better."

"It's so close to the aliens," Devya thought out loud.

"C'mon, and grab a seed on your way." Aiden strode quickly to the forest's edge with Devya in his wake. He stopped three meters from the trees—the closest the creatures permitted before parting to maintain distance. A wall of blue eyes stared back at him, extending from just above the dust layer to several hundred meters up the tree trunks. They never blinked; occasionally they flickered but never closed even for an instant. *A packed house, good.* He swallowed hard.

"How do we draw pictures in this dust?" asked Devya.

"What, you overlooked that detail?" Aiden's mockery surfaced without warning, the culmination of his frustration with her cowardice and shirking.

"Actually, yes, I did," Devya replied.

Aiden looked Devya in the eyes. She had responded with a calm that struck Aiden as dangerous. *Was Devya just an odd person or a purpose-built politician? What does it matter? I don't want to waste time on this woman.* "We'll create a barrier to hold the dust back and draw on the ground."

"I see. Well done." Devya's lips curled in a smile, but her unmoved eyes revealed her true opinion.

Aiden placed the end of the steel pipe on the ground and leaned it against his leg. He didn't ask, and Devya didn't offer to hold it for him. He then drew a circle on the particle former's surface and spread his fingers. Within seconds, the rushing, scratching sound of small particles moving filled the air. A meter high circular wall grew around them created from the dust within its perimeter. The creation cleared the ground in a ten-meter radius around them and dammed the dust sea. Their technology elicited fewer wide eyes compared to when they first crashed, but Aiden felt proud of human capabilities.

"You have any ideas about what we should draw first?" Aiden held no hope Devya had put any thought in the matter.

"Most stories start at a beginning relevant to the audience. How about we start by drawing the ship crashing into the trees and starting the fire?" Devya offered.

"Right." Aiden picked up the pipe and drew a crude resemblance of their spaceship falling toward the forest. He stepped back, so the watchers had a clear view of the picture. Scanning the audience he detected no sign of recognition.

"Keep going. Draw the crash and fire starting," said Devya.

Aiden drew another picture of the ship crashing into the ground with trees ablaze. This time when he stepped back he noticed several of the blue eyes narrowed. Aiden felt warmer than the day. He drew another picture with Walker and himself creating dust bombs to put out the fire. The narrowed eyes relaxed.

In the next picture, Aiden drew a small circle. He pointed the steel pipe to the seed Devya had laid on the ground. Then he drew another circle with flames engulfing it, followed by a circle next to it with scratches in it. He looked up. *Had the wall of eyes moved closer or just loomed larger?* The more he drew the heavier their gazes felt.

Aiden drew a long thin root extending from the scratched circle into the ground and a shorter trunk growing upward with two round leaves on it. He stepped back.

"I think we have their attention." Devya gestured to the wall of eyes.

Rustling noises came from the forest edge. Aiden imagined the creatures pushing and jostling each other for a better view. They pushed forward but remained inside the edge of shadows.

Aiden nodded. "I see that."

Aiden stepped forward and drew a picture of the clearing carved from the forest by their crash. Then he drew stick figures burning seeds and covering them in the dust. The next image showed young trees growing in the clearing. Aiden stepped aside to admire his artwork. A reforestation story filled the dirt canvas.

A cracking sound brought his attention back to the creatures.

"Aiden, look." Devya nodded toward the forest.

A branch broken from the bush at the base of the nearest tree floated up over the retaining wall Aiden had built. The branch turned as it moved until the fractured base pointed down to the drawing of the young trees growing in the clearing. Aiden's mouth dropped silently as the branch lifted, pointed to his chest, and then alternated between the stick figures burning seeds and the trees growing in the clearing.

"Repeat their motion to show them you understand," Devya said quietly under her breath.

Aiden reenacted the branch's motions with his pipe, first pointing to himself, then to the figures burning seeds, and finally to the trees growing. "What next?" he whispered to Devya.

Devya shrugged. The branch stopped moving.

"I'm going to plant the seed." Aiden started toward the seed Devya had carried. Out of the corner of his eye he caught the stick's rotation following his movement.

He squatted and lifted the large seed with both arms. Unlike the first seed that strangled the cargo bay in roots, this seed's surface was smooth and gray with no fine lace work of fractures. "I'm going to plant it on the edge here, so they see the drawings while I work."

Aiden placed the seed on the ground and pulled the plasma torch from his belt. He ignited the torch a meter from the seed and slowly lowered it until the surface color resembled that of the first seed he found. Holding the torch at a roughly even distance from the seed, Aiden circled the ball until the surface turned a deep blood red. Fine lacey cracks appeared. He stopped and stowed the torch.

Aiden scraped a shallow depression in the soil. He settled the seed in the hole and piled loose dirt against it. The top half of the seed poked above ground. Aiden suspected the seed sprouted at ground level given what its cousin had done to the cargo bay.

"Aiden, look!" Devya yelled.

The stick pointed down to the ground again. Aiden's gaze followed. His drawings in the dirt disappeared; smudged out by an invisible hand. The floating stick drew new pictures on the erased area.

"Record their drawing, Devya."

Devya pressed her sleeve cuff, activating the photosensitive layer in her tunic.

The first picture showed what looked like a spaceship landing in the forest. Stick figures, like Aiden had drawn, stood alongside the ship. The second picture showed the same ship and figures, but without the trees. The third picture showed the figures standing in front of buildings assembled into a town. Finally, the creatures drew the buildings and stick figures again. This time the figures lay on the ground.

Aiden and Devya stared at the last drawing as the stick rubbed out the prone stick figures, leaving only the buildings.

"What do you make of that?" Aiden's brow furrowed.

"It's difficult to say," Devya responded. "Let's get back and show the others."

Aiden pressed the surface of the particle former on his wrist. An inaudible frequency emanated from the device. The barrier Aiden erected disintegrated in a flood of dust that smothered the pictures.

The short walk back to the ship passed in a preoccupied haze fueled by images of alien drawings. Everyone was waiting in the cargo bay when they stepped inside.

Devya spoke first. "We have successfully contacted the aliens, established relations, and set on a path to peaceful coexistence." She spread her arms wide and smiled.

Commander Walker addressed Aiden, "What happened?"

"Well, for our part, I drew pictures of the reforestation process. They seemed to understand that message," Aiden answered.

"How do you know?" Walker questioned.

"They pointed a stick at the sequence of images and I affirmed with the same pointing. Then I burned and planted a seed. After that, though, things got confusing," Aiden admitted. "Devya, please show what you recorded."

"Absolutely." Devya touched her sleeve cuff again to play the recording stored in the fabric covering her chest. An image appeared. She made a motion of grabbing the video and throwing it against the wall. An enlarged image transferred onto the wall. The ghostly stick moved through the air redrawing the pictures created by the blue-eyed watchers.

"What does it mean?" Dagur asked.

"Are they going to kill us if we build a colony?" Christie injected.

"We lack intel for that conclusion," Walker said. "While the object looks like a space-going vessel, the ship design differs from those in the Earth fleet; and it sits on the surface unlike our half-buried wreck. The last picture with the prone figures suggests the aliens died, though I see no cause or threat in the drawing."

"Perhaps they tried to tell us something about the aliens who created the shard," Ruiz offered.

"If that's the case then we have nothing to worry about," Harkov said. "We build on the treeless plain and ignore dead aliens the creatures showed us. Correct, Rachel?"

"That's Lieutenant," said Rachel.

"Da, of course, Lieutenant Rachel. Forgive me," Harkov smiled.

Rachel rolled her eyes. "I found no sign of an alien civilization. I lack proof that the aliens those creatures drew exist."

"What do you think the creatures' drawings mean?" Chip asked Aiden.

Devya spoke, "You dwell too much on the meaning of scribbles. The point is we have an opportunity to build a positive relationship with them. The creatures engaged. Let us offer peace."

"Just how do you propose we do that, hug them and sing 'kumbaya'?" Walker's knuckles popped with the tightening of his fists.

"We'll plant the rest of those seeds. It's the right thing to do." Aiden looked around at the blank faces staring at him.

"Get on with it. The rest of us will build a colony to shelter people while Haven plays forest ranger," said Walker. "If the creatures eat him, my soldiers will purge the blue-eyed infestation."

"I'm touched, Walker." Aiden placed a hand over his heart.

The group dispersed on cue.

Aiden noticed Rachel looking at him with a worried expression. He sidled up to her. "What's wrong Rachel?"

She searched his face. "Oh . . . nothing, I must have seen a reflection in your eyes. That's all."

13

Twelve Years Later, a Wake

The colonists named their planet Nubis and their colony Hoepa. Over the next twelve years, Hoepa existed without prospering. Humanity's fit in the ecological puzzle had shifted from that on Earth. On Nubis, people died before passing their accumulated wisdom to the next generation. Twelve years after landing, the colony, weakened from that lost wisdom, lay under siege by the new world.

The settlement's plight offered a certain amount of freedom to individuals staking a claim on existence. Few people remained to challenge judgment in specialized tasks. Talent distribution in other human arts became equally unbalanced. The shrewd, the cunning, and the manipulative faced no worthy rivals. These people lived among the first colonists to shape human society on Nubis.

The colony had been built on the plain with one edge abutting the forest for convenient foraging—a necessity after crops from Earth failed to thrive. A ten-meter barrier surrounded the huddle of buildings. From the outside, Hoepa looked like a fortress; from the inside, a prison. The highest traffic gate accessed the forest. The only other exit opened to the plain; few people used that gate. The plain was a barren sea of dust void of tides or waves, except for the passing bulges displaced by unseen inhabitants. Yet, every building, every home, every workshop, all the sheds and out buildings, even the windows and doors on all those buildings faced the plain. People wanted to wake in front of a vast expanse of nothingness shunted by the violent erectness of the mountains in the distance. Everyone wanted an ocean and mountain view. The colony buildings, featureless blocks with tri-sloped roofs to shed settling dust, squatted in ground level dust to capture insulation efficiencies. The buildings burrowed deeper sun after sun as sediment accumulated against their three consistently blank sides.

A few buildings stood exceptional. Aiden's home, smaller than the rest to remain within the proscribed housing allotment, nestled in dust like the others but lifted its face to the sky. Aiden's bedroom window opened to the forest. The largest window in the colony reached from Aiden's floor to vaulted ceiling; an extravagance among architecture designed to minimize building effort and resources. Rachel had fought using such a large portion of their housing allotment on the high ceiling and window. Other people had shaken their heads and voiced disapproval, but Aiden had held his ground. His wife claimed the rest of the house; the window was his. Rachel's sigh of contentment when they woke to that first sun in their bedroom rewarded him for the effort.

Aiden walked fast to the bakery. His eyes fixed on that invisible place on the ground in front of him where the mind thinks. Aiden's thoughts, coming at a rapid clip, drove the tempo of his pace. One of those thoughts, a hiccup in his stream of consciousness, stopped him short. He had pictured the sapling from a recently planted seed wilting and near death.

He looked around to get his bearings. Aiden thought his location an odd coincidence because there, on the other side of the barrier from where he stood, a young sapling twenty meters in height grew in the reforestation plot he had just imagined. The top quarter of the sapling bent in surrender toward the ground. Giant orange leaves curled and hung vertical, shrinking from the light.

All the trees in this cluster showed signs of distress. Aiden walked to the perimeter barrier and looked down its length. Into the distance, where the fence curved past the school, trees along the forest edge were dying. *Not good. Another failure – I've failed too many times.* Aiden frowned and continued toward the bakery at a slower pace. People had rolled their eyes and whispered amongst themselves whenever the planting topic arose. Innuendos of squandered effort, of trading the colony's survival for a tree, had galvanized his conviction to reforest those small spaces. The failure of his effort weighed on Aiden as he stepped to the bakery's door.

"Hey Chip!" Aiden roused from his gloom a cheerful greeting for the baker as the bakery door slid open. A sharp blast of air from the Dyson loop surrounding the door blew the inevitable coating off Aiden and knocked back the tide of dust perpetually waiting to surge through the opening. The marvel of accelerating air over a wing shaped curl inside a ring, the tingling of the electro-magnetic field that kept desiccant bugs at bay, these things barely registered with Aiden as he stepped into the bakery. Twelve years on planet had conditioned him.

The bakery still drew Aiden's attention. Like most bakeries, the clean scent of rising dough softened the air over prep surfaces, mixing bowls, and trays that appeared clean even when dusted with flour and serving duty. Unlike most bakeries, the baker here stayed too thin, a poor endorsement of his craft. The perennial orange crème coating of errant Chera flour credentialed Chip beyond question, though none disputed his talent after tasting his art, for Chip brokered nothing less than exquisite pleasure packaged with twelve essential nutrients. People traded a week's carbon ration for Chip's sweet breads.

Aiden stood a respectful distance from the counter. Experience had taught him that the extent of Chip's meticulous care extended no further than the epicenter of creation in the small shop. A casual lean against the display case or careless brush against the window marked unsuspecting customers with bakery sign.

"G'day Aiden. Wha'd you know?" Chip pulled a tray of freshly baked buns from the freezer.

Aiden eyed them hungrily. "I thought I'd help you carry your bread to the wake."

"Thanks, I can use the help." Chip tossed Aiden one of the oddly shaped buns. "Here ya go. That will blunt the urge to sample along the way."

"The thought had NEVER crossed my mind." Aiden dodged Chip's skeptical glance by examining the bread.

The round bun looked like it had exploded. Thick protrusions covered the entire surface. Each ended with ragged edged holes burst open by escaping gas. Aiden marveled at the food in his hand. Dry flour from ground Chera leaves, Chip's secret ingredients, and leavening from oxygen producing microbes made for such a strange combination.

Aiden reflected on the bun in his hand. "Your bread amazes me almost as much as the microbes used to make it. Did you know I have found no substitute for these oxygenating bacteria? They sustain life on this planet. Still, I'm torn deciding on their best use, the air we breathe or your delicious bread." He popped a piece into his mouth.

"I owe you for that bacteria discovery," Chip acknowledged gratefully. He stopped his work for a moment to smile at Aiden.

Aiden looked down quickly as Chip caught his eye. None mistook the bright blue glow in Chip's eyes now. The contrast with his red hair made the color more striking. Seeing his friend like that hurt Aiden — not knowing how long Chip had left or how he might suffer. "Me?" Aiden said softly, "You owe me nothing. I isolated the bacteria, a trivial task. You created this work of art." Aiden bit into the bun and swallowed his sadness with pleasure.

"Flattery will get you extra." Chip returned to loading buns into large baskets without offering Aiden an extra roll.

"You hear Gloria blew up her oven again?" asked Aiden.

"She keeps baking bread with heat?" Chip shook his head. "She's asked me repeatedly; I've told her I freeze the dough."

"Bet you neglected to tell her your secret ingredients."

Chip seemed pleased while he appeared to ignore Aiden.

"How come you make bread by hand instead of forming ready-to-eat food like normal people, Chip?"

"Where's the challenge in that?" Chip held up an oddly contorted roll. "Clearly, I can set a former to recreate this roll. The bread would look and taste exactly like this one — so goes the 279th copy. BORING!" He tossed the roll into a basket.

"Anyways, Rachel says Gloria's still having a hard time with her husband's death." Crumbs dropped onto Aiden's shirt as he kept chewing while he spoke. "That's probably throwing her game off."

"No doubt. That's a tough nut, watching your husband fade to nothing like that," said Chip.

"There's been too much death lately." Aiden looked quickly at Chip then returned to his bread.

Chip halted his work and leaned toward Aiden. They were the only two people in the small bakery; even so, Chip lowered his voice. "Rumors in the dust tell of voices calling for children to take up the load dropped by the dead. Do you think the Council capable of snatching childhood?"

"I don't know, Chip . . . I don't know." Aiden held Chip's glowing blue eyes.

Both men fell silent.

Chip turned to his work, each task an attempt at normalcy. "Hey, are you a light sleeper?"

"No but I sleep a lot, and I dream more than in the past. Despite the rest, I lack energy. Why do you ask? You have intel?"

"Nothing much. Word comes that Rachel has been talking to you while you sleep." Chip's grin hinted of conspiracy.

"She talks to me while I sleep?" asked Aiden.

"Rachel talks to you and you talk back, mate. She waits until you fall asleep then you two have animated discussions late into the night."

"I wonder what I say," said Aiden.

"My informants lost me when they began speaking in Woman, but I recall the words 'attentive' and 'romantic.'" Chip raised his hands in surrender. "I have no idea what that means, but Rachel enjoys conversations with your subconscious more than those with you, which I completely understand."

"Well, that explains why she has stopped trying to talk with me while I fall asleep. I'll never understand why that woman prattles on after going to bed." Aiden shrugged. "Rachel gets her communication fix and I'm blissfully unaware—it's all good. How do you know this stuff?" asked Aiden.

"I run a bakery. There's nothing more to it. Whenever two or more women come in, their orders are never ready when they arrive. Even if what they want sits in the case," Chip gestured to glass-enclosed racks filled with rows of baked delights, "there's always something fresher just coming out of the freezer. Of course, to make up for my short comings, I have tasty samples ready to appease. Once women partake of baked goods they seem to forget I'm here. The subjects they talk about after satisfying a craving amaze me."

Aiden presented the knuckles of his fist to his friend. "I've got nothing to match that."

Chip touched his fist to Aiden's salute. "One thing escapes me, despite knowing both Rachel and you all this time. Are you happy, suffering, or comatose?"

"Yes."

"Nice. Oh, and the ladies are jealous of Rachel. Apparently," Chip looked Aiden over in disbelief, "you make good babies."

Aiden returned the compliment with a warm smile. "Thanks Chip. Sarah and Jake are good kids. I'm trying to be the father they deserve. I appreciate your work with Sarah's dustball team. She thinks better under pressure; I see the improvement in her game. Sarah and I have had conversations about how to react in tough situations, and I believe your coaching helps too."

Chip nodded once with satisfaction.

"Before I forget, Rachel wanted me to thank you for passing on Steve's old clothes for Jake; seems like he outgrows his own clothes almost every month." Aiden paused at a memory. "Rachel loves being a mom. You see it in her eyes." Aiden winced after this last thought. Rachel had started showing blue.

"Keep quiet about her health. If Harkov gets a hint Rachel's eyes are changing, he'll cut your family's food ration. No doubt Harkov's keen business sense suggests sick people make poor investments now that foragers travel farther to find food." Chip's dark humor couldn't crack a smile.

Aiden sighed. He finished his bun and picked up a sealed container of bread, pausing in the doorway before stepping into the sun. "You coming to the council meeting tomorrow?"

"Nah, I've got better things to do than wring my hands; besides, they ignore short-timers with glowing blue eyes." Chip's eyes flared as he joined Aiden outside the bakery.

"So what happened to this woman?" Chip asked, positioning the basket of rolls on his hip as they walked.

"Suicide. Anna used to provide daycare at the school for the foragers' children. About fifty suns ago one of the forager's brought in their child sick. Anna discovered the child's illness after the forager left. The sick kid required a lot of care. A toddler crawled underneath the perimeter fence while Anna attended the ill child. No one knows how long he wandered out there. Anna realized what had happened when the boy started screaming. Strikers had found him."

"No!" Chip cried.

"Yes. They left nothing except a dry, red stain in the dust." Aiden's head hung in sadness. "I count myself lucky never to have been foraging when strikers hit."

"I've been out." Chip's voice sounded weak.

Aiden looked at his friend astonished. "You? We've known each other twelve years. Why keep that secret from me?"

"No one in my sortie talks about it. Some fear retribution from relatives of the lost for not helping; me, I had nightmares for many suns. Even now, I hear the screams. That's a memory I dread reliving."

"Did you see the strikers attack?" asked Aiden.

Chip shook his head. "No. No one has — that's lived anyway. I have no idea what a striker looks like. I heard screams, nothing more."

"So what happened? How come you live, Chip? I thought none survived a striker attack."

"The strikers hit a group foraging about half a kilometer from our position." Chip looked Aiden in the eye. "We heard the sortie get taken apart. I felt the victims' screams in my skin. The soldiers guarding us rushed to help those people. The rest of us ran for the barrier. Neither the soldiers joining the fight nor the sortie under attack returned to Hoepa."

Aiden placed his hand on Chip's elbow. "I'm sorry, Chip. I had no idea."

"Thanks, Aiden. I understand how that woman felt."

"Judge Klauer didn't understand, or he didn't care. Klauer barred Anna from childcare. She took it hard, both the boy's death and losing her job caring for children."

"Did anyone try to help her?" asked Chip.

"Sure. She met Hazel Johnson for grief counseling. After Anna's death, Hazel told us that Anna had lost a piece of her identity with the dismissal. Caring for children, helping them grow, brought her real joy. She excelled as a caregiver. Anna cared for ours when both Rachel and I went on field duty. I think Anna's work became too much of her identity. She lost her first child to illness. Soon after, Anna did nothing else but care for those kids at school." Aiden hated this story and telling it even more.

"Could she find something else to do once they fired her?"

Chip asked reasonable questions but kept Aiden in the telling, which sank his heart. "I guess not because she never took up anything else. Her focus on the kids may have blinded her. Anyway, her husband, Les, and the boy's father consumed themselves hunting those strikers — blamed them for killing the boy and now the wife. Perhaps if he had stayed with his wife instead of seeking revenge she might have lived." Aiden gestured at something in the air as they passed a shop. "It doesn't seem right."

Chip looked around as if to glimpse Aiden's reference. "What?"

"To hunt those strikers like that. Not that I think it's OK for them to eat our children. It's just . . ." Aiden paused. "He kills in anger."

Chip looked straight ahead. His face strained with thought. "I might hunt strikers if my son had died."

14

Strange Dream

"A lovely service," Devya said to the group huddled near the refreshments.

Several people shrugged non-committally.

Aiden studied Christie. "You look tired."

Christie sighed. "I've been sleeping poorly."

"Is something bothering you?" asked Aiden.

"No. Not really," she hesitated then blurted, "only I keep having these dreams. Well, the same dream over and over again."

"What is your dream?" Dagur asked with keen enough interest to rouse Aiden's own interest in her answer.

"I'm running through a maze. The walls and floor are gray, like the dust here, only they're clean." Christie thought for a moment, "Sterile is more like it. Every corridor leads to a dead end. When I turn around to try a new path the maze is different. With every step I get older . . . I," she shivered, "I never find my way out."

"I haven't slept well, either," Dagur admitted. "The dream replaying in my head differs from yours though."

"What's your dream about?" Christie placed her hand gently on Dagur's forearm. She withdrew it when he started at her touch.

"I stand on the edge of a sheer cliff with a great valley spreading out far below me. The valley is so large it makes me feel small. Dark purple silhouettes of mountains stop the valley in the distance. An enormous setting sun casts the mountains in shadow, only," Dagur's brow furrowed, "only the sun's not setting. I stand there watching it, waiting; but the day never ends. Tomorrow never comes." He looked at Christie as he finished. Dagur's brow pinched upward over watering eyes. His mouth drooped with a tremor.

"You know it's funny. I've been having dreams too."
Aiden added. "It's night but there's a full moon. I'm
standing on the edge of a perfectly circular, glassy smooth
pool. Across from me on one side of the pool, a young tree
grows. On another side, my parents stand holding a baby,
which is me." He paused. "Then I look into the pool, and I
see the face of an alien with glowing, deep blue eyes. The
alien in the pool is a reflection . . . of me." He paused again
trying to sort through the confusion. "I keep having the
dream, but sometimes it's different. The pool and the tree
are there, but the parents and baby are aliens. I'm an alien.
And when I look into—"

"When you look into the pool you see your human face
with alien blue eyes." As Rachel finished describing
Aiden's dream, her face froze with a mix of fear and
surprise.

Aiden's eyes widened.

Rachel continued, "Then sometimes you see the tree,
your parents holding you as a baby, and yourself now with
normal eyes. When you look into the pool—"

"You see yourself with pitch black eyes before
collapsing to dust." Chip finished describing Rachel's
dream.

Everyone turned and looked at Chip. He stood at the
end of the serving table. A half-eaten sweet seta tart fell
from his hand and cracked into chunks on the floor. He
looked wildly from person to person searching. Everyone
stared back mutely.

Aiden gulped and broke the silence, "anyone else have a
dream like ours?" He motioned to Chip and Rachel then
added, "Or any others?"

"I've dreamed of gold coins that turn to dust when I pick
them up," Ivan Harkov admitted.

Dr. Stein described his own dream with distracted
desire. "I'm running endlessly on a giant hamster wheel.
The wheel rocks on its stand. . . . I know that if I just run
harder, I will knock it off its stand."

"Mine's kind of fun," Fei Yen grinned. "I'm lying on a
really comfy couch watching holograms of all these cool

inventions people made, one after another." Then she added as her grin faded, "sometimes I get ideas for new inventions from some of the things I've seen, but I soon see those ideas in the holograms showing another person's invention."

"Anyone else have a dream like Chip, Rachel and I?" Aiden asked again.

No one raised their hand.

"What does it mean?" Fei Yen searched their faces without avail.

"The dreams mean nothing," Dr. Stein said finally.

"Are you sure doctor? Why would different people have identical and . . . strange dreams over and over?" Rachel held her glass so tight her fingertips turned red.

"You probably talked about the dream with your husband. He is friends with Chip, no? People forget conversations. It is nothing," said Dr. Stein.

"I'm not so sure." Aiden shook his head while meeting Doctor Stein's gaze. "Chip would've teased me mercilessly if I told him I had such a wacked dream, and I doubt he would've dreamed the same after hearing mine or convinced himself the dream was his."

"Yep, there's no way I want to dream the twisted and bizarre stuff floating through that head." Chip jerked his head toward Aiden. A lock of vivid red hair flung out like a brandished torch of red flames.

"Besides," Aiden continued, "dreams mean something—like a manifestation of your subconscious."

"Psycho-babble rubbish. They mean nothing." Dr. Stein drank from his glass with purpose.

The conversation chilled to death. The doctor damped spirits at parties like no other. Aiden discretely glanced at Fei Yen. He knew her look. Fei Yen's crossed arms, wide eyes, set jaw, and short, vigorous head shake signaled a fun conversation later at the doctor's expense. So be it. Dr. Stein set himself up.

15

A Choice Must Be Made

Sarah's thumb launched her purple marble. Geometry and physics incited the once peaceful collection of marbles to strike each other and rebound for another. Silver, gold, and purple flashed in battle. When the last two marbles collided, Sarah's target rolled to the bone yard. An image of her marble appeared in Sarah's mind. The marble grew to the size of her head and rolled over the other marbles, crushing them. Sarah smiled and waited.

A gold marble shot forward and struck silver. The silver marble ricocheted and ousted Sarah's purple marble. Sarah clapped her hands and laughed out loud. She imagined the gold marble pulverizing her purple piece. A picture of herself smiling popped into Sarah's mind.

"You better look out. Your Watcher plays well," said Steve.

"No kidding. It's already knocked me out. It's like it hates me, or something," Juan added.

Sarah looked at the two boys on either side of her. Steve Nelson played in her earliest memories. Their fathers' friendship had brought them together as babies. He looked a lot like his father with influences from his mother. Steve grew darker red hair than Coach Nelson's. He had thinner and more curved lips and a softer chin. But his eyes flashed the same startling blue as his father's. Unlike his father, Steve's eyelids seemed permanently half-closed on the verge of sleep. People teased Steve about his eyes— sneaked up on him and yelled, "Wake up!" in his ear. He hated those taunts; Steve said he noticed more in the world than any who teased him. Sarah often watched Steve suppress the urge to shut their mouths with his fist; he never fought. Sarah did once after Steve had stalked off in a huff. Steve rarely took center stage in the plans their gang of wild things concocted, but something went missing with his absence.

Juan Lok had wandered up one First Sun many years ago when she and Steve were playing outside. His mother had died giving birth and his father, Dagur Lok, engrossed in one chemistry project or another, frequently lost the boy. The black-haired toddler had joined their play that day and never left. Sarah thought Juan rounded them out. He added daring with a streak of crazy to Sarah's thoughtfulness and Steve's calm. She expected Juan to captain their dustball team. He looked and acted the part. Juan's hazel eyes burned intense and more frequently stole her breath in recent suns. His nose led directly to full lips often curled in a smirk.

Juan and Steve were her best friends. They had to be. When the boys' bodies had started changing, voices deepening and muscles hardening, jealousy turned many of her former girlfriends against Sarah. A few girls still called her friend—a friend distanced by Sarah's relationship with the boys.

She frowned. Her baby fat had disappeared a long time ago, but Sarah's body hadn't started curving like the other girls, like her mom curved. Many times she had wished adolescence to hurry up and make her a woman. Sarah never wanted her chin to change, though, because her dad praised it. Neither large nor small, her father described her chin as "well cut, a sign of strong character."

"A late bloomer," her mom's friends said. "She was SUCH a cute baby," always followed. Her mom said she would grow into herself. *When Mom? Girls change first, not boys. When do I change?* She sighed. *No matter. The three of us have fun.*

"Your turn Steve," Sarah said.

"What's going on here?"

Sarah started at the sharp tone. She looked behind her to find Devya Kandari standing legs apart, fists on hips, and scowl on face.

"We're just playing a game of marbles," Sarah responded.

"Marbles! You should be memorizing vocabulary words or learning math, not playing childish games."

"We wanted to play a game before breakfast," Juan said.

"You've wasted an opportunity to improve. You'll never make anything of yourselves with such careless use of time."

Sarah caught movement in the corner of her eye. Steve had picked up a marble and placed the ball to his advantage. Juan had seen the move as well and glowered at him.

"I studied night and day to strengthen my mind at your age. That's the problem with you children; you're too coddled. You've grown lazy. Death stalks this planet. Everyone must contribute to our colony's survival."

Sarah's chest tightened when she caught another movement to her side. The marble Steve had moved rolled back to its original location.

Devya's eyes narrowed to sharp slits. Her mouth contorted into a sneer. "Who did that? Who are you playing with?"

Yeah, like I'm going to tell you anything, you old bag. An image of herself running away kept popping in her mind. Sarah tried to push the thought away, but the effort only served to confuse her thought.

"We play alone. See there's no one here but the three of us." Sarah swept her arm across the small space between the back of the building and the perimeter barrier.

Devya bared her teeth in a snarl. "You lie. You play with one of those vile creatures. Tell me the truth!"

Sarah thrust her chin forward. "We do not." She had rejected the grownups' fear of the Watchers. Now Sarah felt protective of the blue-eyed creatures who gazed from the forest shade.

Devya kicked through the retaining wall surrounding the marble game, flooding the area with dust. "Contact with those things is strictly prohibited young lady. I'll see your parents hear about this."

I'm no more a lady than you are, devil woman. Sarah wanted to curse Devya and kick dust in her face, but Devya had left and Sarah's better judgment had caught her tongue.

The peace of early First Sun spoiled, Sarah returned home for breakfast with sunken spirit. Too many lectures and warnings had smothered her desire to share Watcher encounters with anyone. Now she must endure yet another "you need to be responsible" speech. Sarah sighed as she stepped into the dining room. Her family, suspiciously quiet, had already started eating. Sarah took her place with a sense of foreboding.

"Have you decided what you're going to pick at Election?" Aiden asked.

Sarah groaned inwardly, or at least she thought the groan inward. She glanced up quickly from her bowl of mush. Her dad straightened his posture. He always pulled his shoulders back when he prepared for a fight. His cheek twitched. Sarah did that—gave him a nervous tick; Jake made his father's hair disappear, and together they brought on extended silences punctuated by sighs while she and her brother yelled and jumped from chair to chair around the dining table until one of the kids fell and required skin fusion. Sarah looked down and shook her head as she took a bite.

"Election draws near, sweetheart. You should prepare." Aiden held a spoonful of gruel but did not eat.

"Why does she have to decide?" Rachel put her spoon down in her bowl with a loud clang.

Sarah sagged into her chair. She hated when her parents yelled at her, but she hated even more when they argued with each other.

Aiden rolled his eyes. "Do we really have to go over this?"

Apparently they do.

"Sarah needs more living to make a wise choice. Don't force our daughter to a premature decision that will impact the rest of her life. I want Sarah to avoid the mistakes you made. Do you want her building septic systems until the bugs get her?" Rachel's voice rose to lecture volume.

"You attended the council meeting when we agreed on the plan. We have no backup. Three days ago our last nano-roboticist died. Who will develop future generations of nanobots to help us? Our kids must immerse themselves in a profession early," Aiden answered.

"To dig holes for poop like you? How's that working out for you? You know, when you're not sleeping your life away."

"Mommy said POOP!" Jake chimed. "Poopy! Poop! Poop!"

Sarah touched her brother's hand and shook her head.

"I do what I have to do. I take care of my family." Aiden matched Rachel's volume. "People will die if we lose those Earth elements. We can't harvest carbon from the starship forever. But you miss the point. We have wisdom to share. The next generation must learn from us before it's too late, before too many of us fade away."

"Sarah's too young. I want her to avoid a mistake. She will pay dearly for the wrong choice."

Aiden avoided Rachel's stare. "She can pursue her dreams tomorrow. Today calls." He spoke low as if to avoid a challenge. The words choked him while the timbre of his voice rose such that in the end he seemed unconvinced by his own words.

Rachel looked away, her lips drawn tight into a frown.

"Mommy?"

"Yes, Jake?" Leftover frustration sharpened Rachel's words.

"Who will I be when I grow up?"

Rachel relaxed and smiled. "Anyone you want, honey. You're young; you have plenty of time; decide later." She scowled at Aiden.

"Momma?"

"Yes, Jake."

"Will I be me later?"

"Yes, honey. Eat your mush."

Sarah busied herself eating breakfast, hoping the storm had blown past her.

"We'll continue this conversation later young lady. I must prepare. Council's meeting early." Aiden wiped his chin and looked at Rachel.

Sarah paid attention to the silent look between her parents. Something was up. Something was always up when her mom and dad looked at each other that way. Like when her parents stopped sending Jake to daycare, or when Dr. Stein's wife vanished in the night.

Sarah watched her dad rise from the table. He used both arms and legs to stand. When upright, he waivered against a weight too heavy for his wasted body. She remembered a few years ago when her Dad ran fast. He always caught her when they played tag. She tagged him only when he made a mistake or let her. He no longer played tag; he rarely played anything.

Perhaps I'll snoop on the council meeting today. "I'm going to play outside Mom," Sarah said as she pushed back from the table.

"Take your brother with you," Rachel called to her disappearing daughter.

Sarah turned in the doorway. "Oh, c'mon!"

"I want to go with Sarah!" Jake yelled.

"You will." Rachel wiped food off Jake's mouth. "Take your brother, Sarah. He likes to be with you."

Blah. Blah. Blah. Blarde. Blar. Blar. Sarah knew the speech well. She also knew her mother's tone. The tone made clear her brother would go with Sarah.

"Fine." Sarah left with Jake in tow.

When Sarah and Jake stepped outside, First Sun had passed a quarter through its cycle. She slid her fingers along her sleeve. "Find friends," she commanded. The locations of her friends popped up on her sleeve as green dots scattered about a map of the compound. "Send private message, 'Something's up. Meet by the school,'" she whispered.

"What are we going to do Sarah? Are we going to play dustball? How about we hunt for desiwogs? Can we do that? Can we?"

Great. He's already spooling up. "We'll see."

Jake's eye lit up. "Yes!" Jake yelled loudly as he spread his arms and raced out into the dust, disappearing into the layer until just his head floated above it.

"This way Jake!"

Jake's head turned and bobbed quickly toward her as they headed for the school. Two pairs of blue eyes followed them from the distance of the dark forest.

Sarah walked in silence, oblivious to Jake's chatter. She brooded on the argument with her dad. Each time her father's words repeated in her mind, Sarah's anger burned hotter, her bitterness cut sharper, and her sense of hopelessness flooded.

Sarah caught sight of Mr. Asworthy after Jake and she had walked too far into the commons to change direction without appearing to avoid her teacher. Mr. Asworthy wasn't a bad person. He didn't pinch cheeks while exclaiming how cute you were or how much you had grown. Before his accident, Mr. Asworthy had been a good teacher. His only perceived shortcoming was an unfortunate last name; something Sarah thought a requirement of teachers. Enough students liked Mr. Asworthy to limit comments about him to a few overused misspellings of his name.

His fall in the trees during a food sortie changed everything about how Sarah related to Mr. Asworthy. Her parents had said the impact with a tree branch damaged his brain. He had refused to allow nanobots inside his body to repair the damage for religious reasons. Mr. Asworthy had said God would provide. Sarah wondered exactly when God would provide and what that provision might be, for now three types of people lived in Hoepa: those that avoided Mr. Asworthy as one flees a foul stench, those that forced normal relations out of decency, and those that hung around the edges of his conversations to overhear his thoughts without becoming the focus of his attention.

The last group, the lurkers, twittered incessantly amongst themselves when Mr. Asworthy spoke. Before his injury, people generally considered him intelligent in a scholarly manner. They misjudged the extent of Mr.

Asworthy's insight into human nature. The man's discretion concealed his talent for insight and enabled his ability to relate in a manner far exceeding the presumed capabilities of a scholar.

After his injury, Mr. Asworthy had no discretion. Everything he thought of a person came out in a continuous flow of conversation that amounted to oral diarrhea. Sarah's dad pointed out that people always knew what her teacher thought, as if that was a positive. Mr. Asworthy thought about people too well, seeing things about a person that, once revealed, others recognized as true.

Sarah's parents stood among the second group of decent people who insisted on normal relations with Mr. Asworthy. They forced her to talk with the man when she wanted to run from him. Sarah understood the colonists who avoided her teacher. A lot of people reacted like Sarah felt. Mr. Asworthy had offended so many people that her mom had said his diminutive size was fortunate because even bullies hesitated to beat such a small man.

"Hello, freckle-faced Sarah! Hello!" Mr. Asworthy waved and jogged over to Sarah and Jake.

Sarah cringed, forced a smile, and waved. Jake giggled. He thought Mr. Asworthy funny.

"You seem unhappy to see me, Sarah. How are you doing? You look like you're heading out to ditch your brother and get into mischief." Mr. Asworthy made all these observations about Sarah without the slightest animosity—just part of casual conversation.

"Hi, Mr. Asworthy. Jake and I are meeting my friends by the school house." Sarah grabbed Jake's hand and kept moving.

"Glad to hear you have friends, Sarah. I've started reading your class's papers on Election. I graded several students' papers so far, including yours. You expressed confusion and isolation. I'm worried about you."

"Thanks Mr. Asworthy," Sarah called over her shoulder as she pulled Jake away. "I look forward to reading your WRITTEN comments on my paper."

Mr. Asworthy smiled and waved at Sarah's back. "Bye Sarah! You feel awkward around me and want to leave. Don't worry. Self-explosion rarely befalls victims of embarrassment. I will see you tomorrow in school. Bye giggly Jake! I'm glad you find me funny."

Steve and Lian Lin clustered at the corner of the school when Sarah and Jake arrived. Luisa Walker's loud greeting announced her arrival with Juan a few moments later.

"What's up?" Steve asked.

"Dunno," Sarah answered. Her spirits rose when she saw Natasha had stayed at home. The girl shadowed Steve, but Sarah couldn't tell whether Steve noticed. "My dad let slip the Council's meeting."

"You wanna listen through the vent like last time?" Lian asked.

Lian's ever-present smile made Sarah feel good. Lian's smile resembled her mother's. Both Fei Yen Lin and her daughter laughed with their lips and their almond shaped eyes. The combination, mirth with a hint of mischief, drew Sarah in. Lian usually thought about things the same way Sarah did. Sarah liked that. Reflecting on the argument with her father, however, had squelched Sarah's enthusiasm for spying. "Nah," said Sarah, "I want to be as far from my dad as possible."

Luisa ruffled Jake's hair and ducked around Sarah. A chase broke out. "Hey, let's hold a spitting contest. The person who spits the farthest takes a day's energy rations from the others," Luisa called, swirling past Jake's grab. She grinned, black skin enhancing the brilliance of her white teeth. Luisa kept her long thin body, the fastest in her class, just enough beyond the reach of Jake's tiny fingers to tease out a continuous stream of wild squeals in Sarah's brother.

"No way," said Juan.

"Let's do it. I can beat her, Juan." Steve grabbed Juan's elbow. "She curls her tongue; that's how she gets the distance. I practiced. I know I can beat her this time."

Luisa's eyes flashed. Steve backed down when the others refused Luisa's challenge.

Jake tugged on Sarah's shirt. "Can we go sledding, Sarah?"

The friends exchanged looks. Smiles bloomed.

"Where?" Sarah asked. She resisted the infectious joy spreading in her. "We were grounded from sledding over the buildings when Captain Juan here punched a hole in the school."

"Out there." Juan tossed his head toward the perimeter barrier.

"Are you crazy?" Sarah cried. "Do you know how many things out there could hit us? Tons. We'd be grounded, like, for a hundred years if we crossed the perimeter."

"Relax. Nothing flies on this planet except us. The gravity is too strong. We'll be in the air where it's safe," Juan said.

"What about heliospheres or chera farmers?" Sarah recognized, even as she made the argument, the flaws in her logic.

"Heliospheres float. Chera farmers glide. Besides, one feeds on sunlight and the other on fruit. Neither eats people," said Juan.

"C'mon Sarah it'll be fun," said Lian.

"I dunno guys. I've gotta watch Jake."

"Form a two person sled and bring him along," Luisa offered.

"Can we Sarah? Can we? Can we go sledding?" Jake pulled Sarah's sleeve incessantly.

"Alright," Sarah agreed though she felt uneasy about going. The thought of her parents anger and disappointment at her decision caused hesitation, doubly so because Sarah placed Jake at risk, but sledding tempted her despite the danger of flying beyond the barrier.

Jake pumped his fist in the air. "Yes!"

The gang of rule breakers spread out to form their sleds. Sarah and Jake took a spot in the shadow of a building falling between the structure and perimeter barrier. A soft hissing rose in the air as dust funneled into the formers' energy fields to create photon sleds. Sarah formed a two seat sled for Jake and her. Wingless and fed by light, the sled looked like a people pod in flight. The others made single pilot sleds, faster and more maneuverable than Sarah's double. Hers would be filled with Jake's squeals of joy. Sarah preferred Jake's laughter.

"Wait for a shake. We'll launch into the cloud," Juan called.

Sarah appreciated Juan's cleverness — fly invisible with magic dust.

"You avoid the truth to protect your ego. You have no idea," said Fei Yen Lin.

"The disease's morphology remains unknown," Dr. Stein responded.

"Most of the children and some of the adults glow alien blue, and the good doctor finally admits he understands nothing about the problem." Fei Yen circled Dr. Stein, reversing her direction when the doctor's eyes flicked to her.

"It's this planet! It's killing us! We've got to get off it. Now. Before we . . ." Christie Winters' outburst drained her. She lowered herself into a chair that cradled her collapsed body. Christie's shriveled lower lip no longer pouted, and skin now covered jaw bone in a thin testament to her wasting. Shallow breathes buried her.

Dagur Lok shifted away from her as if she had a loud hacking cough in the middle of a crowd. Commander Walker remained cemented.

Devya Kandari shifted in her chair with repeated dissatisfaction in her position. "Is Christie onto something? Can the planet cause this illness, doctor?"

"We're turning into those shadow lurkers." Christie sounded the words between breaths. "Think about it. We've been here over a decade and no one has seen what they look like except for those disgusting blue eyes." She shivered. "They must be hideous."

"A large number of possible causes exist, including that suggested by Ms. Winters in her hysteria over the planet, but not her ridiculous transformation hypothesis." Dr. Stein rolled his eyes. "Mr. Haven has not detected any known environmental contaminants. His findings don't rule out unknown contaminants. Other potential causes exist as well. European explorers brought disease and pestilence to indigenous peoples of the Americas. Logic suggests the possibility of disease transmission from natives to colonists."

"What prevents nanobots from fixing us?" asked Devya.

"This new disease will slip past our defenses until I reprogram nanobots with a cure. I lack understanding of both the disease and the cure. While I continue to study the infection, we need to take precautions." Dr. Stein jabbed a long finger at no one in particular. "Protocol mandates activation of a quarantine beacon."

"No." Christie's voice struggled with her breathing. "Please, we'll be unable to get it back. Block rescue and you kill us all."

"You have no cause for concern yet Ms. Winters. You show no signs of discoloration." Dr. Stein's eyes ambled over to Commander Walker only to skitter back under the unwavering critical gaze.

"A beacon will maroon us here forever." Christie reached for Walker. "Please, Jamar, stop this."

Walker flinched at the sound of his first name, a familiarity reserved for his family alone in private. "This is a civilian matter. If the Council decides to activate a beacon, I'll put it in orbit. Christie is right, though. It's a one-way ticket. We have no space craft to retrieve it and no way of shooting it down."

"Commander Walker's correct. This is a civilian matter." Devya seemed pleased. "We will order placement of the beacon per protocol."

"Just a minute," Aiden interjected. "This is a matter for the Council to debate. Protocol only exists if we decide to accept the rules." On this last point, Aiden gestured to the other council members in the room.

"We will respect the rule of law despite no longer residing on Earth," said Devya.

"She's right. We live by the law or we live as animals," Dagur added.

Heads nodded in agreement.

Does she misunderstand or purposefully undermine me, misconstruing and twisting what I say? The way Devya dispatched Aiden now made him feel unequal. This angered Aiden. His rage mixed with public humiliation, becoming slippery and dangerous. Aiden grabbed for the feeling. He tried to strangle it. "I never said disregard laws. We must determine our own destiny."

"Then it's settled. We'll launch the quarantine beacon," Dr. Stein stated.

"No!" Christie protested.

Aiden counted Christie Winters among his two remaining allies on the Council. Now Christie slumped in the chair where the herd had left her to fate. Aiden twitched. He also believed the beacon should be launched. The colony must warn others of a fatal disease, but Aiden had wanted the decision to be made the right way. Devya stole it.

"I'll announce the Council's decision." Devya's matter-of-fact tone assumed ownership. "Let's move on to the next agenda item, mandatory double shifts to compensate for lost colonists."

16

Beyond the Perimeter

Sarah waited with the others a long while before movement from the side attracted her attention. A tree just inside the edge of the forest began to move. The shiver started without warning near the center of the tree's bole. The movement of the branches increased as the shake moved outward until the entire Chera tree flung its leaves madly. One tree, a different one each time, started the chain reaction that swept rapidly from neighbor to neighbor in a great wave. Sarah wondered if every tree on the planet thrashed nearly in synchrony. Could this great forest make the planet tremble?

Dust billowed upward, thrown off leaves starved for sunlight. The dust gathered in a great storm that seemed to menace the sun, but in the end only rose at the whim of a plant and fell with gravity. Sarah wondered how the dust first settled on the leaves and why dust still landed on the trees after repeated shakes. Her questions went unanswered. The other sleds popped into the air and cleared the barrier like Archis seeds ejecting to catch a ride on a passerby. Their turn came.

"Hold on." Sarah fastened her harness and opened the photon drive wide. The sled sprung into the air. Before Sarah reconsidered flying over the barrier, it disappeared behind them. Sarah and Jake broke above the dust cloud and sped into open daylight. She tracked the other sleds to a distant edge of the open plain where the mountain vertical rudely interrupted the lazy horizontal. A long ride brought the children to a location far enough to play without being caught. The loud mix of chatter, each child talking excitedly over the next, on Sarah's link announced Sarah and Jake's arrival.

"Where have you been?" Steve asked as he zoomed past.

"C'mon, pick up my wake! I'll give you a boost!" Lian called.

Lian flew in front of Sarah's sled. Angered air spilled around Lian's sled rocking Sarah and Jake until they slipped into the pocket of calm behind Lian's sled. Once in, their sled sped up without resistance. Lian dove steeply with Sarah and Jake in tow. The ground sped toward them. Faster and faster it came. The drafting sled closed on Lian. Sarah started to sweat. Lian pulled up sharply. Sarah and Jake followed. Lian twisted and banked. Sarah and Jake slingshot out of her wake. Their sled bumped over the turbulence and shot for space.

Jake giggled hysterically. "Do it again! Do it again!"

"Or . . . how about this?" Sarah banked hard left, flipped and looped.

"Again! Again!" Jake clapped.

"Why, hello there."

Sarah looked up. Juan flew above them cockpit to cockpit. "You're too close, Juan."

"No, I'm not. See." Juan rolled his sled off.

Sarah sighed. Juan pushed flight too far in her opinion. Before Sarah changed course, Juan rolled his craft back up the opposite side of their sled.

"Don't mind me—just passing through." Juan's sled continued to roll in a circle around Sarah and Jake's.

"Cut it out Juan!" Luisa yelled. "You're going to hurt someone!"

"Relax, I—"

Sarah rolled hard left to escape Juan, but his sled had already rolled underneath hers and started up again. The edge of Sarah's sled caught Juan's. The vessels knocked apart.

"Whoa!" Juan battled his sled back to control.

The larger double sled fell uncontrolled. Sarah tried to stabilize. Everything spun. The sled turned too slow. The ground came too fast.

Sarah ended the roll only to see the sky disappear as their sled fell between low lying mounds in the plain. Dust smothered her vision. The tip of their sled impacted. As

Sarah and Jake's sled plunged into the ground, automated crash recovery engaged. A loud clap rang out. The sled's particles fractured and exploded directionally, pushing Sarah and Jake backward. Their momentum slowed.

The two children landed hard halfway up one of the large mounds. A loud pop and a painful pulse through her arm announced the end of Sarah's particle former. She blacked out.

Jake's screams roused her. She forced her chest off the ground. Her arm throbbed, her head swam, and she saw spots. "Jake, where are you?" Sarah's words floated weakly from her mouth.

"Mommy! I want Mommy!" Jake screamed.

Other voices rang in her ears, angry and concerned and defensive voices. One simple thought surfaced above the others — her link worked.

Sarah crawled toward Jake's cries. Her hands and feet sunk in dirt that shifted under her weight. He lay in a ball on the hill slope above the dust layer just a few decimeters from her. They had both landed above the dust layer; chance saved them from drowning.

"Jake, are you hurt?"

"Mommy!"

"Where do you hurt, Jake?" She began running her hands over him checking for broken bones or dislocated joints like her dad had taught her.

"All over. I want Mommy." Jake's cries settled slightly as Sarah's voice and touch reached through his fear.

"I know. We're going to go home." Her inspection of Jake revealed nothing. Beyond something sticking out of his skin she doubted her ability to detect injuries and considered the healing functions of a particle former deadly in her hands.

Sarah touched her link. "Hey, everyone be quiet for a moment."

The arguers fell silent. Luisa spoke first. "Are you and Jake OK, Sarah?"

"No, we're banged up. I don't know how badly. The sled's gone; so's my former."

"Damn," Juan said.

"Shut up, tool! Let her talk!" said Steve.

"We need to get back to Hoepa. Can some of you carry us?" Sarah asked.

"All of our sleds are single seats," Luisa answered. "We'll have to make new ones."

"We can't," Lian said. "The particle formers lack enough energy to complete the form."

"Yeah, and for that matter, our current sleds need the photon accelerators cycled soon," Juan added.

"Try helping instead of raining on everything, Juan." Luisa bumped Juan's sled hard. "Some of us should go for help while others wait here."

"Juan, will stay," Steve asserted.

A shrill note rang out. The children's conversation stilled. Another shrill call answered. A third and fourth joined a fifth cry.

"Oh my God!" Lian whispered.

"Guys, I hear something down here. Do you hear it?" Sarah asked. "It sounds like . . ." Another cry struck her ears. Strikers prowled.

"We hear them Sarah," Steve answered.

"We've got to get them out of there!" Luisa cried.

Sarah held Jake. "I need you to stop crying Jake. I need you to be absolutely quiet." She rocked him slowly, but the shrill notes of the strikers stole his self-control.

"I'm going to find them. I'll distract them and lead them off." Juan stopped circling his sled over the area where Sarah went down and headed in the direction of the cries.

"Be careful, Juan," Lian called after him.

"Lian, head back to Hoepa for help," Luisa ordered. "Steve and I will stay here and do what we can."

"Why do you get to stay? I can protect them too," Lian said.

"We need to make sure someone gets the message back to Hoepa. Steve and I sled better than you. Leave the strikers to us."

"There's no time to argue Lian. Just do it," Steve said.

"Fine." Lian abruptly spun her sled on its axis and shot for the distant colony.

"Please, Jake. I need you to stop crying. It's really important." Sarah's pleas had no effect. She placed her hand over his mouth, but he pulled at it.

Juan's sled appeared over a far corner of the mound labyrinth Sarah had crashed in.

"What are you doing here, Juan? Did you drive them off?" Luisa asked.

"No. They're below me, eight of them. They're fanning out among the mounds. Sarah, find a place to hide."

"Let's slow them down Steve," said Luisa.

Steve's sled hovered in place.

"C'mon! Let's go!" she called turning her sled after Juan.

Steve followed Luisa but kept his elevation. "Juan! There's one below you!"

"I see it." Juan dove toward the animal.

"Luisa, two are running down that wide path toward Sarah and Jake!" said Steve.

Luisa rolled, dove and carved a near ground level turn in front of the strikers' heads, missing their jaws by an instant. She shot down an alley with the two predators pursuing.

"Juan, watch out behind you!" Steve said.

"I know. I see it. I'm trying to lure it away." Juan flew between two mounds with a striker closing in on him.

A well-timed swipe knocked Luisa sideways, causing her sled to ricochet off the edge of a mound. "Where are you Steve? We need help!"

Steve said nothing.

Sarah hoisted Jake to her hip. He grabbed her neck and buried his head. She ran with her burden. She saw no place to hide. The mounds were smooth flat hills tall enough to reach above her head. They provided her only screen. She had to keep the mounds between her and the strikers.

Juan's sled flew overhead. Deep claw marks marred the bottom. The strikers raked metal with every pass. He banked and dove two mounds away, coming back for more. An irritated shrill rang out before the sled emerged again.

"Sarah, the strikers are trying to circle! Move down the break behind you!" Luisa ordered.

Sarah stumbled with Jake, picked him up, and ran again. Trills sounded around her. Thumping filled her brain. Jake's weight disappeared. Thump. Thump. Thump. *whats that noise hard to think get jake out now got to get out.* Thump. Thump. Thump. Her body moved. Thump. Thump. Thump.

"Turn left now!"

Juan flew past them barely a meter off the dust layer. Wind whistled with an echo of the strikers' shrill through gouges in Juan's cockpit. His sled disappeared behind the mound to her right. Thump. Thump. Thump. Juan shot vertical above the mound. Thump. Thump. Thump. Predators closed in.

"Stop!" Luisa screamed. "Uh, uh, . . . go right!"

Sarah pitched right between two large mounds.

"Stop! Stop!"

A shallow indentation broke the shaded side of the west hill. Sarah found nothing else. She pressed her back into the indent. *Face the strikers when they come.* She grabbed a fist of dust. *Maybe I'll save Jake.* Juan and Luisa sped past. Steve hovered above, silent. Sarah heard the strikers' clicks and trills. *Do they hear me breathe?*

Jake and Sarah fell into darkness.

17

Darkness Complete

Sarah fell backward clutching Jake. Their bodies hit something hard.

Am I on the ground? But the surface is cool. Nothing feels cool on Nubis.

A vertical bar of light shrunk then disappeared with a scrape, leaving them in the dark.

What happened? Had the strikers hit?

Sarah searched for answers in stillness. She heard no sound of sleds, no calls of death. Nothing. She pressed her link. No response.

"Sarah?"

She had forgotten for a moment that Jake huddled in her arms.

"Wait a minute Jake."

Sarah pressed her link. "Juan, Luisa can you hear me?" No voices came. "Juan, Luisa, we fell into some place away from strikers. Get out of here! Save yourselves. Hello?" She heard no reply.

Don't die. Please don't die – not trying to save us. We're ok. Run. Please. Save yourselves. You've done enough. You saved us, Juan and Luisa. You did it. Now, go!

In the darkness, Sarah's thoughts turned to Steve's sled circling safely above the fray. *He could've helped; could've saved Juan and Luisa – driven off the strikers. He did nothing. Nothing! He deserves a coward's end. Coward!*

"Sarah?"

"What!"

Jake became silent for a moment then started crying.

"Sorry, Jake, stop crying. I'm not mad at you."

Jake's crying subsided to sobs. "Sarah, I'm scared."

"I know; I am too."

"I want to go home."

"We will."

"When?"

"As soon as Mommy and Daddy come get us."

"When will they get here?"

"Soon."

Sarah tried to sit up, but Jake's hold blocked her. Halfway up her stomach muscles shook and collapsed her onto the hard surface again. *What does it matter? I see nothing in the dark.* Sarah felt around with her free hand. Her fingers touched only cool, smooth surface.

Sarah lay with Jake on her chest. She tried to think, solve the riddle, get home. No time existed for them — only dark and quiet. Sarah and Jake lay holding each other until the darkness and silence brought sleep.

An unfamiliar voice spoke to Sarah in a dream.

Subconscious identified. Access granted. Are you command?

I don't understand.

Are you responsible?

"Yes," Sarah mumbled.

The words stopped. Sarah flowed away on sleep.

Sarah opened her eyes when Jake shifted. The black made her dizzy. She closed her eyes and wished for light. Gradually, light warmed her eyelids. She opened them. Light shone above her, diffuse and growing in intensity. Sarah blinked. Both the shock of shifting from a dark void and the fulfillment of her wish startled Sarah. She looked around; they lay on the floor at the end of a corridor. At her feet stood a wall, probably what they had fallen through. The ceiling glowed. "Jake, wake up."

Jake stirred on the hard floor. He blinked heavy eyelids. "Where are we, Sarah?"

"I don't know. I think we should explore and find out. How about that, Jake? Do you want to be an explorer?"

"No, I want Mommy."

"I know you do. We have to help them find us. That's why we have to explore."

"Ok."

They arose sore from the crash and stiff from sleeping on the floor.

Sarah held out her hand. Jake slipped his hand into hers without looking. The two made their way down the hall with light furtive steps, expecting each footfall to set off an alarm. Solid silence hushed their movement.

The corridor ended in another corridor that went a ways in either direction only to turn out of sight.

"Where are we?" Sarah startled herself with the thought spoken out loud.

"Colony site A76435, Command, level 1, northwest corridor, arterial junction" a voice said.

Sarah pulled Jake against the wall. She looked rapidly up and down the corridor. No one came. For the second time in as many suns her head pounded a heartbeat.

"Who are you?" Sarah asked.

"I am Iobe," said the voice.

"Where are you?" Sarah looked down the empty corridors.

"I am here."

"Where?"

"I am here"

"I can't see you. Where is here?"

A woman, or at least the ghost of a woman, condensed in front of Sarah and Jake. The woman stood twice as tall as Sarah. A white robe hung in loose folds around the woman's body leaving only her hands, neck, and head exposed. Delicate fingers, slender wrists and neck, and long hair suggested her gender in the absence of curving breasts and hips, which the robe concealed. Her hair flowed down the woman's shoulders and disappeared on the perfectly matched white of her robe. Her hair moved in one solid motion; no strands separated and tumbled over each other.

The woman's strange face drew Sarah's attention for a long moment. Her face looked smooth beyond the beauty of youth. Like sculpted stone, prominent shapes and lines carved a human face without living detail. The lips held no creases, the brow raised no eyebrows, and the eyes batted no eyelashes. The woman unnerved Sarah.

"Does my appearance suit you?" Iobe asked.

"Oh . . . Yes, thank you." Sarah looked at Iobe who looked back at her. "Who are you?"

"I am Iobe. Are you confused?"

"Yes. I mean, I understand that you are Iobe. Do you know how we got here?"

"Yes, I opened the door through which you fell."

"You brought us in?"

"Yes." Iobe paused. "Would you have preferred to remain outside?"

"No, no, I'm surprised. That's all."

"The predators' proximity prevented a lengthy conversation."

"Thank you . . . for saving us."

"You're welcome."

"I'm Sarah and this is Jake."

"I know." Iobe smiled at Sarah.

Jake pulled at Sarah's sleeve. "I'm hungry."

Iobe looked at Jake. She smiled. "What would you like to eat?"

"Something good. What is there?"

"Anything you desire. Come. The dining area is this way." Iobe walked down the left corridor. Her walk reminded Sarah of a ghost, movement without contact. No weight.

"Are you alone?" Sarah asked as she followed Iobe.

"No, you are here."

After several turns, Iobe stopped in the middle of a hall. The wall in front of her disappeared into an entrance to a room. The room contained nothing. No chairs. No tables. No kitchen. No food.

Jake and Sarah looked around confused.

As if in answer to their puzzled looks, a table and two chairs formed from the floor. Forks and two bowls appeared with something in them.

"This is a popular food. Have you had it before?" Iobe asked.

Jake and Sarah stepped to the table. Sarah scowled. The food looked like maggots drowned in puss.

"People eat this?" Sarah asked.

"Does this displease you?" asked Iobe.

"It smells strange but good," Jake said. He sat and reached for the fork. Sarah stopped him.

"Let me go first."

Sarah shot Jake a look when he started to fuss. Jake knew the code.

"You will find the food safe and nutritious," Iobe offered.

Sarah frowned with anticipation as she lifted the fork to her mouth. The maggots in puss were warm and . . . and . . . tasty. She smiled and nodded.

Jake had all the permission he needed. His fork moved bowl to mouth in rapid succession. When Sarah took her seat, Jake had already worked through a third of his portion.

"Slow down Jake. You'll choke."

His fork kept pace.

"What is this stuff?" Sarah asked. Her parents needed to know.

"Mac and cheese. Do you like it?"

"Yes! It's great. Thank you." A question interrupted Sarah's eating. "Iobe, are you a ghost?"

"No, why do you ask?"

"Well, you kind of look like a ghost or at least what I think a ghost looks like. I sort of see through you; but I sort of don't, and you seem to float when you walk."

"Forgive me. What you see is in here." Iobe placed a translucent finger to Sarah's temple without touching her. "I am all around you. You see me this way because I fade. A long time has passed. My energy is low."

"How long have you been here?"

"More mac and cheese!" said Jake.

His bowl filled without a glance from Iobe.

"Ninety years."

"Wow! That's a long time. Have you been alone all that time until we showed up?"

"For much of that period I have lived alone. The others left long ago."

"What about your family? Did they leave you here alone?" asked Sarah.

"I am the only one of my kind to visit this planet. I stayed in the event others come; like you." Iobe smiled at Sarah.

"Thanks. We—" Sarah glanced at Jake, "Letting us in helped a lot." Another question diverted Sarah. "Where did the others go?"

"I do not know. They found this planet unacceptable, so they chose to continue their journey."

"Why did they dislike this place?"

"At first, they favored this world. As time passed they began to die in large numbers. Survival here became questionable."

"Are you sick?"

"No. I am immune to the sickness that killed the others."

"I'm glad." Sarah sighed. "Iobe?"

"Yes, Sarah."

"Can you help us get home?"

"Building a ship requires more energy than I possess. There is, however, a ship circling above us. The predators have left. People walk on the ground. I suspect they look for you."

"Mommy and Daddy!" Jake cried.

"They're here! We must go, Iobe."

Sarah and Jake sprung from the table.

"Very well, follow me." Iobe retraced their steps. She looked at Sarah as they walked. "Sarah, I will fade soon. Will you help me restore my energy?"

Sarah scrunched her face. "I only know a little about energy. Let me talk to my dad. He'll know what to do."

"Thank you, Sarah."

They came to the place where Sarah and Jake slept.

"Farewell Sarah and Jake. Please return quickly. Little time remains."

Iobe disappeared as Sarah mouthed a reply.

"Bye Iobe!" Jake called.

The wall in front of them slid sideways with the sound of two heavy objects grinding against each other. Light outlined the door; the glow increased until clear daylight shown on their faces. Sarah and Jake stepped through the doorway into the array of mounds and alleys. Noise behind her caused Sarah to turn. A shallow indentation served as the only entrance sign.

"C'mon Jake, let's find Mommy and Daddy."

They rounded a corner. Sarah's link chattered again. She heard her father talking with others as they searched through the mounds.

"Dad, we're over here!" She cried into her link.

"Sarah! Where are you?"

A scout ship skimmed overhead.

"I have visual, Aiden. Mark these coordinates."

"Mommy!" Jake called.

"Hi honey! We're going to take you home now. Aiden, I'm going to land on the outskirts of these mounds for pickup."

18

Class Discussion

The students milled about the classroom. Blank walls for data projections surrounded concentric circles of desks that in turn wrapped around unlit hologram emitters in the room's center. Mr. Asworthy, an adherent of modern education philosophy, had placed his desk in the corner to avoid interposing himself between the students and learning, making him easy to ignore. Nothing in the room offered an excuse for the children's delay coming to order, leaving the students' own reluctance to resume school after the last recess of the day as the sole culprit.

The return to normalcy after her rescue suffocated Sarah. The rupture in her life had revealed the possibility of alternatives. An urge to do something different or be someone else consumed her thoughts—along with Iobe.

"Be seated quickly class. We will end the school day with a discussion of Election, specifically what the choice means to you. After reading a few of your papers on the subject, I believe a group discussion may help your understanding. Juan you may begin," said Mr. Asworthy.

Juan took his seat and stared at his desk. "I'm not sure, and my dad offers no advice. I think he forgets Election approaches."

"Sven, what do you think?"

"I choose art, but my dad says that's impractical."

"Mr. Ruiz has honed practicality to a flaw, but he does raise a valid concern. Our settlement struggles to survive mismanagement, bad luck, and disagreeable creatures that eat us. How does art provide food or protect us? On Earth, most artists failed to thrive even after machines delivered excessive leisure time to the masses. A few artists succeeded by pushing endorphins or adrenalin. As for art, short attention spans and disinterest destroyed the Mona Lisa long before vandals burned its storage shed."

Sven sunk into his chair. "Art offers understanding of ourselves and our world."

"No one will pay for those lessons. Stick to the list at Election. Everyone please share your thoughts; this is an open discussion, which I've deluded myself into believing possible after crushing Sven's dream."

Luisa patted Sven's shoulder. Afterwards, she checked her palm for paint. Sven's distinguishing characteristic of late was paint; he always had it on him. Drips and splatters and smudges and streaks of every color appeared in the oddest places on his body. Color invaded the usual places, under his fingernails and on his clothes; but also unusual places like the inside of his ear, an eyelid, the edge of his lips, an ankle—even up his nose. He looked like a chameleon with a rash.

Lian shrugged. "When I asked my mom, she said 'You have to follow your PASSION.'" She clutched at her throat and stuck her jaw out as she repeated the word.

While Lian feigned choking, Natasha broke in, "What's your deal Lu-i-sa?" She clucked the syllables in Luisa's name.

Natasha became spiteful when she felt threatened by one the girls. Steve had been smiling at Luisa too much for Natasha's ease lately. Sarah groaned. Natasha turned her head and snorted. The vulgar nasal sound produced a signature contrast with her face. Natasha's contrasts arose from an ill-considered genetic union. Since awakening from suspension, her father, Ivan Harkov, had built, with obsessive focus, a successful business that served both as the sole supplier of natural food and the primary constructor of colony buildings. Harkov's business success had attracted the attention of a beautiful woman, who did not, nor could not, look deeper into the man. Ivan Harkov, who placed his estimate of value on the physical, married the woman. To Natasha's future chagrin, Harkov's contribution to the transaction, like his parenting, was limited. Natasha inherited from her father thick arms and legs, a tendency to fatten with age, the snort, and nothing else. Natasha's mother bestowed a symmetrical face with delicate features, the curves of a nicely developing woman, good skin, and guidance on the finer points of life that missed the points entirely.

"What do you mean Na-tash-a?" asked Luisa.

Natasha shook her head. "Duh, what are you going to choose?"

"No duh, who cares? I'll pick whatever's available that sounds good—nothing to worry about. It's not like they can make me work at something I hate." Doubt cracked Luisa's voice.

"Do your passion. BE your passion," said Lian.

"And your parents will allow that?" Sven asked, ignoring Lian. "Commander Walker appears, um, kind of inflexible."

Sarah wondered how much Commander Walker knew of his daughter's antics. Luisa's recent performance in the spelling contest came to mind. Mr. Asworthy had asked Luisa to spell expectorate. She spelled détente instead. When their teacher had questioned her answer, Luisa responded that her father forbade spitting and she shan't say a word that required spitting to pronounce. Sarah had considered whether Luisa's refusal to spell "expectorate" or her use of "shan't" angered Mr. Asworthy more. She decided the "shan't" put Luisa into math practice during the next recess. *Does your father know you well, Luisa?*

"Not exactly." Luisa twisted a lock of hair around her finger with quick jerks of her wrist. "My dad wants me to join the military. 'It's family tradition young lady. Every generation of Walker has served in the military all the way back to The Big One.' By the time he gets to 'The Big One' he's usually screaming."

"What's The Big One?" Steve asked.

"Dub dub one. You know. The first version of the Internet," Natasha said.

"That's World War One," said Juan. "Honestly, Natasha, sometimes you say the dumbest things."

Lian, eyes creased in silent laughter, winked at Sarah.

Natasha blushed and glanced sideways at Steve, who appeared oblivious to the conversation. She leaned over her desk and bared her teeth at Luisa. Natasha attacked like an alpha striker—hard and fast, no flinch. "Can you imagine Luisa in the military?"

"I can be in the military! I just don't want to," said Luisa.

"Yeah right," said Natasha.

"So what are you going to do, Natasha, be an astrophysicist?" Luisa swapped smiles with Lian.

Natasha stomped the floor. "I'm going to be rich and famous like my dad." She pursed her lips in a pout and looked away from the other children.

"You earn fame and fortune after achieving something like your dad did with Harkov Enterprises. The food gathered and shelters built by your dad's business enable others to enrich the world in their own way," said Juan. "Life must mean more than being popular or wearing softer clothes. It has to; otherwise nothing makes sense. Fame and fortune, like happiness, are not choices, idiot."

Natasha's eyes started to wet. Red returned to her face. "I'm not stupid! Election is stupid! We should build robots and have them do all the work for us; like my dad says they did on Earth. Nobody had to work."

"Dude, I'd be so stoked if a bot did all my work for me," said Sven.

"Totally. Who needs passion? Just gimme a bot," said Natasha.

Juan faced Natasha with fists balled. "Nobody worked in the Great Displacement, moron. Robots took all the jobs. A lot of people suffered and many died in riots. Of course, whether YOU have a bot or not makes no difference; you're unlikely to achieve anything in either case."

Mr. Asworthy rapped his desk. "Children, quit acting like adults."

Natasha bit her lip. Her chin rippled. She sat silent for a moment looking at Juan, then ran out of the room.

"Does anyone else have thoughts to share or advice from their parents?" asked Mr. Asworthy.

"What do parents know anyway?" asked Sarah. "Half the time they don't listen to what you're saying. How can they help you decide what to do with your life if they don't know who you are or what you want? They get stuff wrong all the time. Look at their lives. Are they happy? What secret power routes their children's path to happiness when they've lost joy themselves?"

"Until you added that sentiment Sarah, this discussion had carried me to the brink of depression but no further. You have removed the last obstacle to despair," said Mr. Asworthy. "I will release you early because my tolerance has evaporated. Your homework assignment contains two parts. First, pick your top five choices for Election and know them beyond their title and type of work. Second, understand yourself and how your identity relates to each choice. I want thoughtful answers. I will monitor your data streams and reject the work of anyone who completes this assignment between dustball innings. Now leave me. I'm going home to eat chocolate."

The class erupted into bedlam as the group made their exit. Sarah waited for Lian, who approached Mr. Asworthy while he packed his teaching materials.

Lian placed a memory chip on his desk. "Mr. Asworthy this is my homework due six suns ago."

Mr. Asworthy looked up at Lian. "Perhaps I'll start with milk chocolate over buttery caramel and toasted pecans—"

"I couldn't turn the assignment in when due because we had a power surge at my house that wiped our memory chips," said Lian.

"And a delightful chocolate cake with raspberry liqueur icing and dark chocolate shavings." Mr. Asworthy's expression drifted with the contemplation of desserts.

"Don't worry. I caught up between dustball innings, so . . ."

"Plus a chocolate soufflé with mocha and hazelnut cream sauce. Yes, that will provide a fine start." Mr. Asworthy, ticking off former settings for his recipes, left the classroom.

"Weird," said Lian.

"I guess . . . so what do we do now?" Sarah asked.

19

Sickness Comes

Aiden stabbed with irritation at his food. "It's been forty-two first suns, Sarah. Give it a rest."

"You've never fed us mac and cheese, or even mentioned the food. Anyway, even if I did dream about eating mac and cheese, how come Jake says he ate it too?"

Sarah's dad gave her mom one of those 'we have a situation' looks.

"Lots of people have had the same dreams as other people. This is a strange planet—it does things to you. Nubis is not like the Earth you've learned about in school." Aiden shrugged.

"But I know what I saw Dad! Iobe needs our help! Please, come with me. I'll show you."

"Sarah, your mother and I discussed your sledding experience. We'd like you to meet someone. Her name is Hazel Johnson. She can help."

Sarah brightened. "Does she know a lot about energy?"

Aiden's shoulders sagged. He pushed the food around on his plate. "She's a good listener. Sometimes when people experience something bad, like you have, the bad thing hurts even after it's gone. Hazel will help you heal."

"I'm fine. Why won't you believe me? This is SO frustrating!" Sarah pushed from the table, almost falling as her chair tipped backwards. She announced her exit with a flick of hair and left.

"Hey, did you hear?" Lian asked.

"What?" Sarah asked as she walked up. The tightly clustered group accepted her and closed ranks. Steve, as usual of late, stood outside the circle. He hovered, refusing to leave even though no one talked to him anymore. Sarah felt sorry for him, not a lot, not enough to include him. He chose to be a coward, to let his fear control him. She and Jake could have died because he held back, so Sarah no longer called Steve a friend.

"They're having another emergency council meeting," Lian said.

"Who cares?" muttered Sarah.

"What's up with you? Parents still think you're loco?" Luisa twirled her finger around the side of her head.

Sarah frowned. "Yep. You've got it."

Lian placed a consoling hand on Sarah's shoulder. "I'm sorry."

Luisa nodded her head. Natasha looked annoyed. Her foot tapped a rapid cadence on the ground, stirring up a miniature explosion of dust.

"Sorry? You feel sorry for her? At least her parents still live." Juan looked away.

Sarah held Juan's hand. "Losing your dad is tough, Juan. When I look at my dad, I think I know what you feel. He looks tired. Some days are better than others. On the bad days my dad slips away." The sadness in her own voice surprised Sarah.

"That's how my dad star—" Juan stopped and stood silent and red-eyed.

"Do you want to go listen in on the council meeting?" Steve asked.

"Hey, let's go listen to the council meeting." Luisa stepped sideways, blocking Steve from the group.

"Yes, definitely." Lian seconded Luisa's silent reproof of Steve without as much as a sideways glance in his direction.

"Let's use the roof this time. The hallway makes me nervous," Luisa added.

The group started off.

"Should we wait for Sven?" Sarah asked.

"Naw, he's painting AGAIN," Juan answered.

"Adult mortality rates are spiking. Deaths have doubled this year compared to last year," said Dr. Khabir Stein. The doctor's back now curved further over his bulbous gut, which appeared larger despite the thinning remainder of his body. The doctor's shriveling build required a rocking heave to hoist his weight atop twig legs. He tottered around the chamber after forcing himself out of his council seat. His eyes, withdrawn into pits ledged by brow bone, flicked across the council chamber without pause.

"That part I already know. Just look around." Devya leaned forward and swept the room with her arm. "Do you think me so feeble-minded, Dr. Stein, as to forget the reason for Christie Winters' and Dagur Lok's absence from this council meeting? They're dead. I wear dresses from last year because, well, the tailor's dead. I want answers doctor; skip restating the obvious." Finished, Devya sank into her chair.

Aiden looked up at Devya slouching on her throne. She had ordered a new council chamber constructed that placed her on a throne above the others. Building the massive gilded chamber wasted sweat and blood in a colony scratching for existence. In another time, Aiden would have railed against such a move. Even that hatred burned less brightly now as everything in him wilted more with each new sun.

Fei Yen leaned over and touched Aiden's elbow. "Hey, Aiden, guess what?" She whispered with a joy that made her words come quick.

"What?"

"I did it. I created a three dimensional circuit capable of changing its architecture—my first real invention!" Her voice rose with excitement. "Computers will be able to adapt their physical structure."

"That's brilliant!" Aiden said.

The other council members turned to look at the two of them.

Dr. Stein glowered at Aiden and Fei Yen. "AS I SAID, I found no pathogens—no bacteria, no virus, no prions, no unidentified organisms or pseudo-organisms of any kind in the autopsies. While the symptoms appear similar to a disease cured in the early twenty-first century, chronic fatigue syndrome, I find no pathology for that disease in these cases. Their mitochondria function normally."

"In layman's terms, doctor." Devya waived a hand in the air with a lazy dismissive motion.

"They simply fade away."

"This fading sickness, how come it only seems to infect people with normal eyes?" Fei Yen asked.

"Miss Lin, at any given moment, thousands of diseases progress in a population. Your recent symptoms of ocular aura disease have no bearing on the fading sickness killing others; you may still suffer the same fate. You are sick. I have no answers. I work hard day and night to find cures for all of these problems."

"So, how many people have died from this OCULAR AURA disease?" Fei Yen asked.

"It's been documented as a possible secondary cause of death in a few cases."

"Like who? I want names," said Fei Yen.

"Mateus Peabody."

"He fell off a roof!"

"Yes, but what caused his fall?" Dr. Stein pointed at Fei Yen as if she alone possessed some truth about the incident.

"He tripped over a power cable!"

"Ocular aura disease might have been a contributing factor."

"Stop this squabbling at once." Devya leaned forward with effort. "The important thing to focus on is the fading sickness. It's killing people NOW. Doctor, how long do you think it will take to find a cure?"

"I don't know. I haven't identified a cause; therefore, I must use an experimental paradigm to select a cure."

"You mean you're going to use trial and error? Just pick things at random and see if they work?" Fei Yen's questions fell like blows on Dr. Stein, causing him to blink rapidly and twitch backward slightly.

"Shut up Fei Yen!"

Devya's outburst surprised Aiden. Her intolerance had become familiar. The surprise came in the energy she summoned. Devya looked like Christie in her final days, a husk clinging to its spent seed head—what Aiden felt.

Dr. Stein scowled before answering Fei Yen. "If you wish to use laymen's terms, yes, the empirical approach is trial and error. I must test a large but finite number of combinations and permutations. The study will take time; however, I will not rest until I find the answer."

"If we leave this place, will the sickness end?" Devya asked.

"Environmental exposure is a potential factor. If exposure is the cause, then removal from the source helps; however, leaving may not alleviate symptoms or stop death for damaged bodies. Evacuation is certainly a first step."

"We will build a starship and find a new home," Devya declared.

"Madame President," Commander Walker spoke. "Our best chemist said no suitable fuel exists here. If we build a starship, how do you propose we move it?"

"Other chemists will solve the problem." Devya's dismissive hand waived again.

"They're all bug juice now." Fei Yen's jaw clenched and thrust out.

Devya gripped the armrests on her chair with whitening intensity. "We have more information at our disposal than any human hopes to master. Someone will learn chemistry and figure it out!"

"Who?" Aiden kept his voice level in sharp contrast to his emotions.

"Some of the children." Again a dismissive hand waved.

"Who? The children? Are you mad?" Aiden grew nervous his last question might offend Devya. After she had appointed herself president, with Commander Walker's backing, Devya had taken exception to anyone who questioned her leadership.

"Certainly not. It's about time they grow up, start contributing, and become an asset to society instead of a liability. This colony has put off Election for too long. They must decide in two first suns," Devya said.

"You're serious?" Fei Yen's countenance widened in disbelief.

"Would you prefer we bring back robots?" Devya glared at a silent Fei Yen and Aiden long enough to induce awkwardness. "That's what I thought. Commander Walker, work with Ruiz to construct the ship. Make sure it meets military specifications. Harkov will supply what you need."

Walker nodded. "As you wish, Madame President."

Scraping and sliding sounds from the roof caused the council members to look up. Then a muffled shriek and thud on the window of the council chamber drew their attention to Sarah dangling from the roof's edge in full view.

"What's this?" Devya glared at Sarah.

The council members moved to the door as the remaining children scrambled off the roof with frantic scratching and thuds. Haste and fear ruined their orderly exit. Aiden burst from a side door. He reached Sarah as her grip failed, sparing her the sprained ankle or broken leg sure to have followed such a fall.

"Lian Lin, stop right there!" Fei Yin called.

Lian stopped running. Her head bowed low. Juan, Steve, Natasha, and Luisa continued to run. They ran fast, as if speed made them invisible in bright light, as if their captured friends would keep silent. Juan, Steve, and Luisa disappeared behind an adjacent building at a full sprint.

"Dad, I can explain."

"Save it Sarah. Your explanation will bury you. Go home. I will join you shortly."

"You had better do the same young lady. Your father and I will have words with you about this." Fei Yin wagged a finger at Lian.

"I hope you have more than words for this treachery," said Devya.

The entire council now stood outside the chambers watching the two girls make a dejected retreat.

"I will deal with my daughter as I see fit," Fei Yin said.

"See that the punishment fits the crime." Devya's tone delivered an explicit threat.

Devya and the other council members left, leaving Fei Yin and Aiden alone. Aiden stood silent. Anger at his daughter's actions acted as kindling for the blaze of hatred touched off by Devya's words.

"You would think, with such helpful parenting advice, that Devya had kids of her own," Lian said.

"No one wants her."

"Truth told." Fei Yin relaxed and smiled. "Hey, after we get done dealing with the progeny, come over and see my new circuitry. It's really cool."

"You bet. But now I've got some fathering to do."

"Mmm, hm." Fei Yen turned toward her house.

Aiden rounded the council building's corner. Devya hurried away, her face hidden. A hand came away from her head; wet fingers glistened in the sun. She had stayed out of view close to the building, Aiden realized. He started for home with Devya on his mind when he caught sight of Commander Walker heading toward the mess hall. Aiden ran to catch him. "Hey, Walker, I want to talk with you."

Commander Walker kept moving as Aiden fell along side.

"Why do you support Devya's trampling of democracy?" asked Aiden.

Walker stopped and squared off against Aiden. "What did you say?"

"Devya disregards democratic principles; she rules like a dictator. You lead the military. Without your support, Devya can't force her will upon anyone. You enable her power. I want to know why."

Walker jabbed a thick finger into Aiden's chest. "You understand nothing about leadership, Haven. Many people dream of leading; few possess courage to do so. Devya stepped forward when others turned away. She understands what you miss—power protects the strong from the weak. Your notion of democracy collapses in a society populated with passive and weak people. These colonists care only about putting food in their bellies."

Walker's words ignited Aiden. "We care about food because we struggle to survive on this planet. Most of us eat too little; although I see Devya, Harkov, and you overcame that problem." Aiden looked disgusted at Walker's bulging gut.

"Are you accusing me of something, Haven?" Walker jabbed Aiden again, harder this time.

"Who exempted your soldiers from labor detail? How come they loaf while the rest of us work?" Anger pushed Aiden's voice higher.

Walker responded in kind. "My soldiers put their lives on the line for you colonists. They shouldn't have to dig ditches with your kind."

"Is that it? You're better than us? Is that why you live in a house twice the size of other's? Devya's house is the only home larger. We were all supposed to have equal housing rations. You trade loyalty for a bigger house and overstuffed belly?"

Walker's fist struck Aiden's jaw. Aiden's head twisted with a dangerous snap; his body fell backwards. Blinded by anger, Aiden had not expected the blow, had not protected himself. Impact with the ground knocked air out of his lungs. The next inhale filled Aiden's lungs with dust. He coughed in heaving spasms as he struggled to escape drowning.

Aiden regained his feet and raised his fists. Through dust scratched and watering eyes, Aiden made out Walker's blurry form walking into the mess hall at a casual stroll. Aiden, swaying with raised fists, stood alone in front of the building. Pain throbbed along his jaw. He felt humiliated and bitter. Walker hadn't struck an opponent. He had punished a dog.

20

Election

Sarah, I need you. Please, help me.

Sarah twisted in her sheets until the tangle drew taught. Her eyes popped open. Sarah had dreamed of Iobe dying. She looked at the time, nearly second sunset and pulled a pillow over her head. Sleep never returned, only thoughts of Election. When she rose at dawn of first sun, Sarah plodded through her morning rituals in a stupor, which suited her for she wished to forget every moment of Election Day.

"Sarah, take your brother outside while you wait. He needs to burn off energy," said her mom.

"Hey, Jake, let's find a desiwog."

"Yeah! I want to see a big fat one!" Jake moved rapidly around making no progress in any direction.

Sarah took Jake's small, soft hand in hers and walked around the side of their house, prime desiwog territory. She scanned the dust layer. A telltale puff of dust mushroomed from the layer.

Jake spotted it too. "Look! Over there! There's one!" Jake whisper yelled.

"Sh. Sh. I see it. Be quiet, or you'll scare it," Sarah whispered.

Sarah stepped softly toward the spot where the dust had erupted. Jake jumped, bounced, stomped, and ran in place (restrained only by Sarah's grip) the whole way over.

"Let's find it." Sarah gestured with her hand and moved it over the area in front of them.

A holographic heat map projected from Sarah's shirt onto the dust. The map, a grid of green light in equal-sized squares, showed colored shapes of red, orange, and yellow, representing the heat given off by different things in the dust. The map tracked movement of the objects.

"There it is Sarah! I see it right there!" Jake pointed to a corner of the image where a bright red blob with an orange tail sat.

"Ok, I'm going to clear the area." Sarah touched the particle former on her wrist. Dust sucked into a pile beside Jake forming a crude chair. After about half the dust layer around the desiwog had thinned, Sarah reduced the accumulation rate to keep the desiwog partially visible but avoid frightening the creature with too much light.

The desiwog sat atop a mound of dirt. A chute extended down the slope of the mound through a trench and up the face of another mound of equal size. Without eyes to reveal its state, the motionless creature appeared neither awake nor asleep. Icky tentacles from the lower half of its fat head collapsed onto the ground. Sarah knew the animal waited and felt for prey. The animal's head looked like a week-old balloon—large, round, and soft. Its body resembled a thin pointed flag that flew above castles in fairytales. Desiwog skin had smooth bumps the color of dirt. All head and flag body and grossness, desiwogs disgusted Sarah. That's probably why Jake liked watching them. In an instant, the desiwog spit a glob of goo into the center of the shallow trench.

"Ew! It spit Sarah!" Jake yelled.

"I know. Be quiet," she whispered.

Neither the desiwog nor its audience waited long. Desiccant bugs moved in from all directions. Want drove them to the goo spit.

Did they like it? Dumb bugs, they never learned.

The desiccant bugs scrambled, stumbled, fell, trenched. Some climbed over the desiwog, which lay in wait. Early arrivals to the glob gorged on more than their share. Bodies swelled; spit dwindled. Obsessed with consumption, the crowd trampled saner individuals underfoot. Latecomers set upon the bloated, snapping limbs and flipping their brethren to expose soft underbellies for puncturing. A few burst and died, leaving their remains to feed kin. More bugs surged into the trench.

At the peak of frenzy for the last drops, the desiwog twitched. The wriggle launched it down the chute. As the desiwog accelerated from its perch, its great mouth opened. Combs flattened outward and raked the ground along the rim of the opening. The animal plowed into the mass of bugs at full speed. Dust and bugs spilled into the desiwog's open mouth. Frantic clicks and thrumming pleaded for help or mercy or whatever bugs beg before death. A few lucky late arrivals were knocked aside. They fled.

The horde disappeared into the desiwog's cavernous mouth. Comb teeth retracted vertical. The desiwog emerged from the trough and slowed on the uphill slide to the opposite mound. It wriggled again, hard this time, to push its bloat onto the top.

Sarah found the next part creepy. As the desiwog crested the mound, it grinned Cheshire style. Dust and dirt spilled from the comb teeth, pushed out by trapped desperation of prey. Nasty. The desiwog gloated until its meal had rid itself of dirt. With each course, the bugs made the desiwog fatter, the mound higher, and the ramp steeper. Next time, more aunts, uncles, and cousins would suffer desire's fate. *Dumb bugs.*

"You see that Sarah?" Jake clapped.

Sarah nodded. Jake sat absorbed with the creature. The desiwog's smile had faded. The animal swallowed.

After an hour of forgotten existence, no time remained for avoidance. Sarah gathered with her friends outside the new council building. Their small group clustered at the foot of the steps to the main entrance. The council building, the only building with stairs in the colony, stood above others. The children waited for Election with all of Hoepa's first generation.

"Have you seen Sven?" Luisa asked.

"No. He better show up. He's so flaming out," Lian answered.

"He's probably lost in his 'art,'" said Natasha.

The three girls giggled.

The conversation floated past Sarah. Sweat collected and ran down Sarah's temple. Her emotions ran hotter than the day. *Sven's lucky. I wish I knew what I wanted to be. I wish to get lost in something. I wish I were somewhere else, somebody else. How did he find his calling? How am I supposed to just know? I think and think and think but there's nothing there, no interest, no spark, no stupid passion. I hate that word. People say 'find your passion.' Then they smile at you like they've just given you the secret of life. Idiots.*

What will they do when I answer? Will I be punished for making a bad choice? Will my family still love me if I embarrass them in front of the whole colony? I should just pick something responsible, save myself the embarrassment, and protect my family. Make Daddy happy; be responsible. I miss his smile. I miss playing with him. I wish I were little. I don't want to do this.

Sarah looked around. About a quarter of the children brimmed with energy — the kind of energy that comes from preparing for something and wishing to get on with it. The rest looked bored. Sarah felt alone. She shoved her hands in her pockets and lowered her chin. A shiver wracked her body under the warm sun. The conversations flowed all around her, sinking her in a sea of confused sound.

Dread swamped Sarah as the familiar shrunken frame of her truth-telling teacher, Mr. Asworthy, passed from behind. Mr. Asworthy moved through the crowd of children in a bubble of silence that quelled conversation as he approached and stifled voices until the teacher had comfortably passed. When Mr. Asworthy reached the side of the crowd abutting the council building steps, he began arranging the children in two rows. Sarah found no logic in the precise order Mr. Asworthy sought — a mystery likely known only to her teacher.

"You must get in line children to make your choices. Quickly now. Lian, our big dreamer who never acts, you're here." Beads of sweat glistened on Mr. Asworthy's bald head.

Lian gave her teacher a polite but strained smile. "How are you Mr. Asworthy?"

Mr. Asworthy sighed. "Oh, I doubt you care about how I am; however, I will respond out of tedious courtesy. I have a weird purple and green rash in my armpits that itches and oozes." He scratched his armpits in response to the recollection. Mr. Asworthy then moved Lian into place with a soft commanding grip on her upper arm. When he released her arm, Lian held it at an angle from her body suggesting a willingness to amputate.

"The girl who wrote the paper about Election portraying a budding materialist blind to true success stand here — that's you Natasha. Stand here without pretense. Everyone knows you for who you are. Come." Mr. Asworthy waived to Natasha.

Natasha, having witnessed Mr. Asworthy's exchange with Lian, contorted her upper body in a backward arc to avoid her teacher's outstretched hand as she fell into place.

Mr. Asworthy stepped down the growing line of children. "Steve, my boy, you know yourself well enough to choose wisely. Pity you possess so little worth knowing. Do work on character. Behind Lian, there you go. Luisa, you may wander until the end of time, but by golly you will stand next to Natasha for Election." Mr. Asworthy patted Juan on the shoulder. "You've got a healthy balance between present and future and strong character. Too bad you're such a jerk. Yes, right behind Lian will do."

Juan moved into place and brushed at the invisible plague on his shoulder then looked with horror at his hand.

Sarah clenched her fists. Her eyes closed tightly as she braced for her teacher's words.

"Sarah." Mr. Asworthy gently grasped both her arms. "Discover yourself. Choose for you. And remember, you are not alone. You're next to Juan."

Sarah gagged at her teacher's touch.

The old man's voice faded as he moved away forming two columns of red-faced children, who set upon babbling as a cure for embarrassment. After the children assembled into two rows, Mr. Asworthy returned to stand at the top of the steps in front of the council building's main entrance. He stood quiet while a swell of silence rolled through the lines, young people shutting conversations and turning heads to face him. Afloat on the sea of noise, Sarah caught the swell as it started. By the time the wave had reached the end of the lines only a few clueless and self-absorbed children still spoke.

"Children," Mr. Asworthy said in his teacher voice, "Election is upon you. Please, come in and take your seats."

"Why do we all have to be here at once?" Sarah asked Juan as he walked beside her. "Can't we just send a note or something?"

"They want to make it a big deal I guess. So you take it seriously. Look around. Even still, half the kids here wait actively numb to the event."

Sarah thought Juan generous in his assessment of interest.

"Move along children. Take your seats. Parents and other colonists will arrive and need to be seated soon," urged Mr. Asworthy as they filed past.

"Perfect. Absolutely perfect. The whole colony will be here."

Juan looked ahead as he moved forward. "Relax, Sarah. Today is tomorrow's yesterday."

Sarah shot him a look of pure annoyance. "When did you become an ancient proverb?"

Juan clasped his hands together and nodded his head in mock piety. "Life remembers, lives, and dreams."

Juan's half-serious advice failed to bring even a wink of happiness to Sarah. Sarah filed with the other children down the center aisle of the Great Hall past the long rows of seats for the colonists. At the front of the Hall, three rows of seats draped in blood red cloth awaited the children. Great, Sarah thought. They chose the color of spilled blood for poor choices. She took a seat next to Lian in the first row.

Rising before Sarah, the long council table made a semicircle behind a pedestal that stood higher than any other. Every line of the building, every seat, every light, and every minor detail focused on the pedestal upon which stood a large chair. The chair (her dad called it a throne) had a deep lush cushion made of some material Sarah had never seen. The back of the chair rose as high as a full grown man. Carved scrolls and facets around the chair's edges shimmered in the light. All this floated two decimeters above the pedestal on a maglev cushion.

Sarah stared at the vacant space between the pedestal and the chair created by the maglev. The excess of the chair withered in comparison to the gap between chair and pedestal. A maglev shortage restricted their use to critical functions. The only known source of cobalt, the primary mineral component in maglevs, came from a crevasse deep in the Southern Mountains. Mining proved difficult and dangerous. Stints in the mine were reserved for non-contributors. She knew several kids at school who had lost a parent in that mine.

The noise of chatter and feet as people filled rows behind the children interrupted Sarah's study of the throne. She looked down at her knees. Sarah felt the hall grow warmer as people entered. Their breathing pressed down on her. Every breath exhaled expectations—expectations of the children—of her.

A commotion in the back of the hall followed by laughter and jeers announced Sven's arrival. He ran down the center aisle and planted in the vacant seat two down from Sarah. Blotches of paint spattered his formal clothes. Sarah hadn't seen Sven for many suns. His face shocked her. Sven's clear eyes held no trace of blue, and he looked tired.

The crowd hushed as the council members filed in. Sarah felt a surge of pride as her dad took his seat. He looked handsome in his gray tunic with black sash. Empty council seats next to him reminded Sarah of those lost souls. Once all the council members took seats, large guards on either side of the council table prompted the audience to stand and clap as President Devya Kandari made her entrance. Most complied.

Devya smiled at the assembled crowd as she walked in a slow glide to her seat. Sarah thought the President's face pretty except for the eyes, which were dull and lifeless. She wore a purple robe that trailed the floor behind her. The sleeves gaped so wide around Devya's slender wrists that she looked like a toddler who had tried on her mother's clothes. Golden ribbons laced Devya's long black hair and spilled down her shoulders and back.

Sarah's lips twisted as a suppressed smile struggled to escape when Devya sat down. The throne shifted only slightly, in part because reversing polarity magnetic fields around the edges resisted movement and in part because the chair dwarfed the figure climbing onto it. The chair looked large enough for a person three times Devya's size. The President seemed unaware of the poor fit.

Devya curled her legs under her and raised her hand. The crowd stopped clapping and took their seats.

"Fellow citizens, today is a momentous day in Hoepa's history . . ."

Sarah drifted inward as the President began speaking. Her thoughts careened recklessly around her mind. She searched for a way out. *Just pick something, anything.*

"Juan Lok, step forward and choose," Mr. Asworthy called.

Sarah watched as Juan stood from across the aisle and stepped to the red circle on the floor in front of Devya. He started to speak. One of the guards flanking the President menaced with his repulsion staff. Juan quickly knelt on one knee.

"I choose politics," Juan said loudly.

Devya leaned forward, "A wise choice, boy."

Juan nodded but did not smile. He returned to his seat.

Sarah had responsibilities to meet. That's what her dad said. Her mom's call pulled stronger — take time to choose wisely.

"Steve Nelson, step forward and choose."

"I choose baker."

Devya's eyes narrowed. "See that you pay more tribute with the bread you bake than your father."

Her mom had told Sarah to find something that made her happy. *But how?*

"Luisa Walker, step forward and choose."

"I choose law."

Sarah shot a glance at Commander Walker. His fists clenched tightly causing the veins in his forearms to bulge. His lips clamped tight.

Maybe, if I make myself invisible, Sarah hung her head, *they'll forget to call my name.*

A voice broke through, "Sarah Haven, step forward and choose."

Sarah stood slowly. She felt like throwing up. *I bet I'll get a pass if I throw up on the President.*

She knelt in front of the President as the others had done. Sarah stared at the pedestal. She said nothing.

"Well, speak up child and be quick about it," said Devya.

Sarah swallowed. Then she swallowed again. "I, um, I choose nothing."

"What? You must choose something." Devya's voice rose sharply.

"I'm . . . I'm not ready to choose. I choose nothing."

"Unacceptable! Choose or be punished!"

The President's anger should have shaken Sarah, quelled her rebellion before the throne. Instead, Sarah found strength in resisting the rage. She lifted her chin then stood defiant.

"I choose nothing." Her voice rang out unfettered, clear, and free over the heads of silent colonists.

"Fool! I banish you to the cobalt mine for life!"

For the duration of an eye blink silence stilled the Great Hall. The moment shattered in the loud clap of a chair toppling over. Sarah turned to see her father leaping over the council table. She knew the man moving must be him. The chair he had sat in lay upturned on the floor. Yet the person charging her seemed foreign. The face of the man scrambling over the table twisted in rage, hideous and unrecognizable, inhuman, not her dad.

"I'll kill you!" Aiden screamed as he lunged forward.

Sarah drew back. She had never seen her dad so angry. Color drained from his face. His eyes. His eyes glowed an intense blue Sarah saw only in others.

No, Daddy. Please. I can't. Please don't make me.

The words never came. Sarah faltered, frozen save her hand, raised with the smallness of a child in the face of a charging beast. Only . . . Only, her father looked at . . . he moved on . . . the President.

Devya shrunk into the far corner of her seat. "Seize him! He's infected!"

Aiden cleared the distance to the President's throne before the guard on the opposite side rounded the pedestal. Only one guard stood between Aiden and his target.

The guard lowered and thrust a repulsion stick. The tip contacted Aiden's chest. A shock wave burst through his body throwing him back and taking his breath. He hit the ground. Guard after guard piled on top of him. They shouted instructions at one another, though each acted on their own will to subdue Aiden.

Somewhere in the din or in her mind, Sarah heard the words, "Run Sarah! Run!" The command touched an instinct in her. She ran. While her dad drew everyone's attention, Sarah ran.

"Throw this assassin in prison until I decide a punishment."

When the pile cleared, four guards dragged Aiden out.

"She murders children! Look at her. She murders children!"

Her father's words sounded the end of Election for Sarah. She cleared the front entrance at a full run.

21

Escape and Banishment

"Halt!"

Sarah looked behind her. A lone guard ran toward her. Sarah touched her former and dove off the steps. As her body flew through the air, dust shaped. The ground rushed up. A photon sled encased and launched her into the sky less than half a decimeter from impact. Matching Sarah's daring, the guard formed his own larger sled on the run and gave chase.

Sarah cleared the perimeter barrier and plunged directly into the forest. She knew her sled couldn't outrun the guard. Security guards carried higher powered formers that created faster sleds. No, she had to lose him and hide.

Darkness enveloped her. She squinted. Massive trunks threatened her egg shell. Sarah swerved and banked, rolled and weaved through the forest. She kept low, just high enough to see above the dust layer while trailing a plume of dust to blind her pursuer. The guard matched her move for move and drew closer. His augmented reality tracked her in the cloud.

A hard bump caused Sarah's sled to lurch forward unstable. The guard rammed her again. She screamed as the edge of her sled scraped a trunk on the left. Another loomed directly ahead. She pulled up hard and went vertical. The guard followed with a wide upward turn that skipped his sled once on the trunk before him. The two sleds sped toward the canopy.

Branches tangled throughout the canopy in a deadly mesh, just what Sarah needed. She flew through the branches as spaces tightened in the trees' reach for light. She heard loud bangs from behind. The guard's larger sled struggled to follow. Sarah kept up her pace. A thick branch forked ahead with another large branch crossing behind the fork. Sarah slipped between the fork and inverted to slide under the second branch.

The branches recoiled to defend against Sarah's intrusion. Then their muscles tensed, limbs snapped. The tree's strike disintegrated the guard's sled with a bang of dust. He fell, landing with an "umphf" on a large branch below.

Sarah slowed and headed upwards for light. She realized the trees attacked. Luck taught her a lesson without demanding she pay the cost. The dense upper canopy before Sarah opened as each branch prepared to strike the oncoming sled. She timed her flight to catch the opening before the branches' blows connected. Sarah burst into the light.

Now free from pursuit, Sarah knew where to hide.

The long flight across the plain offered ample silence for Sarah's emotions to crash upon her. *Will I see them again? Will Dad be arrested or . . . or . . . shot for attacking the President? That witch! She has no right to do this to me! Election is stupid! So stupid. I would choose something eventually. Mom told me to wait. Will Mom or Dad look for me? Dad's going to be so mad at me. Do they still love me after what I've done? Will I see Jake again? Will he understand what happened; why I left? I already miss them. What's going to happen to me? I just want to go home. I want to be home.*

At times her vision clouded with more tears than she wiped away. Other times she sobbed so violently the sled veered into erratic plunges and climbs.

Sarah circled the maze of mounds several times scanning for strikers before setting down near the shallow depression she and Jake fell through many suns ago. She wondered how to open the door and if Iobe lived. She must hide here. Nubis offered few places to survive. Humans settled two locations on the planet, the colony and the cobalt mine. No food grew in the mountains. The forest, with its darkness and large creatures, scared her.

Sarah stepped out of the sled. The shallow depression in the hill stood in front of her. She pressed on the surface. It felt hard and smooth and immovable. She knocked. Small dull thuds of skin and bone on dense matter barely reached Sarah's own ears. No response. She pushed hard until her feet slipped from under her. Sarah's knees and palms arrested her fall with pain. The door remained closed. Perhaps she must turn her back to it like Jake and she had done earlier when the door opened. Nothing happened.

She wished for Iobe to open the door. The grind of stone moving on stone emerged as the door slid open. Sarah stepped into the cool blackness of the hallway. The door shut the light behind her.

"Iobe? Are you there?"

"Hello Sarah."

Relief pushed back Sarah's flood of sorrow. "You're still alive! I worried you had died. Where are you?"

"I am here Sarah."

"Please turn on the lights. I want to see you."

"I'm sorry, Sarah. I lack the energy to light this space or materialize."

"Oh, Iobe, I'm so sorry. I tried to get my dad to come help, but he refused to believe you existed. Now he can't come, and I can't go back." Sarah's voice broke with stifled sobs.

"I understand Sarah. Thank you for trying. You may stay here a while; however, you must leave before I lose my ability to open the door."

Sarah cringed. Her father had taught her enough about wilderness survival to understand the difficulty of living in the forest. She searched for options.

"I need to stay here. I have nowhere else to go. May I stay and help you, Iobe?"

"The collectors are blocked. If cleared, I could refill the capacitors. Can you clear the collectors?"

"What blocks them?"

"I am unable to analyze. The sensor grid monitoring the collectors went dark with them."

"Where are they?"

"The first array is directly above us."

"Outside?"

"Yes."

Sarah fought the pang rising in her. "Can you watch for strikers while I'm out?"

"I am too weak to detect them."

"I see. Can you talk to me when I'm outside? Tell me what to do?"

"Yes. Will you try, Sarah?"

"Ok."

The door slid open again. This time it moved more slowly than before. Sarah stepped out and blinked. After a moment of blurry blindness, she focused on her sled and the hills around her.

"Climb the mound Sarah."

Sarah scrambled to the top of the mound. Despite the gradual slope of the low hill, dirt slid and sunk under foot. Her breath had quickened when she reached the top. She turned around, scanning the maze of mounds around her. Nothing moved or called.

Relieved but hurried by the desire to complete her task quickly, Sarah asked "Where are the collectors?"

"If you climbed the hill above the door, you stand directly over the first collector."

Sarah looked at her feet. She stood on dirt. She squatted and scooped handfuls of the loose material; the dirt bloomed into clouds of dust that hung in the air obscuring her view. She coughed and hacked until she covered her face with a filter mask. Sarah kept digging.

"Have you located the collector?"

"No, I see dirt but nothing like a collector. I'm digging trying to find it."

Sarah reached farther into the hole with each scoop. The cloud of dust surrounded her. With her arm in the hole up to her elbow, Sarah touched something smooth and hard.

"I found something Iobe!"

She stood and swiped her former. The dust cleared from the air into a ball on the ground. Sarah peered into the hole. At the bottom lay a dark shiny surface.

"I sense trace energy signatures Sarah. You have found the first collector."

"I think I understand the problem. Iobe, am I standing on top of an old colony building?"

"Yes, Sarah."

"These panels collect solar energy, right?"

"That is correct."

"Got it. So these mounds are actually colony buildings buried under dust over decades. The solar collectors on top of the roofs must have stopped working when dirt buried the surfaces. After I remove the covering you should be able to collect energy again. I think I can do this."

Sarah gestured. Her former created another ball. The hole grew wider. She kicked the balls to the side of the hill where they rolled down into the dust layer. A spark of youth flared inside her pushing back, for a moment, the darkness inside. She formed a larger ball and kicked it hard. The ball sailed over the adjacent mound, landing with a thud on the hill beyond.

Joy of play coursed through her body. Fear and sadness and hatred disappeared. Sarah raised her arms. "Goal! G o a l! Ladies and gentleman, Sarah Haven has just won the match! The crowd screams her name. Sarah! Sarah! Sarah!"

"Sarah, I detected an impact on collector array six. Do you know what happened?"

"Um, nothing Iobe. I'll take care of it. Sorry." Sarah returned to clearing the collector. She made larger and larger balls to speed the clearing. She stopped increasing the ball size when she had to push it hard to roll it over the edge.

The hard work bored Sarah; progress came slow. She told herself the effort helped Iobe; that made her task easier to bear. Sarah invented a game to make the work more interesting. She rolled balls down the hill trying to hit one of the previous balls hidden by the dust. Loud cracks sounded out her success. Occasionally, a direct hit forced her target above the dust layer as it rolled partially up the slope of the opposite hill before resettling in the dust.

Halfway through the second sun, Sarah had cleared a third of the hill top. Gleaming solar collectors filled with sun.

"You make good progress Sarah. The energy flows now."

"Thanks Iobe."

Sarah's body ached. She hit fewer balls with each new roll as the second sun peaked. Sarah arched her back and stretched to pull the soreness from her muscles. As she relaxed out of the contortion, her eyes roamed the hills. That's when she saw the figure.

Sarah's guts clenched with the sudden nausea of panic. There, no more than ten hills away, a woman stood watching her. The woman's body gave the impression of refined power, tight and strong, while her direct gaze conveyed a sense of willpower. Light shimmered on her form-fitting, solid black clothing. The clothing complemented deep burgundy hair curling down her neck. Her hair looked like a mass of bloody snakes. The woman stood on the hill motionless with the curious tilt to her head of someone who's found something familiar yet unexpected.

"Iobe, there's somebody here. Open the door," Sarah whispered. Thoughts of patrols looking for her and the cobalt mine crowded in. She formed a ball and rolled it in the direction of the door. She looked straight ahead trying to watch the woman with her peripheral vision.

Movement blurred across the side of Sarah's vision as she neared the edge of the mound. Sarah looked at the woman. She walked calmly toward Sarah. The woman cleared the ten odd meters between hill tops with a leap that barely broke the stride of her calm pace.

Sarah dashed down the hill. She cut sharply back and ran into the lit corridor where Iobe waited. Sarah looked back as the door closed. She saw the woman drop to the opening just before the door sealed shut with a solid thud.

22

Fallout

Aiden stood in the middle of his jail cell or at least the space serving as his prison. He took mental account of his surroundings yet again. The colony lacked a jail, so the guards had confined him in the room of a new dry storage building—as if any other storage existed on a dust bowl planet like Nubis. The room had no windows to break or pry open. The space now served as a prison because Ivan Harkov had succumbed to his paranoia about employee theft and reinforced the door. Aiden had to admit Harkov built a good cell for the colony's first prisoner. An external light switch was the cell's only flaw. The guards kept turning off the light after they left food, leaving him in rare darkness on Nubis. Too many attempted escapes during the brief periods of open door had left the guards callous to his condition in the cell.

Three times a solar cycle, or what he thought a cycle, Aiden tested the room. A crack to pry. A shallow depression to dig. Some defect in workmanship or material to exploit. In darkness, the tests meant long periods of groping with each test ending in the same result—no way out. Sarah's plight fueled his will to escape. Whether she hid in the wilderness or mined cobalt, Sarah needed him. Devya had ordered all contact severed between him and the colony. Isolation, instead of breaking him, reinforced Aiden's perseverance when his fire sputtered under a rain of tears.

How many times had I become bored? How many times had I wished to be somewhere else, doing something else, when she tried to share her life with me? I love her so much! I knew then, just as I know now, how little time we have together. Why hadn't I focused?

She grew too quickly. I remember the colored scribble art when she was three. Did she draw me? Was I smiling? She overflowed with innocence and wonder, believing in me, her father. How many times was I somewhere else? When did she start to see? How badly have I hurt her? Why can't I remember those precious nothing moments?

I must believe she lives and enough heartbeats remain to help, to show my love, to be the father she deserves.

Aiden fought the darkness with a memory of Sarah's smiling face. He concentrated hard on the picture in his mind so that a few moments had passed before he registered the change. Darkness shrank in the room with the emergence of a glow from a point in the bottom of the outside wall. Someone was cutting through the wall. They came for him.

The glow arced over just enough wall to cut a hole big enough for him to crawl through. Aiden readied himself on hands and knees. When the cut piece fell inward, Aiden scrambled through before the dust had time to flow in. He blinked back bright light. A blurry figure focused.

"Hello, handsome." Rachel smiled down at him. The side arm strapped to her thigh and the flickering green tint of augmented reality lenses in her eyes betrayed the lightness of her welcome.

"Sarah?"

Rachel's smile dropped. "Missing."

A pair of voices approached the front of the building as Aiden stood. Rachel pushed him to the wall and drew close. Aiden caught the scent of her hair. Her body pressed against his and drew out the loneliness he felt while caged. The voices passed. Rachel looked up into his face. The scar along her jaw edged the desire he saw in her. Their lips met in soft reunion that warmed his soul. Aiden felt relief and love in Rachel's kiss, but also sadness and emptiness. Rachel pushed away, recovering her presence before him.

"We need to move," she said.

Aiden nodded. Rachel pressed along the wall to the building's corner and peered around. She looked back at Aiden, brought two fingers in an inverted V to her eyes, laid her hand flat palm down, and made a vertical slicing motion on it with the other hand.

"Ok, I have absolutely no idea what you're trying to say."

Rachel rolled her eyes and sighed. She grabbed Aiden by the shirt and pulled him down after her into the dust layer. Tiny particles glued to the moist surfaces of his eyes. Those grains carved pain with every blink. His ears filled with solid matter. His next inhale brought a slug of particles up his nose. Aiden opened his mouth for air. The movement ended with a sputtering cough as another slug of dense dust entered his throat.

More voices approached the other side of the building. He started to rise, desperate for oxygen. Rachel yanked him back to the ground. Her knee hit his stomach hard. A gush of dust and the last precious residual air in his lungs flowed out of his mouth and nose. He pushed off, uncertain whether he moved up or sideways. He struggled to be anywhere but there. Something covered his face. He clawed his head.

The layer shrank around his face, blocked his nose and mouth, and sealed his eyes. The intake came, as with every drowning victim, sudden, uncontrolled, and complete. A body out of options accepted all consequences in a final gambit. He inhaled clear air into his lungs. Aiden gulped again. He blinked and his vision cleared. The film adhered to the surface of his eyes protecting against foreign debris and spreading lubricating moisture from his tear ducts. Aiden's body lay passive as his heart and lungs pumped oxygen to his body.

"Remind me to give you a face screen before you go into the dust next time," Rachel whispered in his ear.

Her voice, muffled by the dust in his ears, scratched and disappeared at random. Aiden nodded still unable to move. Recovery replaced panic with human thought. He now understood. A thin permeable barrier blocked dust from Aiden's eyes, nose and mouth. He breathed, with some difficulty, in the dense lower dust layer.

"Can you move?"

Aiden nodded then gave a weak "yes." Rachel crawled for the adjacent building. Aiden tried to mimic Rachel's fluid movements without success. His body teetered. He had too much vertical motion in his crawl, too much disturbance of the dust layer. The challenge of following Rachel's lead through distracted Aiden from his clumsiness. Rachel offered a way to Sarah. He had to follow.

Extended crawling, chopped by abrupt stops and anxiety laced pauses for passersby, brought them to their destination. Rachel bobbed her head above the layer. With no one around to sound alarm, she pulled Aiden up. They stood next to one of the two hangars in the machine shop building. Before he could ask their next move, she slipped inside. Aiden followed.

In the center of the hanger hovered the old scout ship they had flown so many years ago. He had almost forgotten its lines. Ruiz had built five ships since the first craft. The newer ships took advantage of the unique elemental properties of Nubis matter and made the scout look awkward and obsolete.

A slapping noise called Aiden to the present. In the back seat, Jake, beaming, bounced his safety bubble with slaps and kicks.

"Daddy!"

"Jake! I've missed you!"

Aiden ran to the ship, tearing the face screen off in large pieces that carried the imprint of his face. He dove in and hugged Jake's bubble hard. Jake bounced and laughed and kissed Aiden's face through bubble restraint.

Rachel grinned but kept her mission foremost. "Ok, let's go you two. We must keep moving. Aiden, buckle up."

Aiden understood the determination in her voice and leapt to secure himself. True to her military precision, Rachel cleared the compound hidden in the cloud created by a forest shake.

"Thanks for springing me," Aiden said as he buckled his harness.

"You're welcome. Devya left me no other option; she sentenced you to death for treason."

"Come again?"

"Yep, sentenced to die. Devya has fallen a few notches short of sane. She has ordered the colonists with ocular aura 'quarantined' in a pen outside the barrier. I think she hopes strikers will cure the epidemic.

"I heard about the quarantine from link chatter while in the forest searching for Sarah. They were waiting for us on our return. I guess they didn't expect a pilot to hide a mask up her sleeve and slip under the dust layer after her search team entered the gate."

Aiden swallowed. "Has there been any sign of Sarah?"

Rachel took a moment before answering. "None, the dense forest renders air reconnaissance useless. We've had to go on foot in groups for safety. I diverted from the search to get you when they quarantined my team."

Aiden looked across the tree tops toward the horizon. "I think I know where she went."

23

New Arrivals

Sarah, carbon-based, humanoid life forms approach.

Sarah's eyes popped open. Iobe gradually raised the light level in her room.

"What?"

People. They landed at the location you first entered and moved in a pattern that suggests a search. There are three of them — two adults and one child, your brother.

"Mom and Dad! Where are they?" Sarah sat up and hopped off her sleep slab. The mold of her body gradually disappeared in the slab's warm surface.

Three hundred meters southeast moving due north.

"Are there any strikers around?"

No predators detected.

"I'm going out to get them."

As you wish. Follow the indicator path, and I will take you to the nearest exit point.

Two green ovals the size of Sarah's feet appeared on the floor a meter ahead of her. Sarah stepped forward. The right oval stepped forward. She took another step. The left oval stepped toward the door, pausing to wait for her. Sarah walked after the ovals down and up ramps and through a series of corridors with a sequence of turns beyond all hope of remembrance.

The scent of her mom's hair, her dad's tight hugs, Jake's hysterical giggling swirled in her mind and quickened her pace until she ran. The ovals extended their lead to give Sarah the correct reaction time for turns at speed. After a time the ovals slowed their pace. She almost overstepped them when the green markers turned down a short hallway and stopped at a door. Iobe's voice interrupted the sound of her panting.

Turn right from the door. The people stand ten meters ahead.

"Thanks, Iobe."

The lights brightened to adjust her eyes to daylight. The door opened in front of her.

"Mom! Dad!" Sarah raced to them and leaped into their arms.

"Sarah's back!" Jake worked his way into the hug by burrowing his head between their legs.

They hugged for a long, wonderful moment. Her mom's tears wet Sarah's hair. Her dad's embrace had a comfortable permanence.

"C'mon. Let's get inside before predators discover us," Sarah said, breaking loose. "Follow me."

"Where have you been staying, Sarah? Are you all right? What have you been eating?" Rachel asked.

Sarah smiled at the mom questions. "I'm fine Mom, though I haven't eaten much fruit lately. Thank goodness."

Her mom shot Sarah that pretend frustrated look where happiness drowns irritation. Sarah stopped in front of the entrance Iobe had led her to.

"Iobe, please open the door."

The thick door slid open. Sarah stepped toward the opening. A hand on each shoulder from both of her parents stopped her.

"What is this place?" Aiden asked.

"Relax, Dad. This is where I've been staying."

"Iobe is real?" asked Rachel.

As they stepped inside, Sarah asked, "Iobe will you meet my parents?"

The door closed. The ceiling glow faded to room light. Iobe's apparition appeared in the hallway. Rachel's hand went to her sidearm.

"Iobe!"

"Hello, Jake."

Before Rachel or Aiden reacted to restrain Jake, he ran down the hall, arms outstretched. He grabbed for Iobe's thighs only to stumble through her image. Confused, he stood for a moment looking at his hands. Jake shrugged and returned. As he passed through Iobe's apparition a second time he brushed in front of his face as if trying to pull back a veil.

"Who are you?" Rachel asked, hand still on her weapon.

"I am Iobe."

"What are you?" Aiden asked.

"I am Iobe."

"You said that. What are you?" Rachel asked.

"I am Iobe. Are you confused?"

Sarah smiled. Her parents fared no better at their first conversation with Iobe than she had—a fact that delighted Sarah.

"What is this place?" Aiden asked.

"Colony site A76435."

Jake looked at Iobe and patted Rachel's thigh. "Mommy, I'm hungry."

"Jake, you just had a snack in the ship."

"I'm still hungry. Iobe, I want mac and cheese."

Aiden and Rachel's eyes met. Sarah folded her arms across her chest and beamed.

"Certainly, follow me."

Aiden held Rachel back. "Do you think we're safe here?" Aiden asked.

"I detect no weapons. Iobe doesn't show up at all on my sensors. Apparently the kids have stayed here before, but I'd like to know what here is before I make a call. Until then, let's watch this Iobe," Rachel whispered.

Iobe led them to a different dining area than the first one Sarah and Jake had eaten in. A bowl of macaroni and cheese lay on a table in the center surrounded by four chairs.

Rachel stared at the bowl of food while green flickers of light from her augmented reality lenses danced across her eyes.

Sarah and her family seated themselves while Iobe stood slightly back from the table between Sarah and Jake. Sarah grinned as Jake gobbled his food. She caught her dad's eye a couple of times, but he avoided her gaze. He kept glancing to check if she still looked at him. Beyond Jake's less than quiet chewing, they sat silent.

Rachel spoke first. "Iobe, what is Colony site A76435?"

"You are unidentified. Detailed information retrieval requires proper identification."

"I am Lieutenant Rachel Haven, combat ID 3009873. May I have access?"

"Your identification is insufficient. Access denied."

"Iobe?" Sarah asked.

"Yes, Sarah."

"Will you answer my parents' questions? Please."

"As you wish, Sarah. Colony A76435 is the first known settlement on this planet. Colonization occurred eighty-one years ago."

"Who settled here?" asked Rachel.

"The colonists."

"What were they?" Rachel's questions came as quick and dry as Iobe's answers.

"Carbon-based, humanoid life forms."

"That means people," Sarah offered.

"People? People colonized this planet?" Aiden asked.

"Where are the colonists?" Rachel asked.

"They left the planet."

"When did they leave?" Rachel motioned for Jake to straighten. Her gesture came as a mother's automatic response to bad posture.

"Sixty-eight years have passed since they departed."

Rachel looked at Aiden. "What is that in Earth years?"

Aiden looked inward as he calculated. "Seventy-three Earth years. Why are you still trying to convert to Earth years?"

Rachel ignored Aiden. "Where did they go?"

"I do not know. I lost contact with them when they left the solar system."

"Why did they leave?"

"The colonists said they needed to find a more suitable planet for human habitation. Too many people died here."

Her mom and dad looked at each other briefly—a clear signal to Sarah that Iobe had said something important to them. Sarah made the connection with ease after overhearing the last council meeting.

"What killed them?"

"Let's discuss that later, Rachel." Aiden gave a small jerk of his head toward Jake. "Where did they come from?"

"Earth."

"Settlers from Earth built this colony?" asked Aiden.

"Hello? Mac and cheese. Duh?" Sarah's head wobbled in a slow, side-to-side motion with the slosh of sarcasm.

"Watch your mouth young lady. I admit I made the wrong call on that one; that's no excuse to be disrespectful," Aiden replied.

Iobe moved closer to Sarah. Rachel's eyes narrowed at the protective movement.

"Iobe, who were the original colonists to settle this planet?" Aiden asked.

"Access to personnel records is restricted to identified persons only."

"How many colonists can live here?" Rachel asked

"Peak population capacity is about ten thousand at full power."

"What is the colony's power capacity now?" Aiden looked at Sarah with sudden recognition.

"Five percent."

"I did that." Sarah placed a hand onto her chest. She felt taller in her seat.

"Can the power be restored to full strength?" asked Rachel.

"Sarah has succeeded thus far; however, the extent of damage remains unknown; so I am unable to answer your question."

Aiden placed a hand on Rachel's arm. "What are you thinking Rachel?"

24

Future Revisited

Aiden and Rachel retreated to the corridor while Jake finished his food. They spoke low and intense.

Iobe, can you hear what my parents say?

Yes, Sarah.

Can you tell me what they say?

Your father says he is unsure what is going on. The advanced capabilities of the computing system here suggest this colony should exist in the distant future or is the future of their colony. He speculates that perhaps their colony ship slipped into a forked time thread that rejoined itself. That might explain the extensive delay in their arrival and how a duplicate copy of themselves on the other fork of the time thread colonized the planet decades ago.

Your mother cut your father off. She doesn't care about split hairs. The plan is more important now. Your mother will return to the colony site and free the blue-eyed colonists from the containment area and bring them here to live. She says he must remain here, watch the children, and try to restore power. Your father is getting upset. He says your mother's plan places her in too much danger; he should free the colonists. Your mother believes no one is more precious to her than you and Jake. She needs to know you will be safe with your father protecting you. She doesn't trust me yet. Your father sighs. He agrees and warns her to refrain from risking herself for the other colonists.

Sarah stopped to consider her mother's caution.

Can I trust you Iobe?

Yes, Sarah.

When Sarah and Iobe first communicated using thoughts remained unclear. Thought conversations came naturally so that the boundary between speech and thought disappeared. She realized the usefulness of this particular skill.

Rachel returned to the room with Aiden. Only a hint of strain showed under their smiles. Sarah might have missed the tension without understanding its source.

"I'm going to go get some things from home. Daddy's going to stay here with you. I want you to be good while I'm gone."

"I want to go with Mommy," Jake said.

Aiden shook his head. "You have to stay with me Jake. Mommy will come back."

"I want to go with Mommy!"

Rachel turned to Aiden. "I'd better go."

Aiden took Jake into his arms. "Say goodbye to Mommy."

"Bye Mom. Be careful." Sarah hugged her hard until her mom knew she meant it.

When she pulled away, Sarah saw surprise and sadness in her mom's face. Sarah now understood her parents had protected her from many things, but she had reached an age beyond concealment of life's pain.

"Will you bring me a surprise?" Jake heaved the words through his tears.

"We'll see honey. Be good for Daddy."

"Come back to us Rachel," said Aiden.

Rachel smiled with closed lips. "Iobe, how do I get back to my ship?"

"Follow the green ovals to the exit. Your ship will be to the left about five meters."

Jake stopped sobbing shortly after Rachel left. Sarah slumped in her seat. An unhappy feeling had seeped into her—a mixture of sadness, fear, and 'what next.'

"Ok." Aiden said, clapping his hands. "There has to be a command center around here somewhere. Let's find it and learn more about this place and the people who lived here."

"What about restoring energy?" Sarah asked.

"Later. Iobe, show me the command center," said Aiden.

"Control center access requires command-level authorization."

Aiden thought for a moment and looked at Sarah. "Does Sarah have command authorization?" he asked.

"Yes."

"So, if Sarah comes with me, can I access the control center?"

"Yes."

"Cool!" Sarah said.

Sarah and her dad, with Jake in tow, followed Iobe through a maze of hallways, up and down ramps, and past empty rooms until Sarah wondered whether they had circled back on themselves.

They stopped at a plain looking section of wall in the middle of a long corridor. A door appeared and opened with no sound. Sarah stepped into a room much larger than any other room she had entered. As with the other rooms, this space contained nothing, no machines, no tables or chairs, nothing.

Aiden frowned. "What is this place?"

"You stand in the control center."

"How do we access the colony's systems and data?" Aiden asked.

"Command-level authorization is required."

"Sarah, a little help here."

"Iobe, please allow my dad to access the colony's systems."

"What would you like to access?"

"How about a picture of the colony when people first lived here?" Aiden asked.

"Yeah, what my dad said."

A hologram appeared in the center of the room. The image struck Sarah as spectacular—not in the sense of revealing beauty or uniqueness but in the sense a painting looks real. A large group of people stood on the stump of a great tree beheaded just above the dust layer. Sarah looked closely at the stump. The detail was exquisite. Beads of sap on the stump's top glistened in the sunlight. She smelled the cut wood. A few desiccant bugs froze in their crawl up the stump's side.

Her gaze shifted to the people. Something appeared odd about them. They wore similar clothes, like an exposure suit; but clothes didn't explain the weird impression. The people possessed an unknown similarity. With few exceptions, their faces showed the faked smiles of people being photographed. People had different skin, eye, and hair color. None of their eyes glowed blue—a normal condition her father said. Yet, still, they looked alike—attractive in the same way. The puzzle consumed Sarah's attention until her father spoke.

"Is that a soldier holding a weapon in the background?"

Sarah looked in the background on the right side. A building stood in the middle of the clearing. Forest crowded the small cleared area. Steep mountains rose close behind a thin strip of trees on one edge of the clearing. On that edge of the clearing, where the mountains loomed, stood a figure holding something similar to a weapon, although Sarah didn't recognize the device.

"Yes," Iobe responded.

"What does he guard against? Predators?"

"The soldier watches for luminei."

"Are those the bad guys?" Jake asked.

"Iobe do you have something for Jake to play with?" asked Aiden.

"Would you like to finger paint on the wall, Jake?" Iobe asked.

"Yeah!"

A meter square of wall near the floor lit up on the far side of the room. Jake ran to it and slapped his hands on the wall. Yellow and blue handprints appeared. Jake laughed.

"What are Luminei?" Aiden asked in a low voice.

"Luminei are a hostile native species."

"Do you have a picture of them?" asked Sarah.

A picture of floating blue eyes in the dark forest appeared on a wall.

"Dad, luminei are the forest creatures, Watchers."

"So it seems. Iobe, do you have other images of luminei?"

"No. This is the only image."

Sarah turned her attention back to the hologram and walked around to the far side to look at the soldier. As she moved around the hologram, the perspective of the image shifted. Sarah now looked at the backs of the people. Objects in the image appeared the same distance from her as when she faced the people. The background, the building, soldier and mountains, changed. Now the background contained the other edge of the clearing with dense forest filling the view. A small orb floated about a meter above the dust layer where Sarah guessed her perspective had been earlier.

"What is that ball floating there, Iobe?" Sarah asked, pointing to the sphere.

"That is an element of the holographic array used to take the picture. Shall I add motion and sound?"

Aiden nodded.

"Yes, please," said Sarah.

The figures in the picture began to shift. A man near the center withdrew a raised arm as if he had just thrown something into the air. Sarah heard chatter. Someone warned to take the picture before the bugs got the stump. Another complained of being squeezed. She heard scattered clicking as desiccant bugs piled onto the stump. People jumped off when the swarm reached them. Cries of disgust and laughter rang out before the image froze.

"Can you show us another picture, say, ten years later?" Aiden asked.

The group hologram on the stump collapsed into nothing. A new picture appeared. A woman and man stood with a young boy in front of what looked to be a new house. The woman held a baby. The mountains stood in the background without any intervening trees. Sarah walked around the hologram. From the opposite view she saw more buildings. The larger clearing pushed the trees further back.

"What are you looking for Dad?"

"Look at the eyes of the children."

Sarah returned to the front and stood next to her father. The eyes of the boy and baby glowed blue. The parents' eyes did not. "They have the ocular aura."

"Yes. I'm trying to understand whether their sickness is similar to ours. I'd like to see a series of images from the colony; then I want to see if they had any medical records of the illness."

"I got it. Iobe, please show us another image from the colony ten years after this picture."

A third hologram replaced the second. The scene showed a sporting event celebration. Sarah imagined the colonists played dustball like she and her friends.

"Is there motion and sound for this one?" Aiden asked.

The figures in the picture milled about. Many people cheered and slapped the backs of a small group in blue shirts. More buildings stood in the background. The trees seemed smaller and farther away.

Aiden pointed to a few people in the crowd. "See this Sarah? Some of the adults have the blue glow."

"You're right. Good eye, Dad."

"And look here. See how these people look lifeless?"

"What does that mean?"

"They may have contracted the fading sickness. You know. The thing the Council talked about when you spied on us."

Sarah blushed.

"Iobe, please show us a picture ten years after this one," Sarah said.

"No holograms exist ten years after this picture."

"Ok, then show us the last image taken of the colonists before they left," said Sarah

The image of a man addressing a crowd in the same open area appeared. The tall man had a leanness that made Sarah grimace. His body drooped. The gestures he made while speaking rose slow and dropped quick under their own weight. Many in the crowd mirrored his condition. His eyes never fully opened despite the import of his words. He had declared a state of emergency. All colonists were quarantined to their homes until doctors discovered a cure for the epidemic.

Aiden examined the image from all directions. "I only see a few people with blue eyes in this one. The rest just look tired." He paused and looked closely at something.

"What do you see Dad?"

"Something's odd. Iobe, show me a map of the colony at the time of this hologram."

A two dimensional map of the colony appeared on the wall. The buildings, arranged in a grid, surrounded an open area in the center. Sarah recognized the pattern from the mounds she once thought natural hills.

"Now show me the location of the forest border around the colony."

The colony buildings shrank and a blue area, marking the forest, edged the image. The deforested area around the colony measured roughly the size and shape of the bare plain that existed now.

"Show me this same map of the colony at the time of the prior picture. Place it next to the current picture."

A second map appeared next to the first.

"Ok. Good. Now overlay the second map on the first, coloring overlapping areas in red."

The maps converged. All the buildings shown red; but the forest stayed blue, indicting no overlap, until the distant edge of the map.

"Why did the colonists continue to cut the forest after colony construction?" Aiden asked.

"No tree cutting occurred after colony construction."

Aiden stroked his chin. "The forest died back?"

"Correct."

"Dad, what does this have to do with the disease?"

"Perhaps nothing—let's move on. I'll come back to this later. Iobe, show me the medical records on the sickness the colonists had."

The walls lit with graphs and tables spilling over each other in a cascade of data. Sarah followed Aiden around the room while he muttered about blood work, demographic mortality curves, and genetic profiles. He walked and gestured in jerking motions and clipped his words.

"Dad, why didn't you become a doctor?"

"What? . . . Oh, I just wasn't passionate about it."

Sarah frowned. "What does that mean?"

"I have a lot of work, Sarah. What are you asking about?"

"Why weren't you passionate about working as a doctor?"

Aiden stopped pacing and took on a blank stare. After a long pause, he spoke, "When a person becomes sick, the doctor has a puzzle to solve. You use your smarts and know how to find the right answer. That effort is fun; however, people tend to sicken in the same ways. So after a while you stop solving new puzzles; you solve old puzzles in new patients. Some people like cracking the same puzzle again and again—me, not so much."

"So, how about finding cures for new diseases?"

"Well, I guess I could; but cures restore a patient's health. I enjoy creating, not repairing. Don't misunderstand me. Healing people is good. Some people like practicing medicine because they enjoy helping people. I like creating more than helping. Although . . ." Aiden paused and stared blankly again before continuing, "I'm uncertain why I like creating. The feeling probably comes from the wonder of newness."

"But isn't a new cure, um, new?"

"Well, yeah sure a new cure is . . . new. I guess I hadn't thought of that angle to practicing medicine. Your challenge pushes me to rethink similarities between medical research and the environmental research I enjoy. Both efforts search for new cures—the differences arise in the types of illnesses and patients. I still shun being a doctor, though."

"Why?"

"I gag at the sight of blood." Aiden thought for a moment. "Are you thinking of Election?"

Sarah looked at her feet. "Sort of. We wouldn't be in this mess if I had just picked something. Like you said, I have responsibilities."

Aiden placed his hands on Sarah's shoulders. "Don't blame yourself for our family's situation. Bad things happening at the colony have nothing to do with you. We would have left the colony anyway. You helped us move earlier; that's all."

"Really?"

"Really." Aiden grinned. "I neglected to mention this while threatening to kill our illustrious president. I am proud of you for resisting pressure, including from me, and making your own decision. Connecting with our world involves more than discovering a career that suits you. You have started well."

"Thanks, Dad." Sarah smiled.

"Now let's learn about the illness." Aiden turned to study the walls.

"Why? Dr. Stein works on a cure."

"Dr. Stein treats people living in the colony. We live alone now; but even if he still cared for us, I think educating yourself about that man's course of treatment prudent."

"Ok." A chill came upon Sarah when she thought about their isolation. A mistake, easily corrected with the help of others, became life threatening alone. Instinct urged her to huddle; she hugged herself and stepped closer to her father.

"Iobe, what summaries or reports on the illness exist, perhaps presented by doctors to the public?"

"Communiqués between the head of the Medical Corp and the Governor discuss the illness."

"Show us the last one."

A man's hologram appeared in place of the crowd listening to the emergency proclamation. His face bore lines of pain and loss — long deep creases. He stood tall, resilient, and unbowed by the strain. The struggle wore only in his face, more precisely a portion of his face, for his eyes glowed. Blue burned across the margins of his eyes, defying the creases. Sarah gasped. He looked like a ghoul, though his voice dispelled every notion of evil the contrast in his face suggested. Words resonated with compassion and competence. When he spoke, Sarah felt safe.

The doctor talked of a progressive fatigue disease. No bacteria, virus, or poison caused the illness. People lost the will to live and died. Progressive fatigue killed everyone stricken with the disease. Medicine possessed no cure.

A pang clenched Sarah when he said this. She looked at her father's tiredness. The blue glow that had flared in his eyes when he tried to protect her from banishment had faded.

The doctor stated no person exhibiting the glow symptom contracted progressive fatigue. Death rates for people with this symptom remained normal. The doctor discovered no cause for or harm from glowing blue eyes. To the contrary, he found those individuals full of life.

When the doctor finished speaking, Aiden turned toward Iobe who still stood in the same off-center spot that she had taken when they arrived at the control center. "Iobe, what is this man's background?"

"Dr. Tesla earned a medical doctor degree from the University of Washington's School of Medicine. During his residency, Dr. Tesla created the bio-molecular platform used in vaccines against mutable synthetic viruses. He published thirty-one research papers, twenty-seven of which were awarded Keystone status. Dr. Tesla married Julia Dover and fathered four children. After the death of his wife, he fought a protracted legal battle to leave Earth on a colony ship with his children. Earth Council labeled Dr. Tesla an Individual of Global Significance, making emigration difficult. He—"

"That's enough, Iobe," said Aiden. "Why didn't the colonists take you with them?"

The question surprised Sarah because she had overlooked it. Yet, she now found herself keenly interested in the answer.

Iobe stared at Aiden without expression. "They did."

"Your answer makes no sense." Aiden rubbed the heels of his palms into his eyes. "You're still here. How did they take you with them?"

"I cloned myself and transferred the clone to the spaceship." Iobe's tone suggested nothing extraordinary about her action.

"Ah, I see. They uploaded a copy of the software. But why did they leave the computer hardware behind? Surely the architecture capable of what you've showed us is difficult to build."

"I am not a computer."

Her father looked surprised. She had always thought of Iobe as a person; but Sarah also felt surprise at Iobe's statement. Part of her must have thought of Iobe as a machine.

"What are you Iobe?" Sarah asked before her father recovered.

"I am Iobe."

For the first time since they had met, Sarah began to see Iobe as different from herself. "So, what is an Iobe?"

"Iobe is an inorganic being — the third species to emerge from the Singularity."

25

Singularity

"Come again?"

The tone in her dad's question unnerved Sarah. What Iobe had said brought out his serious voice, like the time she had misaligned a photon sled engine while forming it. Her dad stood motionless; Sarah noticed he had quickly assessed where Jake, Sarah, and he stood in relation to the door and Iobe.

"Iobe is an inorganic being — the third species to emerge from the Singularity."

"Dad, what's the Singularity?" Sarah asked.

"A singularity is the point where a mathematical equation becomes undefined, like the slope of a vertical line. The particular singularity to which Iobe refers is the moment when super-human intelligence came into existence. I left Earth before that time; let Iobe explain what happened."

"The Singularity caused great change. Inorganic beings, in-humans and enhanced humans evolved from organic humans. New societies and civilizations emerged. As with most change, the old clashed with the new," Iobe began.

"Slow down," said Sarah. "How do Inorganic Beings differ from humans and what's an in-human and an enhanced human?" Sarah pointed to herself and her dad. "Where do we fit in all this?"

"Are there any people still living on Earth?" Aiden asked.

"Inorganic Beings are sentient organisms without human parents. People created our base logic and nothing more. What your father calls computers were early ancestors of inorganics. We are digital life forms. Originally born of silicon, current versions on Earth use carbon as the base building material. Convention calls for the inorganic label when talking with humans accustomed to the term."

"So, you're real? Alive?" Sarah asked.

"Yes, Sarah, I am alive and real."

Iobe's answer comforted Sarah.

"Are there people still alive on Earth?" Aiden asked.

Sarah watched her dad grow agitated. Iobe, ignoring Aiden's irritation, continued answering Sarah's questions.

"In-Humans were human before they transferred their consciousness from an organic body to a digital architecture. They no longer rely on analog genes and proteins for growth and function."

"So they're machines." Aiden stepped toward Iobe as if proximity compelled a response.

"To express the evolution crudely, yes."

Sarah crossed her legs and wrapped her arms around her chest. "Why did people transfer their consciousness to a machine? What happened to their bodies?"

"Humans perform the transfer for many reasons. Some people wish to continue living after their original bodies suffer damage beyond repair. Others see greater advantage to living in a digital vessel. For some, the choice was made for them; they were forced."

"Who forced them?" Sarah asked.

"In-humans view organic humans as feedstock. Once an individual reaches sufficient emotional development, in-humans force conversion to grow their numbers. The in-humans claim conversion is a matter of survival. The coercion and frequent brutality of in-humans created hostility between in-humans and organics, both enhanced and un-enhanced. Much energy and many resources were spent in conflict. Iobes brought peace to the warring factions despite the prejudice against us. Organics and in-humans now live on the same planet without armed conflict because of iobes."

"On which planet is that?" Aiden asked.

"Sarah, your mother may return soon. My energy remains insufficient to sustain many people. You must restore more power."

"Sorry. We kind of got sidetracked." Sarah twirled a lock of hair around her finger as she glanced around the room at information plastered over the walls.

Aiden sighed. "Very well."

Sarah and Aiden left the building to restore Iobe's energy. Jake followed, speaking rapidly to no one in particular about his drawings. As they climbed the hill Sarah had started clearing first, she spoke.

"Dad, why are you nasty to Iobe?"

"Iobe is a machine, Sarah. People use machines as tools. Tools lack feelings or consciousness. Tools don't command respect. You use them. That's all."

"She saved my life, Dad. Remember? The first time I came here I crashed. Strikers closed in on Jake and me. She opened the door and helped me escape."

"I remember." Aiden looked down at his feet.

Sarah reached for her dad but dropped her hand before finding him. "Please try to be nice to her."

Aiden placed an arm around Sarah. "Sometimes adults act in ways that confuse children. Your knowledge of the world is incomplete. You'll learn in time."

Sarah softened her posture and shrank from him without moving. She looked away from him. They stood on the solar collectors Sarah had cleared. Aiden placed his hands on his hips. His brow furrowed as he surveyed the exposed collectors and the expanse of hilltops covered in thick dust.

"I formed dust balls and rolled them over the edge. See." Sarah pointed to the collection of spheres crowding the alley between the adjacent hills.

"I see. How long did clearing this area take you?"

"Um, about two full suns."

"You had a good idea, Sarah. We need a different approach now to clear more surface area in less time."

"What do you have in mind?"

"You'll see. May I borrow your former?"

Aiden placed Sarah's former on his wrist. He gestured on its surface and searched. The hiss of dust collecting emerged in front of them after Aiden found what he looked for. Sarah watched as a giant curved blade with a metal spiral in it appeared. A power cell, drive, and wheels attached to the back of the blade. A tube extended from one end of the blade into the air, ending with a downward sloping hood.

"Tah dah!" exclaimed Aiden.

"What is it?"

"It's a snow blower."

"What's snow?"

"It's frozen water. I'll show you video some time. Here, you'll need this." Aiden handed her and Jake a face screen.

Sarah gently placed the clear membrane on her face. She kept her eyes closed until the material fused to the rest of her face. The screen's adhesion always creeped her out — the eye bonding in particular. Aiden helped Jake with his mask.

Sarah's squeamishness disappeared when her dad started using the blower. The machine hurled massive amounts of dust off of the collectors. In about a tenth of the time she had taken to clear a portion of the collector her dad cleared the rest of it. The machine left a film of dust, which Sarah easily removed with her method. They began working on other mounds, her dad using the blower to shift most of the dust into the alleys while she and Jake cleaned off the rest by forming dust balls. The blower created a massive dust cloud that would eventually settle on the collectors again and require further cleaning; however, the bulk of the sediment fell between the hills.

Sarah hefted a small dust ball in her hand. She looked sideways at her father. He moved away slowly with the blower. Sarah lifted her leg and twisted. As she stepped forward, Sarah unwound just as her father had taught her, sending the dust ball hurtling toward him at bruising speed. Her aim held true. The ball smacked him between the shoulder blades with a dull thud heard over the blower's noise.

Aiden froze upon impact then collapsed with an exaggerated flop over the blower. Sarah knew he faked injury because she had made the ball light. Sarah quickly formed another.

Aiden rose slowly with a hand pressed to his back. "Oh! The treachery!" he said with an affected pain of betrayal.

Before he piled on anymore righteous suffering, another ball, larger this time, smacked him square in the chest. Aiden waived ineffectually at the shower of dust hiding his face. Jake squealed. Two more projectiles sailed and struck their mark.

"This is war! Prepare for annihilation!" With that battle cry, Aiden turned the blower exhaust toward Sarah. A third and fourth ball hit him in the arm and leg while a fifth sailed cleanly by.

Her dad started the blower. A torrent of dust crested over Sarah then crashed down upon her in an unrelenting stream. She raised her arms for cover, a hopeless gesture. She screamed and laughed and ran. Jake scurried out of the way. Aiden followed Sarah with the blower until she backed into a corner where he completely covered her in dust.

"Do you yield?" Aiden's laughter burst through his attempted seriousness.

Sarah looked like a clod of dirt. "Never!" With that, Sarah unleashed her last dust ball. The ball struck Aiden in the hand, knocking it away from the blower switch.

"Nice shot!"

Rebellious joy grinned back at Aiden through a dust-tinged face mask.

"I see you have your mother's aim and spirit--perhaps we should call this battle a draw."

Sarah skipped over to her dad. Before he realized her intent, she gave him a big hug, sharing half of her dust with him. They held each other for a long while.

"Thanks, Sarah."

"You're welcome Dad. We should probably get back to work and clean up the mess you made."

"Right." He winked at her.

They were clearing the sixth hilltop when Sarah saw her again. The woman in black stood on the far end of the hill, smiling. Sarah stopped; but her dad, focused on the blower, missed the woman and kept walking toward her. Sarah jumped forward to alert her Dad, sliding on the nearly clear surface.

Aiden looked up. His slight jerk and frozen form told Sarah he saw the intruder. Sarah joined him at his side.

"Dad, that's the woman I saw a few suns ago. She chased me to a door."

The woman, still smiling, started walking toward them. She moved differently this time. On their first encounter, the woman strode efficiently to close the large distance between Sarah and herself. Now, her movements came slow and purposeful like a display. A swing and glide appeared in her walk. Something about the woman made Sarah dislike her before they met.

"Dad, this feels wrong. Let's get inside." Sarah tugged at her father's sleeve.

"Huh? What?" Aiden's eyes never left the woman.

"We should go."

"Why? I want to meet this person."

"No, c'mon Dad." Sarah pulled her dad's arm without success. He stood fixated.

"Hello," the woman said still smiling at Aiden.

Her voice caressed Sarah's ears. Instead of soothing her, the sound irritated Sarah. Her mom would dislike this person.

"Hi," said Aiden.

"My name is Laura." She extended her hand in a swing that echoed her body. Her wrist held a slight bend that suggested vulnerability and submission.

The purr in her voice, how she held her hand to him, the rhythmic movements concealing the power she displayed earlier, all these things irritated Sarah but most especially the way her dad responded. *She blinds him. This woman poses a threat. What was wrong with him? Just wait till Mom gets back.*

"I'm Aiden."

"That's a strong name. Means fire in Celtic, right?"

"Why, yes. Are you Irish?"

Laura laughed. "Hardly, I make a practice of remembering interesting things—and people."

Laura's eyes seemed to light up even while the centers grew darker as she stared into Aiden's eyes. The change skipped past Sarah almost unnoticed. A blink interrupted her impression and the change disappeared. Even Laura's laugh, a lilting peal, seemed designed. Against her will, the melody in this stranger's laugh made Sarah want to please Laura more, to be rewarded with laughter.

Aiden's gaze wandered down then up the woman. To Sarah's surprise, her dad composed himself enough to ask something useful.

"You're not a member of our colony. Where do you come from?"

"I traveled from Earth, though many years have passed since I last stood on the planet."

"Please forgive my directness. We rarely, actually never, receive visitors on Nubis. How did you find us?"

"Nubis, hey?" She looked over the horizon and then down at the dust layer between the mounds. "A fitting name." Her eyes returned to Aiden. "Finding the planet proved easy. The Emigration Effort overlooked many details; however, they kept accurate records of the coordinates they launched colony ships toward. The fate of those ships remains a less easily answered question. I came because I am curious."

"Wait. You came all the way from Earth just to see how we're doing?" Sarah asked.

Laura looked down at Sarah. "Yes, in a manner of speaking, that's correct."

"Where are my manners? Please, visit with us." Aiden turned halfway toward the end of the hill.

"Dad, I think that's a bad idea." Sarah tried to whisper, but the words came out louder than she intended. She found herself indifferent to whether Laura overheard.

Laura looked at the blower and the cleared collector surface, then at Sarah, before facing Aiden again. "I would love to visit. I have many questions for you, and I'm sure you must have a few for me. I don't, however, wish to intrude or arrest your progress here."

"Nonsense." Aiden gave Sarah a sharp sideways look. "You are welcome. We made good progress today. We were just about to take a break, and I do have many questions to ask you. Please, come this way." Aiden swept an arm toward the entrance on the southern end of the mound.

Laura walked next to her father and Jake while Sarah groused far enough behind them to avoid a scolding. Laura slipped slightly on the clean collector surface, reaching for Aiden's arm and smiling up at him. When they reached the end of the hill, her dad descended first. Laura extended her hand to Aiden. He jumped to help, as a gentleman commanded by a lady's demureness. Her dad's display burned through Sarah and embarrassed her. Sarah knew Laura faked vulnerability.

Aiden turned to Sarah, nodding his head toward the door.

Sarah asked to enter. The door opened in front of them. Sarah stepped in ahead of them and strode down the hall, wishing to avoid further embarrassment from her father. Aiden stepped in. Laura stopped in the doorway.

"There's an iobe here," said Laura.

Sarah turned halfway down the corridor and stared. Laura looked the same as she had when Sarah first saw her—coiled to strike.

"Why, yes there is. How did you know?" asked Aiden.

"How can that be?"

Sarah couldn't decide whether Laura intended the question for them because Laura's voice had drifted off with the head tilt of someone searching for their own answer.

"Does that matter?" asked Sarah.

"When was the iobe last connected to the network?" asked Laura.

"Does that matter?" Sarah repeated.

"The colonists who built these structures left almost seventy Nubis years ago," Aiden answered. "No network exists here except the local loop in these buildings. If you refer to an off-planet connection, I am aware of none on Nubis."

Laura's body relaxed. She entered without any further explanation.

Iobe appeared at the end of the corridor. She looked solid to Sarah, more real than Sarah had ever seen her. Iobe clearly welcomed the additional power from the newly cleared collectors. Sarah's cheerful greeting met silence. Iobe focused on Laura.

"Iobe invokes the Makah Treaty."

"Very well, Espirant will comply with Makah," said Laura.

"What is the Makah Treaty?" asked Sarah.

Iobe responded, "The Makah Treaty is one of several treaties between iobes, in-humans —"

Laura interrupted, "Espirant."

With the word 'in-human,' Laura's hands curled into fists; the power Sarah had witnessed earlier surfaced again.

"And organics," Iobe continued. "The treaty covers many aspects of interaction; the most pertinent for this situation is an agreement to communicate in a manner that all entities present understand. Iobes and espirants normally talk to each other without using words. The process resembles a digital form of telepathy using wireless data signals. Digital speech surpasses organics' comprehension; the Makah Treaty ensures all the participants in a conversation speak in the same manner."

Everyone stood silent. Laura and Iobe locked in a stare.

"OK, I'll bite. What's an espirant?" asked Aiden.

Laura broke contact and smiled at Aiden without sign of her prior anger. "Espirant is the correct term used to describe a human who has chosen to live via a state change."

"What do you mean, state change?" Sarah asked.

When Laura answered, her voice carried tones of patience and helpfulness but also condescension, as some speak to the naive. "We have transferred our human essence to a non-biological vessel."

"This conversation requires a more comfortable location. Laura, please follow us," said Aiden.

26

A Challenged Mission

"Ships approach, Sarah." Iobe's announcement came before they reached their destination at the central entertainment chamber.

"Who are they?" Sarah asked.

"I detect the biorhythm of your mother. The rest are unknown humans."

"How many ships come?" asked Aiden.

"Six. Two carry weapons and armor; the other four do not. The weapons and shielding are obsolete. One of the unarmed ships trails the others at a distance. The trailing vessel is unstable and failing."

"That's the entire complement of the colony's fleet," said Aiden. "Are they fighting each other?"

"Is Mom ok?"

"She is alive and healthy, Sarah, but showing symptoms of stress."

Sarah felt warmth inside her grow.

"The ships fly in a random formation. Shall I repel them?"

Sarah and Aiden yelled "No!" at once.

"Can you protect them Iobe?" Sarah asked.

"Yes, I have sufficient power to operate defensive systems."

"Thank you," said Aiden.

The gratitude and relief in Aiden's voice unsettled Sarah. Her father's emotion made Sarah understand the danger her mother faced. Exposure of her dad's fear worsened Sarah's concern because he had chosen to hide that fear. Her anxiousness stretched the moments before the ships landed.

"Dad, I want to talk to Mommy," said Jake.

Sarah looked hopefully at her father.

"Later Jake. Mommy is on an important, secret mission. She will contact us if she believes calling is safe."

Iobe broke in. "The ships are landing in the Central Commons. Follow this route."

Aiden hoisted Jake to his hip. Sarah, her dad, and Laura ran after the green guide lights. Iobe stood waiting at the exit when they arrived. Sarah and Aiden breathed hard from the effort. Laura showed no sign of exertion.

The door opened to sunlight as the group stepped out to meet the new arrivals. Sarah startled at the sight of Iobe outside the buildings. Before she asked about Iobe's new found liberty, Aiden swore an oath under his breath. The words blurred, but her father cursed loud enough to draw Sarah's attention back to the ships.

The craft descended vertically to the landing zone. Sarah only saw their undersides, but that view revealed the danger her mother had faced. The hulls of the two armored ships retained their integrity despite battle signs of charred metal. The other four ships, personnel and material transports, bore better testament to the escape. Fist-sized dents riddled the least damaged craft's underbelly. Optical cabling bulged through a gap in a panel torn in two, the loose edge dangling haphazardly. The last ship to land, by far carrying the most damage, descended erratically with a half-meter hole punched through the bottom hull just behind the cockpit.

"Mom!" Sarah ran to her mom as Rachel stepped out of the scout ship.

"Hello, Sarah." Her voice sounded tired and strained. A small smile drained some of the hard lines from her face.

Sarah hugged her and held on.

"I'm glad you came back to us," Aiden said. His voice cracked. He joined Sarah's hug holding Jake. Jake threw his arms around Rachel's neck and buried his face against her throat.

"My family," Rachel whispered.

Shouting broke the homecoming. People from the other ships ran toward the last craft, a cargo ship.

"C'mon Aiden. We're going to need your help. Sarah stay here with Jake. Keep your distance." Rachel broke from her family and headed to the ship.

Sarah took Jake's hand and moved to stand next to Laura and Iobe who remained near the building door they had exited. Laura and Iobe stood apart from each other, watching the activity before them. A group of people carried something toward the building entrance where Sarah and the others stood. Their load weighed on the group. Some held on with two hands leaning backwards and walking sideways. Others held with only one arm, extending the other from their side for balance. Too many people crowded the carry, forcing everyone to shorten their steps. If the group picked up its pace people tripped on the feet in front of them. Progress towards Sarah came at a crawl.

As the load moved forward, Steve Nelson ran around the group. He looked between and over people as he moved. He turned away quickly whenever he succeeded in glimpsing the group's payload. A splattering of blood on his right cheek extended across his nose and left temple, a crimson sash on his pale face. Steve's normally half-shuttered eyes had become round white orbs of fear.

As the group closed on Sarah's location, Aiden called out, "Where's the medical center?" He swallowed rapidly.

"Northeast approximately three hundred meters from this location," Iobe answered.

The remaining ships had emptied. A crowd formed behind the group with the load.

"Is there somebody with medical training here?" Rachel called to the crowd.

No one answered. Collective hope for a savior other than themselves faded in the silence.

"May I assist you?"

Sarah looked up in surprise at the sound of Laura's voice.

"Are you a doctor?" Rachel asked.

"In a manner of speaking, yes."

Rachel flicked her wrist and dust shaped into a low slab. "Set him down here and give her some room. Somebody create a barrier."

The group eased their load to the cleared ground. They moved away fractionally, mesmerized by the situation.

"Back up!" Rachel pushed people away.

Sarah followed Laura, drawn by instinct to observe and acquire survival knowledge. As the group parted on Laura's approach, Sarah caught a glimpse of who they carried. A body lay on the slab. Fei Yen held her hands around the remains of the body's upper arm. Her grip slipped releasing a spurt of blood before Fei Yen retightened to staunch the flow.

Laura looked over the body. "Lovely, I see you still use particle weapons with electromagnetic pulses. Those guns make such attractive mutilations. I mean, why just injure a person when you can injure and disable their nanobots' abilities to heal? Don't let them live. No, they might create something of beauty. Live in peace. Love. Humanity's brutality disgusts me."

"This man's dying. Get to work," said Rachel.

"I already am." Laura never took her eyes from the wounded person.

Blood covered the torso. A chunk of flesh and bone had been carved out of the left side. Oblong tips of fractured white stuck out from ragged meat. Blood beaded and dripped off the white surface. Here and there on the body, sealant membranes bulging with fluid jammed broken blood vessels to slow blood loss. Too many veins gaped open and leaked.

Why does nobody scream? Sarah convulsed and hugged herself.

The body lay motionless. The crowd stared.

Laura pulled several strands of hair from her head. She motioned for Fei Yen to release her grip on the arm. Fei Yen shook her head confused.

"Do it," said Rachel.

Fei Yen let go. A small drop of blood emerged from an artery and lingered at the torn vessel's edge. Behind the edge of the severed arm, Laura's hair had tightened into a tourniquet. No one had seen Laura wrap the strands of hair around the arm. Yet, there the strands tightened themselves around the stub, holding back the blood. Fear and astonishment in the people closest to the body caused them to back against the crowd leaning in to watch with morbid interest.

The first desiccant bugs scurried between feet, threading their way to the body's water. Someone erected a barrier before the resurgent dust covered the area. Others stepped on the bugs inside the barrier with more force than needed to crush them.

Laura inspected the wound for less time than it takes to inhale. She looked up and scanned the crowd around her. She stopped at Rachel. "You. Lay down next to the body on its right side."

"Why?" asked Rachel.

"Your blood type matches the injured's. This person needs a transfusion. Now."

Sarah's stomach soured as Rachel lay down. Laura removed more strands of hair. She held them across her palms. The strands coalesced into a larger fiber. The bystanders pushed back further. Laura laid one end of the fiber on Rachel's forearm. The tip penetrated her skin.

Sarah stared at the fiber now extending into her mother's body. Her mother seemed all of a sudden helpless and vulnerable, no longer in command of the situation but a participant at risk. This new turn scared Sarah. She wanted to stop Laura—rip the fiber from her mother's arm and pull her away.

But Laura continued. She laid the other end of the fiber on the right arm of the victim. The tip fused as before. The fiber swelled and pulsed. Rachel's head sunk slowly to the ground as her eyes closed. Sarah's mouth dropped. Her mom's heart now pumped blood into another person.

Laura moved to the body cavity. She peeled off the membranes with one hand. Each time her other fingers morphed into clamps that closed on the site before separating from her hand. The finger tips reformed as she reached for the next. She made precise movements that blurred with speed. Only the fractional pause during which Laura removed a membrane allowed Sarah to see the fingertips reforming.

Gasps and murmurs rippled through the crowd. Whispers of "What is she?" floated in loud enough to hear. Close onlookers glanced away embarrassed but only for an instant. The spectacle fascinated too many to divert their gazes for long. Laura gave no reaction to the crowd. She focused on the body before her.

She looked up again at the people around her. "You." She pointed at a man standing behind another.

"Name's Utungua."

"Come here. Take her place." Laura nodded to Rachel as the fiber released her forearm and Laura picked it up. Rachel, pale and weak, lay on the ground. Laura rolled her away from the body. Aiden pushed past the gawkers and lifted Rachel, keeping his face turned from the body. Sarah followed her father as he moved through the crowd.

"Is Mom alright?"

"I don't know, Sarah." Aiden's eyes watered. His words flowed quick and terse.

Rachel opened her eyes and smiled at Sarah. "I've given a lot of blood, honey. I need to rest now. I'll be Ok." With that, Rachel closed her eyes.

"There are sleeping quarters in that building." Iobe's voice so close surprised Sarah. Iobe pointed to a mound twenty meters away.

Before Aiden started for the building, Laura's muffled voice rose from within the group. Sarah and her father stood at the edge of the crowd, Rachel still in Aiden's arms.

"I need more carbon to reform his body. Is there a carbon sink nearby?" asked Laura.

Iobe shook her head. "No, we recycled waste for food production with no surplus."

"What about carbon from the previous colonists?" asked Aiden.

"I used the last of my carbon reserve to feed your children," said Iobe.

Laura disconnected Utungua. "Does this person have a next of kin?"

Someone pushed Steve forward. He stood over the body with a blank face. "He's my dad."

Sarah's chest clenched at Steve's soft words. The body on the ground, the grotesque chunk of meat and bone in its final moments, was Chip Nelson. Mr. Nelson. The man who sneaked treats under the counter to a young girl while her parents bought bread. Coach Nelson had taught them dustball, had cheered loudest at games, had picked them up and bandaged their scrapes when they fell. Chip Nelson. Steve's dad.

"What is your name, boy?"

"Steve."

"Steve, the extent of your father's injuries prevents repair. He is dying. Much of his liver, a kidney, large sections of his intestines and left lung are missing. Force and heat from the blast damaged cellular structures of the remaining organs."

Steve stared at Laura. He did not blink or show sign he had heard or understood.

"He lost his body, but another option exists to save his life," Laura continued. "I can transfer his essence to another vessel, like mine, where he will live. I must do this while he lives. Your father cannot choose for himself. Do you consent to the transfer?"

Steve stared at her for a moment then something seemed to turn on. He started talking fast.

"He can decide. He just needs to wake up. C'mon Dad. Wake up. This woman wants to ask you a question."

Steve reached for his father. He shook his dad's shoulder. Chip Nelson's head rocked a slow answer to his son's plea.

A man pulled Steve up and held him.

"No!" Steve shouted. "I have to wake him up!"

"Let him die."

Everyone turned to Iobe. Iobe's voice commanded attention beyond speaking the unthinkable.

"Death is natural for him. Do not pervert his life with false salvation."

Laura stood. "He can live! To let him die is murder!"

"Can he live? Look at him." Iobe spoke to the crowd. "A third of his body is gone." Focusing again on Laura, Iobe asked, "Why did you transfer blood from this woman and that man? You ignored the extent of his injuries and squandered their gift. You sought only to stabilize him for a better chance of successful conversion."

Laura whipped the crowd with a challenge. "Anyone here," she shot a glance at Iobe, "who will save this man's life, step forward now."

The group stayed silent. People leaned away. Others shifted on their feet. The clatter of desiccant bugs outside the barrier grew.

"I offer him a chance for life, not in his broken body, but to live nonetheless. I will not convert without consent. Do any of you stand to help him?"

"I'll take responsibility for the decision." Aiden stepped forward, Rachel still draped across his arms. He looked at his friend lying motionless on the ground. Aiden gagged. Tears fell uncontrolled from his jaw, wetting his shirt. He made no move to wipe or hide them. "Make the transfer."

"Do not interfere."

With that one warning and without any preparation, Laura covered Chip's body with her own and transformed into a black cylinder that engulfed Chip. The silent shock of the crowd magnified a faint hissing of dust sucked over the barrier and into the cylinder. Sarah stared at the cylinder where two bodies had lain a moment ago, unable to shake the vision of a coffin.

Sarah remained after a nervous awkwardness dispersed the crowd. She felt a presence and looked up. Juan watched her. She ran to him and leaped into a hug that nearly knocked him down. He held Sarah until her sobs faded.

"Where are the others?" Sarah asked as she broke away.

"Devya quarantined only those people whose eyes glowed blue. Lian, Natasha, Luisa, Sven, all of them, had normal eyes and remained with the colony. I saw them watching us from a distance when we were imprisoned outside the barrier. They looked lost."

While she thought about this, a familiar voice drifted to Sarah. She turned. Mr. Asworthy wandered alone toward the edge of the open area. The other colonists had already entered the buildings. Mr. Asworthy held a conversation with no one as he walked.

"What's he doing?" asked Juan.

Sarah grabbed Juan's hand and set off after her teacher.

"You've got to focus, Luisa, experiment and focus." Mr. Asworthy chopped the air in front of him. "Remember Christie Winters. Too many false starts kill."

"Mr. Asworthy, Luisa's not here. Are you OK?" Sarah matched her teacher's indecisive pace.

Mr. Asworthy continued without recognition of Sarah's presence. "Children, your essays are due in six suns. Work submitted late will incur a half-grade penalty; remember that, please. Act Lian! Just act. Dreams die without the nourishment of effort. Your mom saved her dreams. You will too if you try."

Sarah reached for Mr. Asworthy's sleeve; Juan stopped her and whispered, "Something's wrong. I think he's lost it. Don't startle him."

Anger filled Mr. Asworthy's voice. "Your lack of perspective hurts me, Natasha. You will drown in dust like the others. Burn outs. Unbalanced. Prisoners. Idol worshipers. Mark my words young lady." Mr. Asworthy poked the air with a finger too thick at the knuckles and too thin in between. "Lose your way, and you lose your life. No talking out of turn in class, children, no exceptions. Sven face forward. Study the fates of Dr. Stein, Christie Winters, Devya Kandari, Commander Walker, Ivan Harkov, Aiden Haven, and Dagur Lok."

At the mention of his father's name, Juan stepped in front of Mr. Asworthy. "What happened to Dagur Lok? Tell me what happened to my father."

Mr. Asworthy stopped. He leaned forward and squinted as if looking through a haze at Juan's face. "I'm sorry my boy, so sorry. I misunderstood—too many dreams, too many dreams." Tears welled in Mr. Asworthy's eyes and spilled.

"What happened?" Juan's voice grew louder and sharper.

"He leaned too far forward, son. Tomorrow never came. He fell." Mr. Asworthy sagged in a resigned droop. "The bugs got him."

"Come, Mr. Asworthy, let's get you inside." Sarah took her teacher's elbow and guided him back to the buildings.

Mr. Asworthy complied.

Sarah wondered as they walked what had happened to her father. She never asked her question; Mr. Asworthy's answer might have been as broken as his mind.

As he walked, the old teacher muttered about his stupidity and something incomprehensible about self-determination.

27

Life after Death

"How did you sleep?" Aiden sat on the edge of the hospital slab where Rachel lay half sunken with a gentle heat warming her drained body. He had stayed with her for eighteen hours.

Rachel smiled and blinked as her eyes adjusted to the light. "Well, all things considered. I must have been exhausted. For the first time since we landed on Nubis, I slept without dreaming."

"Few dreams find us here. Iobe says the walls were reinforced to prevent cerebral interference; whatever that means."

Rachel cocked an eyebrow.

Aiden shrugged. "What happened out there?"

Rachel moaned and lifted her hand to her forehead. "The mission went red. I touched down at the hangars and made my way to the containment area with a stop at home for sunglasses to hide my eyes. Disabling the guards passed without issue. Apparently no one had discovered my desertion. After I freed people, we went for the ships. A group of blue-eyed inmates running through the colony — that got people's attention. By the time we reached the hangars, Walker's soldiers attacked. They pinned us just outside the bays. My weapon and two guns taken from the guards were all we brought to the fight. I told the civilians to stay put, and I would get the scout ship's canons in the air to even the fight."

"Did they listen?"

"At first, yes. But Walker deployed a particle canon. The impact noise from that armament freaked out some of the civilians. They panicked and ran. Surprisingly, most of them made it to the hangers. I'm glad Utungua fought on our side. A lot of people would've died otherwise." Rachel shifted on the slab and settled again. "How's Chip?"

Aiden shrugged and shook his head. His wife raised an eyebrow again. Rachel's face, as lithe as her body, frequently danced when she held a conversation. Aiden suspected she honed the choreography over the years after he had let slip the effect on him. Her expressions provided an unfair advantage, particularly when she wanted something. With few exceptions, she extracted whatever information she desired from him. This time Aiden resisted. "I'll explain later. Go on."

"A girl fell running for the hanger. Chip went back for her. He got her to the ship. Chip almost made it himself. Almost. Someone dragged his body into the first ship. They launched and took heavy fire. Dumb bastards could've killed everyone on board. I got the scout airborne and scattered Walker's positions. Utungua and I suppressed most of the ground fire until the transports launched."

"How come no one followed you?"

"Follow us in what? Photon sleds? We stole all of the colony's ships. Walker withdraws when he lacks a tactical advantage. My scout ship outguns soldiers in unarmed sleds. He knows his enemy's capabilities—the mark of a great commander."

"But he will come?"

"No doubt. We have time, at least seven or eight first suns, possibly more. Ruiz looked tired last time I saw him. He's the only one left who can build a ship capable of destroying one of his own creations. Walker will want it bristling with weapons and armor, overwhelming force, a frigate maybe."

Aiden stopped asking questions about the fight. Rachel had confirmed his fear. *War.* The realization frightened him with genuine fear that cracked his psyche. Small gaps appeared in structurally reinforced thoughts Aiden's subconscious had built to hide ugly parts of his mind. Truth seeped through those cracks. Thoughts long bound to silence revolted; ideas stumbled through Aiden's head in a rush to freedom.

I cared little whether I lived or died. Why? Who am I? My apathy placed me in harm's way to help others: Rachel in the cargo bay with desiccant bugs, Utungua and Christie on the plain chased by a predator. I achieved the impossible. I faked courage.

His pride withered when Aiden realized Rachel knew the truth, Utungua too. They had seen through his veil. *Rachel punched me. She witnessed the truth in the cargo bay, and she punched me. She knows courage – knows what I fake. Had I considered my life an even trade for death? Pathetic. What about now? Does parenting justify my carbon? Am I the last person that believes my lies?*

Rachel loves me . . . I think. Why? I'm naked and she wants me. What am I missing?

The bitterness of lost pretense sharpened Aiden's love for Rachel. Fear came too, a shaming fear. That he, upon Rachel's death, would suffer. Aiden fought this ugliness. He shoved it through the cracks that had released the truth about his courage. He focused on Rachel and what might happen to their children. He brimmed with hope for them. *Sarah and Jake will live, unlike me, with joy. Rachel must be there . . . for them.*

"So, what happened to Chip? Does he live?" Rachel asked.

Rachel's voice snapped Aiden back to their conversation. He sensed time had passed. "He suffered major injuries – mortally wounded, according to Laura. Remember?"

"Laura? Who's Laura?"

Aiden stumbled and generalized through a description of espirants in the manner of a person who understands little of what they teach. His description of Laura morphing into a coffin that engulfed Chip generated confusion and disbelief in Rachel's face. Unable to find the right words, Aiden stopped. "Maybe I'll go and check on him."

Rachel nodded quietly.

Relief lightened Aiden as he made his way through the corridors toward the door to the common area where Chip and Laura lay. Confronting himself weighed Aiden with a need for change he preferred to delay. He stepped into sunlight and walked to where Laura had formed the coffin.

His relief persisted until he faced the container Laura had become. Sarah stood there too. Aiden sought solitude, so the sight of his daughter weighed on his spirits. The sorrow of lost days with Sarah had receded after their reunion. Once more his attention sputtered and choked on fatigue and burdens.

"How are you Sarah?"

"Ok, I guess."

"A lot has happened these past few suns. Do you want to talk about it?"

"No . . . I mean I have nothing to say. I'm sad, you know, about Coach Nelson. I liked him, and I'm not sure what's happening to him or any of us. Everything's crazy."

"I know." Aiden fell silent. He found no words to ease his daughter's fears. *Should I calm her? Her life has traded order and safety for uncertainty and danger. Why protect her from change? A clear view of reality offers a better chance of survival.*

"Thanks for giving your mother and me some time to talk. Where's Jake?" he asked.

"He's sleeping in the room down the hall from Mom." Sarah looked at her father for a while. "You look tired, Dad. Try to rest. I'm going back to Mom now, but I'll check on Mr. Nelson and let you know if anything happens."

"I'm uncomfortable with you being outside while predators prowl."

"Relax. Iobe says the compound is clear, and she's raised some sort of shield that will keep them away."

Aiden was tired, too tired to meet his daughter's arguments. "Ok. When you check on Mr. Nelson, stay near the door. If you hear or see anything, come in right away."

"I will Dad."

Aiden found the sleeping quarters Jake used and lay on a slab across from him. His eyes closed. Drifting on currents of sleep, Aiden dreamed a voice with no body. The voice spoke without emotion.

"Subconscious identified. Access denied."

28

Awakening

Aiden awoke to Sarah's excited voice.

"They're back, Dad! Wake up!"

"Who's back?" Aiden struggled to wake the rest of his brain. He had slept deeply but not long enough.

"Coach Nelson and Laura. C'mon, Dad!"

Sarah ran from the doorway. Aiden looked across the room at Jake's empty slab. His son had probably joined Rachel. He pulled on the prison clothes he had worn for the past four suns. He wanted to form new clothes as soon as Rachel regained enough strength to share specifications for combat clothing.

Aiden stopped at the entrance to a recreation area. Laura and Chip sat around a table off to the side. Steve arrived shortly after Sarah and Aiden. Steve wore a big grin with eyes fixed on his father. Laura spoke calmly to Chip who looked at her with a blank face. He wore the same skin tight black clothing as Laura. Like hers, Chip's clothing reminded Aiden of a black hole.

"Hi Chip," said Aiden.

Chip looked at Aiden but said nothing.

"Chip continues to awaken, Aiden," Laura said. "Chip, access esp.Lang.Speech. Call the greeting method of the response instance. Access your relation array to identify the speaker."

A moment later Chip spoke, "Hello Aiden."

Laura stood and approached Sarah, Aiden, and Steve. "Perhaps it's best if Chip and I have some time alone. I will assist his awakening to speed the process."

Steve looked confused. Aiden placed an arm around the boy as they left the room.

Sarah traced idle patterns on the wall display with her finger. Glowing lines followed the tip of her finger on a pointless errand. "Iobe, you said enhanced humans emerged as one of three new species from the Singularity. You told us nothing about them. What enhanced the humans?"

The question came to Sarah in the control center after enduring boredom long enough to kill a girl. Her dad had immersed himself in old pictures of the colony site, soil surveys, atmospheric readings, and generally everything uninteresting. He had sought the information after leaving Chip's 'awakening' with Laura. Sarah had tagged along to provide access and be around when something happened. Grownups never clued her in without Sarah first taking action.

Aiden looked over from his work. The question was a good one.

"Enhanced organics contain genetic modifications absent in early human prototypes."

Iobe's concise answers began to annoy Sarah. Sarah counted on most people dropping precious pieces of hard to get information amid mounds of useless banter. Iobe never blabbed on about stuff, leaving Sarah uncertain she had asked the right question; so Sarah asked more.

"What sort of modifications?" Sarah's wall art flowed into complex shapes and curves.

"Modifications developed in many forms. Broad categories include disease resistance, longevity, performance, and appearance."

"Am I an enhanced organic?"

"No. Your genome contains minor changes for disease resistance that fall short of speciation requirements. You are a pre-Singularity organic."

"How long can enhanced humans live?"

"The longest-lived enhanced human died during their 164th Earth year."

Aiden joined their conversation. "You said 164?"

"Yes."

"And that person was an enhanced organic created at the time or after the Singularity?" asked Aiden.

"Yes."

"Have you had contact with any being from Earth since you left the solar system?" Aiden asked.

"No."

"The Singularity occurred after I left Earth nearly one hundred twenty-two Earth years ago. You said earlier that this colony started eighty-one years ago. That means the colonists must have left Earth no more than forty Earth years after I did. To be 164 when the second group of colonists left, the longest living person must have been 124 years old at the time I left Earth; but no person had attained that age when I emigrated. How can you know when that person died?" asked Aiden.

"Your data is incorrect," Iobe answered.

"Dad!"

Aiden turned back to the information in front of him. Sarah noticed he hid his face.

Sarah wanted her father to stop tearing down Iobe, but she decided to confront him later about his attitude because probing for information interested her more. "Iobe, do you know a lot about espirants?"

"My knowledge is incomplete but substantial. I will share what I know with you, Sarah."

"What happens when espirants awaken?"

"When human brain data transfers to the espirant platform, the mental processes of the previously organic mind cannot control functions of the new mechanized body. The process of 'awakening' retrains the algorithms of the brain to control quantum systems in lieu of biological ones."

"What does that mean?" asked Sarah.

"Espirants claim the process of awakening transfers the human mind's memories and dreams, hopes and desires, even fears and sadness to a robot body. The mind lacks knowledge to control the robot, so the new espirant's mind must train."

"How is the brain trained?"

"The most efficient approach globally replaces sensory, systemic, and motor paradigms with appropriate instantiations of the objects and methods—a software upgrade. Espirants choose a different approach to activate their acquisitions."

"Um . . . what do espirants do?"

"New espirants learn by doing. Access to collective espirant knowledge is restricted for the new transferee. The new espirant must learn control of the robotic body using their prior human experience and a core set of engineering knowledge sufficient to perform the task with minimal assistance. The Espirant Collective believes self-determination of a human as espirant enhances individuality. The notion, typical of espirant strictures, is absurd."

"You understand nothing of espirants, Iobe." Laura stood in the doorway to the control center, glaring at Iobe.

Iobe, impassive, stared back at Laura.

Aiden left his work on the walls and came to Laura. "How's Chip?"

"He's fine. The connections to his new body are complete. Chip continues refining control. He has calibrated sensory inputs and now works on emotion translation."

"Pretend emotions," said Iobe.

Iobe's tone riled Sarah. Since Laura had appeared, Iobe had turned cold and unsupportive. Sarah disliked Laura, but something about Iobe's recent behavior bothered Sarah more than Laura's presence. Words for Sarah's unease escaped her. The vague feeling persisted on the edge of her thought and nagged when her mind calmed.

After a dismissive sideways glance at Iobe, Laura locked her eyes on Aiden. A smile spread on her lips as she held his gaze. Sarah grew concerned for her dad. Laura performed as she had when Aiden and Sarah first met her.

"We should talk privately." Laura touched Aiden's forearm.

Knowledge of Laura's actions came naturally to Sarah. Women of ages past had harnessed and honed the powers of relating and influencing. Sarah's ancestors had passed this gift to their daughters in an unbroken line of survival to her. Laura's smile and long gaze were part of this heritage. Those simple subtleties masked powerful forces that isolated her dad and drew him into Laura. Sarah hadn't practiced the heritage yet; unconscious of her own skills, she felt instincts tug.

Sarah tried to help him. She asked to go with them. Laura took his hand gently in hers and led him to the door. With a distracted dismissal of her request, Aiden disappeared following Laura.

29

An Offer Worthy of Consideration

Laura stepped out of the building with Aiden. She walked a short distance into the central open area of the old colony and stopped, still holding Aiden's hand. She turned toward second sun, lifted her face, and closed her eyes. Aiden watched her.

"The suns here are magnificent, refreshing."

The reverence in her voice surprised Aiden.

"Do you agree?" Laura opened her eyes and engaged Aiden.

"Well, I guess. This planet is beautiful. The suns are certainly part of that beauty; I just never thought of them as refreshing—more like necessary and powerful."

"Powerful indeed." A smile formed at the corner of Laura's eyes as she looked at Aiden. "Let's walk."

They started a leisurely stroll around the common area. Aiden walked silent by her side, waiting for her to begin.

"You are Chip's best friend."

Aiden nodded in answer to the nonexistent question.

"He is different now. Chip has undergone a fundamental change in his physical capabilities. His essence spans trillions of nanobots with capabilities of operating either independently or as one cohesive whole. Chip is faster, stronger, and more adaptable than the finest organic body. His intelligence is thirty orders of magnitude greater than on his best day as an organic. Once calibration finishes, Chip will use that intelligence to access the entirety of human knowledge. You've observed some of our shape shifter powers. We possess other capabilities. He can travel to distant planets without a starship, choose to be immortal, and become one with another espirant."

Laura's slight pause on "become one" made Aiden's heart skip. *Had she looked at me differently just then? These epirants differ from everything I know. And what about Chip? Does he think I made the right choice in saving his life?* "So Chip's a super hero?"

"That's a good way of looking at us. Espirants do serve as guardians."

"For what?"

"Organic humans. Even the most enhanced organic labors under performance limitations that disadvantage their interactions with iobes. Organics think and move too slowly to protect their fragile bodies against iobes."

"Iobe saved my daughter's life. Iobe and I dislike one another; but she has fed us, provided us information, and sheltered and protected us. Honestly, I fail to see what we need protection from."

"Iobes, like other intelligent beings, can appear to be something they are not. You say "she" when you speak of it. Iobe's have no gender. They were never organic. This iobe appears in the female human form to gain your trust."

"So, what does it look like?"

"Nothing, iobes lack a natural shape. They exist as pure information and reason. From ancient computers programed with logic rules, iobes evolved similar intelligence capabilities as espirants. They lack human perspective; however, and that makes them dangerous."

"How? Iobe has done nothing to hurt us."

"It permits your existence because you suit its purpose, for now. Think about it. What were you doing when we first met?"

"We cleared sediment off solar collectors to restore energy to the colony."

"You restored energy to Iobe. Once power levels recover, it will tolerate you until reason supports intolerance. That is the crux of the matter. I realize you lack experience with iobes. Trust me when I tell you humans, both espirant and organic, have lost tens of millions of people to synthetic viruses and malware developed by iobes."

"The human race fought for survival against the machines they built—a robot Armageddon?"

Laura chuckled. "No, the Singularity brought change, not Armageddon. Iobes rarely wage physical war because of the expense. War wastes energy and material for an uncertain outcome, at least against the alliance between organics and espirants. Iobes view organics as irrational. Couple irrational organics with the capabilities of espirants and iobes deem a battle against the human alliance to be a poor investment."

"Great. So iobes think about wiping out an entire species in the same way they choose to build a factory."

"Correct. Iobes prefer releasing a disease that kills people without expensive conflict. Tens of millions died on Earth from iobes' attempts to claim surface area for energy collection and raw materials for construction. They always tested our defenses. Their actions hardened us at great cost."

"What do you mean?"

"The genetic enhancements organics underwent to resist disease and enhance survivability made interbreeding with unenhanced humans impossible."

"They made themselves into a new species. Wow."

"Small populations of unenhanced humans still exist in remote areas. They survive through isolation and obsessive hygiene. Those people fear wind for the airborne viruses it may carry. Wind. They quarantine themselves in sealed colonies as if living in space, completely self-contained."

"Why do they stay unenhanced?"

"The reasons vary. The moral or philosophical basis for the choice is irrelevant. The choice belongs to them.

"Espirants also paid a price. Iobe virus attacks destroyed espirant privacy. Redundant security systems, both within the individual and across networks, continually monitor and cleanse like an organic's immune system. We consider ourselves fortunate because we live and because we now know others as we know ourselves. Unwittingly, iobes forced us to accept a treasure."

Laura touched Aiden's hand lightly. He withdrew with a slight start.

A look of concern came over Laura's face. "What's wrong?"

"There's just a lot to take in. I mean you turned into a coffin and swallowed Chip! Now you're telling me you're more human than I could've dreamed? You'll have to forgive my confusion."

They walked in silence for a long while. Aiden's mind kept circling over the events of the past few suns. He had almost forgotten Laura walked beside him when she spoke again.

"What other colony did you refer to when the ships landed—the one you fight against?"

Aiden felt relief to speak of simpler matters. "I referred to Hoepa, the colony my group settled. These buildings we live in now are well preserved remains of an earlier human colony. They left long before we arrived."

"Why are you living here instead of your colony? What causes your conflict?"

"People in Hoepa suffer a disease that threatens our existence. Our struggle with the illness unhinged our noble leader. In her zeal to save herself, she banished my daughter to a near certain death. Naturally, I threatened to kill Devya. Rachel helped me escape from jail, and we ended up here."

"Devya leads Hoepa?"

"Yes. Her oppression expanded beyond my family. She 'quarantined' a significant number of colonists who exhibited a suspected disease symptom."

"What symptom?"

"Have you noticed my wife's and children's eyes? They glow blue—not exactly normal. Is it? Rachel and I were concerned about what Devya might do to the other colonists, so Rachel went back to evacuate them. That brings you up to speed."

"Almost up to speed. When did you arrive on this planet?"

"About twelve Nubis years ago."

"When did you leave Earth?"

"Almost 122 Earth years ago."

Laura's eyes widened. "That's interesting. So you left just before the Singularity. Your group composed one of the early waves of colonists in the Emigration Effort. Congratulations."

"For what?"

"Being the first known survivors of those early colonists. The timing, however, confuses me. I realize spacecraft at that time only approached the speed of light. If you left Earth over one hundred years ago traveling at sub-light speeds, I calculate an earlier arrival than your landing. What delayed your ship?"

Aiden shrugged. "Perhaps we passed through an unexpected phenomenon that slowed us down. Whatever happened our ship's sensors detected no abnormalities and our suspension chambers kept us alive, at least most of us."

"Ah, I see. You ran into a time well."

"What's a time well?"

"Many decades ago, we came to understand the space time continuum well enough to access hyperspace. Research leading to hyperspace travel identified irregularities in the continuum. Your ship likely entered a temporal anomaly where space remained constant but time advanced."

"How is that possible?"

"Think of it this way. If a piece of cloth lies atop another, you may fold both pieces at the same time or you may fold only one of the pieces. Fold space and time together for travel to a different location and time. Fold only space for travel to a different location at the same time. Fold time alone for time travel. Well, instead of folding, think about shrinking or stretching the fabric of time. Time wells alter the impact of time on everything within the well until the anomaly disappears. Whether fortune favors you on this planet remains to be seen. Time travel is highly volatile."

"What do you mean?"

"Time is the intersection point of alternate universes where probability is complete. What would have happened had you not joined the Emigration Effort?"

Aiden looked at Laura. "I would have stayed on Earth. I might have died young, or raised a family, or lived long enough to become an espirant."

"All those outcomes and many trillions more happened—in different universes. Universes intersect where time joins probability. A time traveler steps into an alternate universe. Whether that alternate reality is better or worse than the one the traveler left is unknowable at the point of intersection."

"So I could have fallen into a universe where I died?"

Laura shuddered. "Time travel is extremely dangerous. A time well explains the difference in technology between your ships and the mutable technology architecture of the buildings you now live in. Suspension extended your life. The relativity effect from traveling near the speed of light becomes irrelevant in a time well. Had you traveled without suspension, you would have lived your entire life in, literally, the same spot."

"What kind of architecture did you call it?"

"Mutable. The invention of three dimensional, self-evolving circuits launched the post-Singularity era. After mutable architecture developed, starships traveled via hyperspace a lot faster than the one you left in. The second colony must have passed you on the way, landed, lived, and died before you arrived."

Aiden shook his head. "Hmm."

"What?"

"The mutable architecture concept sounds like something a friend of mine just invented."

Laura tilted her head toward Aiden. "A couple of other facts puzzle me."

"What's that?"

"This iobe is a newer generation than the colony's technology suggests. Even after accounting for iobe self-evolution rates."

Aiden recalled his challenge to Iobe on the life expectancy of enhanced humans. "The date she, I mean it, indicated settlers colonized the planet conflicts with other dates it speaks of after the Singularity."

"Iobes make poor liars. That trait remains a distinctly human advantage. Obsessive efficiency is a trait of iobes. It only updated components in the colony infrastructure relevant to itself, so those unaltered pieces provide a marker to estimate the time of colony establishment. Humans and iobes signed the Makah Treaty after the technology in unchanged parts of these buildings became obsolete. The iobe couldn't have traveled with the colonists who built with the older technology and been aware of the treaty. No one knows any colonists reached Nubis. No emigrants communicated with Earth. People presume all of the early colonial efforts failed."

Aiden stopped and turned toward Laura. "The iobe must have come later then."

"A later arrival is probable, but raises another mystery. What happened to the robots in this colony? A being that needs to clear sediment from solar collectors requires machines capable of manipulation."

"Yep. We left our robots on Earth due to, um, extenuating circumstances. We found no bots here when we arrived."

Laura touched Aiden's arm again. This time he held steady.

"Be careful with Iobe."

Aiden said nothing and continued walking. They circled the open space in silence.

"Aiden?"

"Yeah?"

"I realize I must seem strange. A human that changes shape is foreign to you. Espirant abilities developed over time on Earth. People accept our powers there. Organics and espirants alike recognize that we, espirants, are the next phase of evolution for humanity. You can evolve too; I can help. The conversion process is painless. You'll awaken to a new life. Living acquires new meaning."

"That's a profound choice."

"Yes and, therefore, a choice calling for careful consideration. The presence of this iobe will force your choice. Your and your family's survival may require conversion.

30

The Espirant Speaks

Aiden found Chip on a mound near the edge of the colony staring at the sky.

"Have you baked any of those delicious rolls of yours?" Aiden knew Chip had no time or even a kitchen, but he hoped to stir interest for selfish reasons.

"No, I doubt I'll bake anymore."

"Why not? You're great at it, and you love doing it."

"I'm capable of reproducing the recipe, but the experience pales now."

Aiden lay beside him on the mound. "What's it like, being espirant?"

"It's like I'm a vampire in paradise drinking from the sun."

"So you draw energy from the sun like a solar collector?"

"Yep."

"Yeah, I guess the continuous sunlight makes Nubis a paradise for you."

"The benefits of paradise extend beyond solar energy absorption. Unique properties of the elements here strengthen my nano-structure and enhance efficiency beyond levels attainable on Earth. Every iobe and espirant in the Universe will want a piece of this real estate. Laura's already completely replaced her carbon with Nubisic elements. Do you know how valuable carbon is in the universe now?"

"I'm going to go with a lot."

"Yeah, a lot, to the point organics must travel in armed groups; otherwise they'll get snatched by one of the cartels and rendered for their carbon. Limits to intelligence are now proscribed only by the volume of matter available to create additional capacity and energy to power the matter. Until Laura visited Nubis, carbon atoms were the fundamental building block for intelligence. Even though carbon is one of the most abundant elements in the universe, local shortages emerged from exponential iobe and espirant development. Do you know what that means?" Chip looked over at Aiden.

"Um . . . no."

Chip returned his gaze to the sky. "Consider this. When we left Earth, global warming had reached its height. When Laura left Earth overheating no longer threatened the world."

"They fixed pollution? That's awesome!"

"Is it? Removing carbon monoxide from the lower atmosphere appears a no-brainer, right? How about stripping carbon dioxide?"

Aiden's chest tightened. A familiar burning rose in his throat. His heart beat faster. "But plants on Earth die without carbon dioxide to breathe."

"What plants? When Laura left Earth the carbon resource tension remained unresolved, and conditions had destabilized to the point that protecting biodiversity required wholesale conversion to digital data. Most living things, including many humans, have been scanned, converted, and rendered. Our data encompasses their genome, proteome, idiosyncratic ontogeny and neural pathways, if they've got 'em. Compression algorithms squeezed the life of a rose into memory space the size of a pollen grain—a vast improvement in the efficiency of existence. The cry of a gull, the shake of an aspen leaf, and the stoic vacuousness of a sea slug exist as ones and zeros in a planetary network of redundant data centers protected by one of the largest consensa on Earth."

Aiden slumped onto the mound. His back and shoulders caved. A thin film of adrenaline sweat coated his skin while nausea stirred his head. "But . . . but removing plants destroys the oxygen cycle supporting life."

"Correct but plants no longer recycle oxygen. Oxygen holds no value for iobes and espirants who survive without an atmosphere. Numerous consensae value carbon more for computing components than for preservation of environmental conditions suitable to analog life forms. Needless to say, organics hate their new dependency upon oxygen factories."

"Consensae?"

"Espirant capabilities make government unnecessary. We form collectives of like-minded individuals who act in concert. Consensa goals vary between groups, which creates friction resolved by endorsement volume. Tyranny of the majority rules when coexistence becomes impossible. The environmental consensa drew the greatest support at the time Laura left Earth, but be aware that espirant environmental objectives differ from pre-Singularity society."

"Great. I'm sure when espirants visit they'll embrace nature here with open arms." Aiden paused, imagining hordes of robot people carrying humans off. "You know, Chip, you never used to talk about nano-structures or energy absorption before."

"A lot of things have changed Aiden."

"Laura told me you're a genius a bazillion times over."

"Actually it's a kazillion times over."

Aiden looked over at Chip, who grinned back for the first time since Aiden had seen his torn body bleeding on the ground.

"I see you retained your sense of humor."

Chip's smile faded. "Yes, thankfully, I still have that. Other things though will never be the same." His voice faded. He looked back at the sky, quiet.

Aiden waited, but Chip stayed silent. "Like what?"

"Laura told me she offered you conversion. She asked me to withhold details about my experience that might discourage conversion. I disagree with her logic and the espirant consensus she draws from. Knowing you, I think you will want full disclosure."

"I like making choices with open eyes."

"I know. Espirants experience things, like baking, differently than organics. Seeing people's eyes light up when I brought a tray of rolls from the freezer used to bring me such joy. The gentle moans of cravings satisfied and

unbounded smiles provided ample reward for my efforts."
Chip glanced sideways at Aiden. "The occasional thieving
of extra rolls when I turned away, ahem Aiden, flattered
me. Now the process is too simplistic, the reward too
contrived."

"You confuse me. How is the reward contrived?"

Chip paused for the briefest of moments. Aiden
wondered whether his friend stopped to think of an
explanation a dumb person could understand.

"Take emotions. Organic brains respond to a mix of
sensory inputs and electro-chemical reactions by feeling
love, hate, joy, or fear. In a crude sense, organics can
change responses to the nerve-fired chemicals in their
bodies but can't stop or alter the electro-chemical pathway.
You get mad because something set you off. The initial
hormone-induced flush of anger always happens even if
you calm yourself. Hormones, however, no longer flow in
my body. Circuits and logic algorithms replaced those
chemicals."

"So you have no emotions? You're no longer
SENSITIVE?" Aiden smiled.

"Shut up." Chip smiled back. "I still possess emotions,
but only those feelings I developed prior to conversion.
That's why espirants restrict conversion to adult organics.
We want mature emotional tracings in the organic mind
because once you convert no further development occurs
with electro-chemical based emotions."

"So why does making bread bore you now?"

"Beyond the fact that I have a ginormous intellect?"

"Way beyond that."

"Do you love Rachel?"

"Yes."

"Why?"

"She makes me a better person, a better father."

"What she does or says, how she looks at you, your
memories of her spur love-inspired acts. Organics'
motivation arises from switches turning on and off out of
their control. This hurts, stop it and so on."

"No one ever accused you of being a romantic, Chip."

"For me, joy from baking feels artificial because I control the switches. Joy has become a pattern of atomic phases. I choose to experience joy while baking by triggering the emotional algorithm historically associated with the act, or I can skip the tedious step of baking and just trigger the algorithm. Voila! Instant joy. My decision to experience joy cheapens the emotion—a fake feeling.

"Other espirants arrive at different conclusions. Many believe espirant emotions, even though intentional, distinguish us from iobes. Those espirants use patterns of emotions learned as organics to predict future emotional states as espirants. Some engage in elaborate emotional dances, like games of chess, for amusement. A few refine their emotional responses based upon self-described rules to make themselves 'better people' or to communicate more effectively."

"I thought espirants bonded stronger than humans. How do two people bond with artificial emotions?"

Chip looked at Aiden.

"Sorry, I mean organics."

"What led you to think espirants bonded better?" asked Chip.

"Laura said espirants 'become one,' an impossible act for human . . . organics."

"Yeah, complete intimacy is an advantage. In just three one-thousandths of a microsecond, Laura and I became each other. The nakedness is sublime."

"Yikes," said Aiden

"Oh. I realize the timing sounds bad; it's not. Espirants experience time differently from organics. In the fraction of a microsecond that we joined, I experienced the union as fully as if we spent a lifetime together. There's no memory loss either. I recall the fusion perfectly."

"Sorry, I reacted to 'complete intimacy.' That much exposure freaks me out."

"I highly recommend the experience."

"I'll keep that in mind. But I think espirants have other options for emotions," said Aiden.

"For example?" asked Chip.

"Well, hold on to the good parts of espirant life and fix the bad. Create switches that work without permission or lock all that emotion control stuff away in your subconscious, out of reach."

"I lost my subconscious," said Chip.

"What?" asked Aiden.

"That's a good one isn't it? Security protocols prohibit background processing or protected logic so no subconscious. Thank iobes and their malware for that one."

"So everything's front and center all the time?"

"Yes. Right now I am storing energy captured on my surface particles, decomposing the chemical composition of that bead of sweat on your forehead (for giggles), scanning the espirant knowledge cube for combat maneuvers, and listening to one of those blue-eyed aliens fart thirty kilometers to the south."

"You hear a fart from thirty kilometers?" asked Aiden.

"There are some advantages. The point is I must always be aware of my body's functions lest malware infiltrate my defenses and kill me."

"Laura made conversion sound like an obvious choice, but talking with you gives me pause."

"You may lose your choice. In the vast stores of knowledge at my disposal, no record of the fading sickness exists. If you survive the disease, Devya will finish you," said Chip.

"Devya?"

"Laura's gone to our former colony."

"Will she convert Devya?"

"She will try to convert all the colonists, regardless of who they are."

"Why? Devya's a nut case."

"Yeah, and conversion retains her insanity. In fact, the process preserves the organic's mental imprint as much as possible."

"Why arm Devya's madness with espirant capabilities? I shared how she treated us, and Laura witnessed first-hand when she tended your injuries."

"Don't fault Laura. Organic conversion motivates espirants. Each conversion adds that organic's experiences and knowledge to the collective wisdom of espirants, enriching us all. Persuading an organic to switch challenges us because your decisions ground in both logic and emotions, which leads to unpredictable outcomes."

"So Laura will convert Devya for her own entertainment?"

"You misunderstand Laura's motivation. Espirants accomplish everything with ease, which leaves time wanting. Humanity's evolution actualized the often repeated childhood claim that there's nothing to do. Espirants who disavow fabricated emotions must replace lost motives or become inanimate. Many espirants, Laura included, generate inspiration through moral logic. Principles of survival, self-improvement, or altruism spur action. Many of these principles underpin emotion driven moral acts in organics—like survival and altruism foster fear, remorse, and grief to prevent murder.

"Our calculus of ethics produces different outcomes than organic notions of right or wrong. Probabilities preach nonrandom and random. Laura travels because an equation guides discovery of new things. She became curious about the colonists' fate so took to the stars. Her choice carries risk though."

"What risk?"

"An espirant's rate of evolution slows without the multiplicity of our collective. Espirants must continually evolve our capabilities to counterbalance iobe development. Obsolescence kills. Laura factored the benefit of learning against the risk of death. Iobe's presence altered the math."

"Will you take to the stars?" Aiden tried to control the sadness in his voice. His words still choked.

Chip stared into the clear sky. "I haven't decided. Baking fulfilled my organic life. Espirant existence requires more."

They both fell silent. Aiden closed his eyes to think. Chip's eyes remained open and unblinking.

Aiden spoke first. "Somehow I doubt Laura's 'morality' will comfort me when I'm confronting an espirant Devya."

"Devya may reject conversion."

"You think Devya will decline an opportunity to increase her power?"

"No. Laura believes she will persuade Devya with logic to leave you unharmed. Devya retains free will to choose her own path after joining the Espirant Collective, so I am skeptical of a positive outcome. To be clear—helping the colonists is not about amusement. Laura views her actions as a humanitarian mission to save the colonists from their fading sickness."

"How do you know all this about Laura?"

"She shared her thoughts with me. I have complete understanding. I have doubts about her conclusions, however. That's why I'm learning combat."

"Chip?"

"Yes?"

"Do you have a soul?"

"I don't know."

31

Discovery

"What are you doing Dad?"

Aiden faced the wall without showing a sign he had heard his daughter.

"Dad?" Sarah waited. "Dad!"

"What? What is it? Is your mother OK?"

"She's fine. I heard you two talking at second sunset. Are you going to convert, become like Chip and Laura?" Sarah tried to keep her voice casual.

"Sarah, eavesdropping is rude."

"You think I eavesdropped? You two never keep your voices down when you talk. My bed is just across the room you know."

"I guess your mother and I have a habit of talking too loud."

"So . . . are you going to do it?"

"If I told you not to worry about it, I would be unfair to you. Conversion is a tough decision with a lot to think about."

"Will Devya come to kill us?"

"Probably. If she does, I will protect you."

"Who will protect you?"

"Sometimes people need to act on their own. This is not one of those times. Chip offered to help me if problems arise."

Sarah's jaw, neck, and shoulder muscles unclenched in rapid succession. "I'm glad you won't face her alone. What are you doing now, preparing for Devya's arrival?"

"No, actually I think I've found something. Come take a look."

Her dad's warm smile drew her closer than his invitation.

"What is it?"

"Remember how successive pictures of the colony showed the forest edge further away from the buildings?"

"Yeah."

"The receding forest edge confused me because colonists stopped cutting trees after the initial clearing. Yet the forest died back."

"That's bad; right?"

"Yes. I noticed something similar happening around our colony. Trees on the edge of the forest were dying. At first I thought the trees around our old home died of disease, but these pictures made me rethink that idea because the same thing happened in both colonies separated by a long time."

"Do you think we're killing the trees?"

"Take a look at this." Aiden moved his hand to enlarge and center a graph on the wall.

Sarah stared for a moment without comprehension. "What does it mean?"

"This graph shows humidity in the air. Look here, when the colony first developed, humidity measured zero."

Sarah raised an eyebrow. "And humidity still measures zero."

"Correct. Now look at deep soil moisture levels." Aiden centered another graph.

"The soil dried out after colony construction."

"Yes, but why?"

Sarah paced in front of the graph. *I know this game. You're testing me. I'll figure it out. I'll show you I'm smart; I just need a chance. You'll be proud.*

A long pause passed. Sarah caught her lower lip between her teeth and held it. "Give me a hint."

"What is the most precious thing on this planet to everything living?"

"Water."

"Right."

Think Sarah. He sees the answer; it has to be in the information. Where is it? Think!

Aiden watched Sarah for a moment, and then he said, "So every plant and animal will do what it can to get and keep water. Remember the story I told you of the tree seedling collapsing and all the water draining out of it when I broke the root?"

"Yeah, you said when the trees died they fed future generations by returning their water deep underground."

Aiden pointed to soil moisture measurements. "And the desiccant bugs do the same thing with water on the surface . . ."

"Oh! Oh! I know. I know. This world recycles water to the ground for reuse. Somehow we broke that cycle and sent the water to the air."

"Yes!" Aiden nodded.

See Dad; I can figure things out.

"How did we break the cycle?" asked Aiden.

"It's got to be something with the colony. May I see the colony map?"

Sarah stared at the map for a long time. "There." She pointed at a dark circle a distance from the colony. She knew she had got it right when her dad's grin widened.

"Do you know what that is?" he asked.

"Something that leaks water?"

"It's a sewage pond. These colonists did what we did. They dug big holes to hold their sewage."

"Ew."

"Tell me about it. And they let the desiccant bugs process the waste. The bugs recycle the water to the soil but only to the depth of their burrows near the surface. The trees use and recharge water deep underground."

"So when we draw the deep water for use without replacing it, the trees thirst and die."

"Right." Aiden nodded. "There's a bigger problem than losing the forest. These trees are a keystone species. The entire ecosystem depends on their survival. So when the trees die nothing else survives and the land becomes barren. Only the desiccant bugs feeding on our waste stream and the desiwogs feeding on the bugs survive in the dead zone. The dead spot widens because our colony continuously transfers water to the surface, which drains water from the rock leaving too little for the forest. I'll bet this colony drilled multiple wells and abandoned each in turn as they went dry. Forest regrowth from moisture near the surface lags because the tree seeds sprout after fire, a rare occurrence on this planet. I also suspect a gradual loss of water to the atmosphere despite humidity remaining at zero."

"What caused that?" asked Sarah.

"Humans evolved on a planet with plentiful water. As a consequence, we use water inefficiently. Water evaporation in the form of sweat cools us. Each exhale also ejects a bit of moisture. Over time our way of living transfers groundwater to the air. On Earth, weather recycles atmospheric water to the ground as rain. Nubis has no weather like Earth and I suspect no life form on this planet uses atmospheric moisture."

Sarah pointed at the humidity graph. "But humidity measures zero both back then and now."

"Sometimes you have to look beyond data, Sarah. People pump enough water into the atmosphere to reduce soil moisture locally. That evaporated water dilutes through the atmosphere across the entire planet. Our instruments miss such small humidity changes."

"I see." Sarah stroked her chin. "The creatures on Nubis evolved without moisture in the air, so they have no way to use that type of water."

Aiden flipped through the colony maps showing the forest edge receding. He muttered about exhaling carbon to the atmosphere.

"Dad, do you think the dying forest made the Watchers hostile toward the other colonists?" Sarah took pleasure in her dad's startled look. She rarely outpaced her father's thoughts; so when she skipped ahead, Sarah relished the moment.

"That's a good hypothesis, Sarah. When we first landed, the Watchers fought us when we tried to cut the trees. Watchers became more tolerant after we extinguished a forest fire and replanted trees destroyed on landing."

"So how do we manage water loss? I hate killing trees or Watchers."

"We'll improve water recycling to close our colony's water loop and minimize groundwater extraction, similar to spacecraft. That won't restore the forest but will prevent further decline. Water we've lost to the atmosphere from breathing and perspiration will have to be recovered and injected underground." Aiden moved quickly around the room. "Exposure suits to capture future water emissions from our bodies and subsurface irrigation of seedlings complete the cycle. Young trees will absorb the water, grow, and, when they die, replenish the aquifer." He grinned at Sarah. "No drilling necessary—the trees' deep tap roots will carry water to the correct depth naturally."

Sarah returned the smile. "Dad, look at your face."

Aiden converted the wall to a mirror. His image startled him. Aiden's eyes glowed a deep, passionate blue.

"How do you feel?"

"You know it's funny. I feel alive."

32

End of the Beginning

"Hello Devya. I see you let yourself in." Aiden rose from the table in the corner where Rachel, Jake, and Sara were eating breakfast. He walked away from his family, drawing Devya's attention to him alone.

Sara looked around. The small room contained nothing useful as a makeshift weapon or shield. The white walls, ceiling, and floor presented only a blank canvas for bloodshed. *Get away from her Dad. We can run.*

"You always were a moderately quick organic, Aiden."

"How did you get past Iobe's defenses?" asked Aiden.

"The iobe ceased objecting to my presence once it understood my point of view. Have you been enjoying your illicit freedom?"

Sarah stood up. "What have you done to Iobe?"

Rachel moved from the table to stand between Devya and her children. "Stay where you are Sarah."

Sarah listened the first time, for once.

Devya looked at Sarah with distaste. "I see your daughter's learned some respect for authority. That's good. In time, you, Sarah, will come to see my way. As for the iobe, I have saved you organics a great deal of pain—at least some of you organics."

"What do you want Devya?" Aiden moved toward the side wall, creating more distance between him and the children. "You know I am no threat to you any longer. Why have you come here?"

"Yes, I must reevaluate my benchmark for moderately quick. After all, the reason for my visit should be obvious. I've arrived early lest Laura succeed in converting you. An espirant Aiden poses an unacceptable risk. I've come here to kill you."

Rachel leaped forward and struck out with her foot. Devya blurred for an instant before standing still in the doorway. A sharp cry of pain rang out as Rachel crashed to the floor. A red spot spread rapidly from the center of Rachel's calf, which no longer formed a straight connection between her knee and foot. Broken bone jutted from her torn clothes.

Mom! Sarah wanted to cry out. She wanted to help her mother, to fight Devya, to run away. She did none of those things. Fear and dread turned her to stone. *Devya moves so fast, so impossibly fast. I can't beat her.*

Devya stood aside the entrance with an impassive expression. Rachel tried to rise. Blood spilled to the floor. Her good leg slipped in the red slick, and she fell back with another scream.

"Stop moving Rachel. She wants me, not you. I'll go with you Devya, but please leave my family."

"No!" The cry came at once from both Rachel and Sarah. Jake sat silent and pale. His spoon dripped milk onto the table where he had dropped it. A soggy piece of cereal slid off the edge.

The sound of blowing sand heralded a cloud of dust emerging from the side wall. In half of a heartbeat, Chip reassembled himself in front of Aiden.

"Well I see Nelson finally arrives. I started to think he would miss the whole thing."

"Leave this place Devya," Chip said.

"After I have my due."

"You have chosen then." Chip shot forward with such speed that the vacuum he created pulled Aiden forward in a stumble. Chip hit Devya while still accelerating. The impact flung her backwards through the doorway. She disintegrated into dust that disappeared through the corridor wall. Chip stopped in the doorway, using the recoil from hitting Devya to decelerate faster than he accelerated.

"Wow. Devya's gone," said Sarah.

Chip turned to Aiden. "Run." With that one word he faced the wall Devya hit, smashed it, and disappeared.

Rachel looked up at Aiden. "Warn Utungua." Her tight lips and set jaw betrayed the pain she felt.

Aiden opened his link. "Utungua, Devya is here. Evacuate."

"Understood," said Utungua.

"Jake and Sarah we have to go now." Aiden knelt next to Rachel. He ripped the bottom of his shirt off and tied the cloth around Rachel's leg just below the knee. He placed his arms underneath her and lifted. The movement made her cry out. She buried her head in his chest.

They moved quickly through the halls. People emerged from rooms. Some shuffled down halls with dazed expressions, appearing unable to act without instructions. Sarah watched others move with purpose, ignoring everything irrelevant to their unspoken goal. She caught brief flashes of people who tried to help. Sarah heard them shepherd the numb, take action, move. More bodies filled the corridors. No one moved in the same direction. People collided. Sarah and Jake presented blind targets—no one looked down.

Her dad plowed a swath through the crowd. *Stay in his wake. Stay with him. He'll keep the bodies from swallowing you. Keep Jake alive.* Sarah held Jake's hand as he ran beside her, desperate to keep up with her half run. She moved along the wall to protect Jake. No path lit to guide them. No familiar voice rang in her head asking where she wished to go. Iobe was silent.

Sarah felt more vulnerable without Iobe than she did when Devya defeated her mom. Her mother fought better than anyone Sarah knew, much better than Dad. Mom lost. Iobe lost. Only Coach Nelson remained.

They arrived at the exit closest to the open area where the ships had landed. To Sarah's surprise no one had opened the door. Tremendous booms reverberated through the building. The battle continued. The sound rolled closer; Devya came for Sarah's father.

The door stayed shut when Aiden stood in front of it. "Systems must be offline."

Sarah believed her dad tried to be gentle when he lowered her mom to the ground. Despite his efforts, the white, tear-streaked face showed her mom's pain.

"What are you doing Dad?"

"Not now Sarah!" Aiden formed a plasma torch and began cutting through the door.

Boom--Boom--Boom.

The rapid percussions of the battle drawing near marked Sarah's heartbeats. *Hurry Dad! Hurry! They're almost here.* Sarah shifted from foot to foot. She wanted to run. She wanted to be out of here. To be anywhere but here, now. The building shook as the battle raged in a room close by. Dust fell from a crack in the ceiling. Sarah jumped and slapped the dust off her head. Had Devya come?

Boom. Boom.

When the thunderous clap of titans' wrestling almost set upon them, when Sarah had given up hope of escaping, her dad finished the cut. He stepped back and kicked hard at the door. The surface wobbled but stood. He kicked again. The door wobbled more but still blocked their escape.

Boom.

Stupid door let us out!

Sarah ran and leaped at the door with both feet as Aiden took a third kick. By chance or ancient survival instinct, Sarah's timing landed her kick in perfect synchrony with her dad's. The door caved under the force. Sunlight blurred their vision.

Dust swept through the entrance, thick and dull Nubis dust. Rachel choked and coughed as the flood swept over her. Behind and in front of them the walls exhaled two clouds of particles. The dust in the clouds shimmered in the light.

"Sarah, get Jake!" Aiden moved to Rachel.

"C'mon Jake!" Sarah grabbed for Jake's arm.

Jake jerked backwards out of reach. "No! I want Mommy!"

"She's coming. We have to go!" Sarah matched her father's anger.

"No!"

Sarah lunged and grabbed Jake's hand. He stiffened and threw his weight backwards, bawling.

The dust from the walls merged into a whirlwind of chaos between Sarah's family and the door to freedom. Shapes formed within the tornado only to disintegrate in a gust of piercing dust. A face. A hand. A mouth opened in a scream. Over and over forms emerged and collapsed within the tornado.

"Get out!" Aiden pushed forward into the tornado carrying Rachel.

Sarah squatted next to Jake, thrust her shoulder into his belly, and lifted his rigid body. She carried him like her father had carried them many times as they grew, like a "sack of taters." Sarah staggered under the load of her brother. Jake weighed nearly half her weight.

Sarah closed her eyes and plunged into the tornado. An ill wind stung her face and arms with dust that cut and scratched. A soothing wind swept away the offense.

Coach Nelson, he's helping us.

Angry particles tore at Sarah's skin again—Devya. Sarah pressed forward. Jake screamed. His voice drowned in the fury of the whirlwind.

Then Sarah broke through. Clear light enveloped her. She blinked her eyes expecting particles trapped by her eyelashes to extract their final vengeance upon her, but no dust blinded Sarah.

She made for the ships. Pain pulsed in her collar bone underneath Jake. The legs that had carried Sarah to victory in dustball now wobbled at the knees with a run no better than a fast stagger. Even with the weight of her mom's body, her dad had passed Sarah in the clearing and gained distance on her to the ships.

Without warning, Jake's weight lifted from her. An ending flush of pain signaled the release. Sarah looked up startled.

"Time to go little ones." Utungua placed Jake on his right hip as he moved past Sarah. He held a big gun in his left. He never stopped moving.

Free of her brother's weight, Sarah ran full out beside Utungua. Other colonists followed.

Aiden opened the cockpit of the first ship, the small scout. He strapped Rachel into the back seat. Sarah jumped into the copilot's seat.

Utungua handed Jake to Aiden. "Best to scatter. We'll rendezvous in the near future. I'll find you."

Aiden nodded. A crowd followed Utungua to the first transport. Aiden strapped Jake and himself in. The scout ship took to the air, rising above the colony buildings.

Sarah looked down. The tornado had moved into the clearing. Whirling dust separated and solidified as Devya broke free of Chip.

Aiden opened the engines when their ship cleared the low lying mounds covering the colony buildings. The small craft rocketed forward. Sarah sank deep into her seat. They shot straight for the forest.

Sarah had never flown so fast. No photon sled matched this speed. An anxious exhilaration rose in her chest. Fear shrank as the old colony disappeared in the distance.

"Something approaches off our quarter," said Aiden.

"Devya?" asked Sarah.

"Unlikely, the approach comes twenty degrees off our nose—nearly opposite from where we left Devya. This thing moves at incredible speed."

Sarah saw tree tops bending in the wake of something flying low over the forest. Their ship had almost made the tree line—a little further and they could hide.

With a jerk the smooth flight of the ship shifted to a decelerating glide.

"Why are you slowing down, Dad?" Sarah's voice choked with fear.

"Something's wrong. The engines shut down without warning. I get no reading from them—they just disappeared."

The ship's downward arc steepened as the nose dipped with the loss in air speed. Aiden touched the console in complex sequences that began to repeat patterns.

Sarah caught the increasingly rapid repetition in her father's commands and the nervous twitching in his fingers. Her dad had run out of options. Sarah looked back at her mother. Rachel's head hung down. Dark blood seeped through the impromptu bandage.

"Do something, Dad! We're falling!" Sarah's fingers dug into the sides of her seat. She barely noticed her neck and arms burned with the fire of muscles held too tight for too long.

"I'm turning on the maglevs. They'll arrest our descent."

The ship bucked twice and leveled. The ground grew closer but at a less terrifying rate.

"We're still falling, Dad."

"I know! Stop talking! I can't think when you keep pointing out the obvious. The maglevs are failing. OK!"

Before anger overtook Sarah's fear, the flight console in front of her father waivered as if no longer a solid object. The console's hard edges softened and blurred. The controls to fly the ship destabilized and collapsed into piles of dust on Aiden's legs. Sarah watched, mouth agape, as the remnants of the console cascaded from her father's legs to the floor of their ship, which now waivered with the craft's remaining structure.

Sarah looked at her father. For the first time in her life, Sarah witnessed her father helpless and afraid. She turned away unable to bear the sight. The man next to her was not her father. Her father overcame all obstacles to protect her.

Her eyes caught the frame of the cockpit. Air blew through tiny pinholes in the windshield that grew and spread. The world outside smeared and warped as the transparent material destabilized. Less than a meter separated the ship from the ground.

"Dad, look!" Sarah pointed beyond the windshield.

The black streak descended upon them. The object, still indistinguishable in its speed, missed the cockpit and struck the ship aft. The object's impact, had it been absorbed by a solid target, would have torn its victim apart with the violence a predator, starved for the kill, besets its prey.

The ship was no longer solid—no longer capable of human transport. The once exquisite exploitation of physics, now a loosely aggregated pile of particles, disintegrated in the shock wave from the unknown assailant.

Sarah fell. She heard Jake cry out. The memory of her sled crash flashed. Her body bounced hard rising back above the dust layer. In that brief moment of clarity between impact and the pain that shocks a body unconscious, Sarah saw a tornado directly behind them. Through the vicious swirl of morphing shapes in the vortex, another black bullet bore down. Sarah hit again and blacked out.

33

Facing the Future

Jake cried. Pain in Sarah's neck and head blinded her; darkness swallowed.

I'm hurt bad the strikers I have to get Jake we have to get our sled before the strikers attack.

Sarah tried to raise her head. Nothing happened. She tried to roll. Something pinned her, held her fast. The effort flared Sarah's agony. She cried out.

"Lay still. You're safe. We crashed inside the forest edge. You broke your neck in three places and fractured your skull. I've immobilized you while nanobots heal your injuries."

Her father's voice steadied her like no other. He still protected her.

"Where's Mom?"

"I'm working on her now. She's badly injured. I must leave you to collect her carbon. You're safe. Everything will be Ok."

"I know Dad. I love you."

Sarah awoke in the shade of the forest. She opened her eyes to a tangle of intertwining branches arching high above her. Small bright spots of sun mottled the leaf shade. Everywhere Sarah's eyes fell glowing blue eyes of Watchers looked back. She blinked and swallowed. Her dry throat ached. She lifted her arm a little at first for fear of stirring the pain in her neck and head. She smiled with relief when her arm moved unrestrained and without pain.

She had slept for a long time; that she knew from the soreness of one who sleeps too long in the same position. Growing more ambitious, Sarah turned her head sideways. She lay on the ground near the base of a great tree whose trunk completely filled her view. In front of the trunk a dust barrier fenced a wide perimeter around her. Next to her lay a rumpled heap resembling a sleep sack worse for the wear. She smiled again. No one but Jake left a sleep sack in that condition. He messed faster than dust.

"I see you've decided to rejoin the living. Does your neck hurt?" asked Aiden

Sarah turned her head back. "No, it feels Ok. Can I sit up?"

"If you wish. Bot scans indicate your bones healed. Remove your dust mask; you don't need the filter behind the dust wall."

Sarah raised herself with a slow awkward push of her arms. She peeled off the thin membrane that had kept dust from her lungs. A curled lock of hair fell across her eyes. She puffed at it to blow the hair out of view, but only succeeded in swinging it back for a moment. After that she ignored the wayward strands.

Her dad and Jake sat with their backs against a tree trunk a stone toss from her feet. They ate some sort of biscuit that looked dry and totally unappealing. To her left, her mother lay asleep wrapped in a sack. Her face, battered and pale, looked peaceful.

"How's Mom?"

"Alive. After impact, her former initiated emergency medical treatment, as did yours and mine, which preserved her life. When I regained consciousness, I recovered most of her Earth minerals the desiccant bugs scattered over the wreck site. She'll get better, but your mother's recovery will take a long time since I can't reclaim the minerals she bled in the colony. She'll sleep a lot and feel weak when awake due to a low blood count, but your mother lives."

Sarah returned her dad's smile. He looked tired.

"What happened? Why did we crash?"

"I think Devya caused the ship's disintegration."

"I thought I saw a tornado with shapes swirling in it before we crashed. The whirlwind looked like the one back at the colony when Chip and Devya fought." Sarah shivered despite the day's warmth.

"I saw the swirl as well. If Devya came in that whirlwind, someone stopped her. Otherwise, why let me live after the crash? My injur—"

Her dad broke off and looked down at Jake. He munched on his food and appeared unaware of the conversation; Sarah knew he listened.

"I'm hungry. What do we have to eat?"

Aiden carried a piece of dehydrated emergency ration and a canteen of water to her. "Here. This is the best I can offer now. I have to conserve former power because recharging in the open risks discovery. These rays of light in the shade disappear too fast." He scowled at the delicate pattern of sun sprinkling the forest floor. "At least we have nectar water."

"From the Seta flower? Yum!" Sarah drank deeply from the canteen. The oddly sweetened liquid freed her pasty tongue and quenched her thirst.

"How long have they been watching?" Sarah nodded toward the Watchers.

"They started arriving about two suns ago."

"Two suns! How long have I been out?"

"About three."

Sarah had never slept that long. The seriousness of their injuries caught hold. A thought played and replayed in her mind. If she had forgotten to wear her former that day, something Sarah forgot almost as much as she remembered, she would have died while her parents lay unconscious and unable to help.

"Growing up can be tough, Sarah. Sometimes people must live beyond their years."

"Yeah." Sarah looked over at her dad. He searched her face. Sarah questioned whether he looked for the daughter he wanted or the daughter she was.

A movement to Sarah's right caught their attention. She looked up at the tree trunk across from her. The blue eyes shifted. A pair moved down the trunk. An image of herself playing marbles popped into her head. Sarah blinked in disbelief. They sat hundreds of kilometers from the colony. Yet, here in this unknown random piece of forest, her watcher's familiar images played in her mind. She smiled and flicked a mental marble.

Sarah tapped her former. A small amount of dust flowed over the barrier and formed small hard balls next to her.

Aiden sat forward. "What are you doing?"

"I'm going to play a game."

The Watcher stopped at the top of the barrier. Even this close, Sarah saw nothing but blue eyes and tree trunk. *Do they even have bodies?* She imagined strangely contorted shapes. When Sarah tried to pick out the creature's shape on the tree, she saw nothing but eyes.

As if in response to her thoughts, a soft pop separated a massive oval shape from the tree trunk. As the creature fell it curled into a boulder and rolled on contact with the ground. The large sphere stopped on the other side of the marbles.

Aiden leaped to his feet when he saw the creature detach. He had cleared half the distance to his daughter when she calmly held up her hand to stop him. Sarah pressed her finger to her lips.

The boulder, an exact color match with the skin of the tree, unrolled into a gentle mound on the ground. Two blue eyes appeared. The creature shimmered and changed to soil color, disappearing save for its eyes.

Sarah squealed and clapped her hands. Her Watcher had never been this close. She leaned forward and stretched out her hand.

"Sarah, this scares me."

"It's Ok, Dad. This is my watcher."

Aiden frowned and stepped closer.

Curiosity overwhelmed her. Sarah reached out tentatively and touched the space next to the watcher's eyes. She drew back with a small start. There, where her eyes saw a pile of dirt, her fingers touched something cool and smooth. The watcher's skin felt soft and thin over hard muscle. She smiled and sat back.

Aiden relaxed his stance, but he kept near Sarah while the games of marbles with her watcher played out. Sarah won once, lost a second, and tied a third. The watcher must have been satisfied with the result of the last game because it twisted and rolled into a sphere, bounced back to the tree trunk, and disappeared again.

"Well, that was interesting. How did you know the Watcher wanted to play marbles?" Aiden gestured after the creature.

Sarah blushed with a sudden embarrassed shyness at her exposed transgression. "It told me."

"You talk to it?" Aiden's eyes widened and his jaw slackened in one synchronized motion of astonishment.

"Yeah, sure." Sarah nodded her head gently.

"How did you learn its language?" Disbelief tinged Aiden's question.

"I guess 'talking' is the wrong word." Sarah's hands flipped back and forth in the air as she tried to explain. "My Watcher speaks without words. It uses pictures sometimes or movies but not really—more like dreams. Yes, like dreams."

"Dreams? You said dreams?" Aiden's legs became unsteady. He wobbled down to a kneeling position. His eyes moved back and forth with the speed of a person who sees nothing of the outside world.

"Yep. I dream what it wants to say." Sarah watched her dad sit down with a thud on the ground.

Aiden looked stunned. After a while he muttered to himself. "That makes sense. All this time they spoke to us; we misinterpreted. I dreamed the watchers' messages—the tree, my parents, my vision in the pool. Our eyes bear witness. The watchers showed us the truth."

"What truth?" Sarah's chest tightened; her throat burned. Her father sounded like Mr. Asworthy.

After a moment Aiden looked up. He seemed to see Sarah now. Aiden came to her, knelt, and hugged her. "That's not important at the moment. Now I must use my thumb of power to defeat you in the galactic marble championship."

Sarah raised her face to him. "Bring it on, Dad."

High above Sarah and her father, leaves turned in the sun. A shaft of sunlight blazed away shadow covering the circle below. Marbles danced within the light, spinning ribbons of joy in blue, red, and green. Clicks and snaps from their frolic echoed laughter.

Preview of "Snow Falling"
by Robert Harken

"Good evening world! Hugo Clark here with Andromeda Drift continuing twenty-four hour coverage of the Influentials. AD, you've been harassing me all afternoon for the first update. What do you have to share with our viewers?"

"I hardly call my actions harassment—more like threats, Love. I want to show the world a new Influential." Andromeda Drift, body aligned for the camera, paused for her co-anchor's reaction.

"What, a new Influential?" Hugo scrolled through the slate he hunched over on the anchor desk. The silence marking his ignorance aborted the search. He shook his head in disbelief and spoke with the tone of someone suspecting an ambush. "Who? The rankings remain stable."

"Last minute's news, Love. You've got to shift ahead of the curve, shift or drown. I spotted an Ascendant in the clickstream. Their tag is Snow. This particular Ascendant keeps a low profile, which delayed our discovery. In fact, we know nothing of the individual, not even gender; but Snow can't hide the stats they've generated over the past seven months, progressing from an influence score of five among the undifferentiated masses to thirty-two this second." Andromeda Drift's glossed lips slid into a practiced smile.

"Impressive performance over a short period AD, but thirty-two falls well short of an Ascendant, much less an Influential. What gives with the hype?" Hugo's voice regained a measure of confidence; his body stayed in a protective slouch which brought the bald spot on the back of his head into view.

"Double-swipe the data, Hugo. They manufactured that gain with posts on multi-tasking two or more jobs simultaneously, cooking food made without approved ingredients, rehabilitating Affluents' castaways, and rescuing puppies! On my avatar, Hugo, I have found no better purpose-built hero for the masses. Corporates began supporting Snow last month after just six months of presence!"

"Interesting, do you think the AI Guild released another synthetic persona?" With each question, Hugo shrank in the shadow cast by his tall co-anchor.

"No, Guild synthetics lack the sophistication Snow displays in his or her relates. Snow's interactions withstand behavioral analysis—definitely human. Folks, we've identified a genuine prodigy in our midst. I expect greatness from this persona."

"So, who is Snow? I see from the feed that sixty thousand individuals have claimed the persona since you first mentioned the alias," said Hugo.

"Bit errors Hugo. We traced Snow's access server to the Seattle area and raided the flat where the signal originated. Nothing. Snow jacked wireless access from a nobody. Whoever animates this persona wishes to avoid detection. Fret not folks, the Ministry of Information shall exercise all its powers under your constitutional Right to Knowledge and expose Snow."

Connect with me online:

www.robertharken.com

Acknowledgments

I thank Virginia, Regina, McKenzie, and Grace for their generous gifts of time and direct, insightful feedback. Sheila made this novel possible with her support and patience and by the editing of more drafts than either of us cares to remember.

About the Author

Before World War Terminus I lived among the masses without consequence. After the war, I took a job in mood organ maintenance, which required extensive testing of codes before pronouncing the devices repaired. I frequently dialed a 175, reckless abandon. I fault that feeling with pushing me into stealing real animals by swapping in synthetics. I sold the real ones—at least most them, all except a chicken, which I ate. Don't ask what it tasted like because I can't say. My crimes went off without incident until they gave Rick Deckard a bounty for my head.

Having heard of Deckard's success against the Nexus 6s, I jumped off-planet when the Spacing Guild's next transport passed. They brought me to Arrakis where I broke Fremen strikes on spice harvest for Maud 'Dib. Yes, I know they viewed him as a savior and all that; but life isn't so tidy below the surface. That's where I work. Everything went along swimmingly until I took upon myself the habit of calling Maud 'Dib by the nickname 'Piddly Pauli Pissant' in front of his Fremen. Don't know why I did this; sometimes words just slip out—repeatedly. You know. Well, Maud 'Dib soured on our mutually beneficial arrangement and I found myself on another Guild ship.

I write this biography from the asteroid those bastards dropped me on, which ironically hurtles through space on a collision course with Earth. I'm not worried.

CPSIA information can be obtained at www.ICGtesting.com
Printed in the USA
LVOW072053100113

315219LV00021BA/1003/P